Lasting Impressions

A Boss's Daughter Lesbian Romance

Cassidy Langue

ALSO BY CASSIDY LANGUE

<u>as Cassidy Langue</u>
Sophie and the Sea
Freedom
Lasting Impressions

~

<u>Love Enough for More series</u>
(writing sapphic poly romance as Polly Emorie)
All the Oceans #1
All the Water #2
All the Words #3

~

To sign up for my newsletter to hear about new books
go to cassidylangue.com
If you enjoy a book, please consider leaving a rating or review.
It helps other readers find great books!

1

SARAH

Something soft and warm rubs up against my bare stomach, and I groan. "No," I mumble, smacking her softly and rolling over to face the other side of the bed. "Not now." I am not in the mood for Monday morning yet—not ready to be awake.

As if on cue, my alarm blares, and I'm nudged insistently from behind again. "Oh, quit already," I grumble to Missy. I reach for the alarm clock and feel for the snooze button, even though I know better than to think I can squeeze in another few minutes of sleep. I lean back and give her a quick kiss before dragging myself out of bed. We have a busy day today, and the sooner we get moving, the sooner shit'll get done.

I brush my teeth and turn the shower on. Missy hops into the bathroom behind me, and I give her a playful nudge with my foot, just hard enough to knock her over. Laughing, I pick her up and give her cuddles and a quick kiss between her ears. Her gray fur and green eyes always give me warm fuzzies.

We got her from the rescue five years ago. She was in an accident when she was a kitten, and they had to amputate one of her back legs at the hip. She gets around just fine, but if I nudge her from just the right angle, I can topple her. She loves it, mostly because she ends up with extra snuggles. She loves bare-skin snuggles the best—which is probably why the damn cat sleeps by me every night. She also has the internal clock of a rooster inside her thick skull that prompts her to wake me up five minutes before my alarm. Every damn day. Without fail.

I put Missy down and step into the hot stream of water with a silent exhale of pleasure. *Ten minutes,* I remind myself. I need to get ready, get Lily ready, make sure everything is ready for school and work, make breakfast for humans and felines. *Sarah, stop. One thing at a time.*

I take a deep breath and rinse out my long, chestnut brown hair. I let my hands slide over my wet body with a sigh before turning the water off. After drying my hair and putting on makeup, I pull a navy pencil skirt out of the closet and pair it with a crisp white blouse—always the consummate professional. I usually dress up a little more than everyone else in our small office. As the architect and project manager for our two biggest jobs, the clothes tend to earn me a little more respect from the men. I add a simple silver necklace and view myself in the mirror with a nod, satisfied.

Ready to take on the day, I head into my daughter's room. "Lilybug, it's time to wake up." I lean down to drop a soft kiss on her forehead before shaking her shoulder. Sometimes, my twelve-year-old almost-teenager can be a challenge, but when she's sleeping, she's so innocent.

She peeks one eye open. "Five more minutes," she mumbles in protest. I chuckle. Like mother, like daughter—at least when it comes to sleep.

"No sweetie. I already let you sleep an extra few minutes. We need to eat and be out the door in twenty minutes."

Rolling her eyes, she sits up at the side of her bed. "Don't forget we need to feed the cats, too."

I laugh. "Yes. You need to feed the cats. What do you want for breakfast? Get dressed and brush your teeth. Let's go." I gently drop another kiss on the top of her head.

"Pancakes and eggs?" She glances at me in question.

"You better move fast then," I warn her before leaving her alone. She's normally pretty good at getting herself ready, once she's up, but Monday's can be a little more of a challenge than the rest of the week.

I walk into the kitchen after glancing at her backpack on the couch. It looks like her flute and everything else is already packed and ready to go. Thank God for routines, or it would take us forever to get out the door in the morning. Grabbing a frozen ice pack from the freezer, I stick it in her lunchbox and set it on the couch next to her bag.

Keurig. Pancakes out of the freezer and into the toaster. Egg cup in the microwave.

I pull out two servings of wet cat food and put them on the counter for Lily to open for the cats. Oliver, the older one, hauls his ancient orange ass off the cat bed in the corner next to the heater and saunters over to greet me.

"Morning, Ollie," I coo softly, reaching down to give him a scratch under the chin. I grab my coffee off the Keurig as Lily comes out of her room. Right on time.

She feeds the cats and tosses the empty containers into the trash, turning to wash her hands. "Can I have butter on my 'cakes?"

I nod, grabbing the butter off the counter and pulling the pancakes out of the toaster to pop them onto a small plate. I butter them in record time and grab her egg cup from the microwave. I set the plate on the table in front of her as she sits down, and I sit down across from her.

"Your flute is already in your backpack, right?" I ask her, mentally ticking off boxes of all our activities for the day.

"Yep, everything for school is ready to go. My ballet slippers are in my dance bag and ready to go this afternoon." She digs into her egg cup first. I swear, this child is half my size and eats like a teenage boy. "My key is in my backpack, so I can get in after school."

I nod thoughtfully. Lily normally goes to Beth and Sophie's place after school. She uses the key when she has ballet in the afternoons so she doesn't have to take her dance stuff to school. Beth has a spare key, but I'm trying to give Lily more responsibility.

"It's go time!" her phone chirps. We both roll our eyes. She rinses off her plate, taking a paper towel to hold her plain pancakes, and grabs her backpack off the couch. I drain my coffee, rinse the cup out, and grab my purse.

"It's go time!" We laugh in unison as we head out the door.

I walk into the office four minutes before eight with a happy sigh. Lily's usually carefree, but she knows she has to play by my rules in the morning—or I'll have to get her butt out of bed earlier. The girl loves her sleep as much as I do. We're a well-oiled machine, though, and I'm right on time. I pull the bottom drawer of my desk open and stick my purse inside.

"Morning, Sarah." Bob Parker smiles at me. "How was your weekend?"

I glance up at our other Project Manager. Although we don't work on the same projects, we're always working together in some capacity. We've been working together for almost a decade now, and he and his wife Teresa are two of my favorite people in the world.

"Morning, Bob. It was nice," I tell him. "Beth and I took the girls to the Farmer's Market Saturday afternoon. Lily loves to explore the arts and crafts stuff. Then we saw the latest Disney movie."

He chuckles softly. "We took Brooke and Mia yesterday. They didn't stop singing until they were asleep last night." He looks up and nods at our media manager. "Morning, Emily."

"Hey, you two." She nods to both of us as she slips into her cubicle across from me.

"Sarah." Bob taps twice on his desk with his index finger. It's a nervous tick he has when he talks about the boss. "Richard asked to see you as soon as you got in."

I frown. "Did he say what about?" He pulls me into his office at least once or twice a week, but it's always about one of the projects I'm working on—and it's never been the minute I walked in the door before.

Bob shakes his head. "It sounded important, but I don't think anything's wrong."

I nod slowly, pushing my chair back and standing up. Mr. Tomsen has always been a fair man to work for, and I've never had a complaint about my work for him. The cultural center is on track. The bridge project we're getting started with has hit a few snags, but it's so early in the game he's probably not even aware of them. My team and I have worked through everything we've come up against so far.

I anxiously bite my lower lip and knock on his office door. He's the only person in the office who has a door that closes. The rest of us share an open floor area. We have cubicles, but they're only four feet high, so they don't really serve a purpose, other than giving us a sense of our own space.

"Come," his deep voice calls through the door.

I open the door and poke my head in. "Bob said you wanted to see me right away, sir?"

"Sarah, come in. Close the door."

2

CARMEN

"Happy anniversary, beautiful!" Olivia pulls me into a tight hug. "Can you believe I've put up with you for ten years?"

"You'll be stuck with me for the next fifty, at least," I say, laughing. "You're a few minutes early. I need to change." I motion for her to follow me.

She chuckles, her laugh throaty, and follows me up to my suite on the second floor. She parks herself on the couch in my sitting room. "If you need to take a shower, I can wait. I know I'm early. I didn't know you'd be working out."

"I was just stretching," I tell her from the doorway as I head into my room. "I just hate doing it in jeans."

"You still need to stretch every day?"

I pull a pair of skinny jeans out of my drawer and a baby blue top from the closet, talking to her through the open door. "Without fail. I can skip a day, but then it's harder to get back on track. My dad says he notices my gait if I miss a day. Abuela says two."

"What do *you* say? How do *you* feel?"

I sit on my bed and pull my leggings off, slipping my jeans on. I wiggle into them and change my top. "I notice in the morning, regardless." I shrug, coming back into the sitting room.

She eyes me and whistles. "Literally two minutes, and you go from hot exercise bod to pretty as a picture."

I throw a pillow at her, laughing. *"Cállate,"* I shush her. "Don't let your husband hear you talk like that. He might get jealous."

She snorts. "He won't get jealous of you, don't worry. As much as I love you, you don't set my panties on fire like he does. Sorry to disappoint you."

I pout playfully, and she stands up to wrap me in a hug. "Did I hurt your feelings?" She plants a kiss on my forehead in faux apology.

"For about three seconds—ten years ago. But I'm over it." I shove her shoulder and roll my eyes. "Abuela is making dinner tonight. Dad's home, too. Come on." I head toward the door.

"What's she making?" Olivia asks as we head down the stairs.

"Bandeja paisa." One of my favorite Colombian dishes of meat, beans, and rice. "She figured we'd be hungry. Are Miguel and the *niños* coming? She made enough for everyone," I tell her. Somehow, between being a busy lawyer and a wife, she and Miguel found time to create little humans, too. Three of them.

"Nah. He said that tonight is a celebration of you and me. He's going to make hot dogs and put cartoons on for the kids."

Abuela looks up at us from the kitchen. "Oh, no you don't. You call that man up and tell him to bring the whole gang over here—right now. I'll feed them."

Olivia glances at abuela. *"Abuela, no es necesario,* really."

Abuela dries her hands on a kitchen towel and comes into the living room. She gives Olivia a hug before taking her chin in her hands. She stares into her eyes, almost defiant. "Those are my great-grandbabies, and I don't see them enough. Don't deny a *bisabuela* the chance to see her great-grandbabies." It's a challenge Olivia won't win.

I snort at my best friend and pull out my phone. To be fair, they're not really abuela's blood kin, but they might as well be. Three of my aunts and uncles still live in Colombia, so most of her grandkids are half a world away. My tía María and tío Fredo live nearby, but the grandkids don't see her as often as she'd like.

I dial Miguel's number, stepping out of Olivia's reach. *"Ciao,* Miguel. It's Carmen. Abuela says to get your ass, and your posse, over here as soon as possible. Don't worry about clean or dressed or fed. Just pack them up and head over here."

"Tell him I love him." Laughing, Olivia tries to grab the phone from me.

"Your wife says she loves you—even though she just left you alone with three toddlers. I'm not sure I believe her." I laugh. "Honk when you get here. We'll come out and help you with them."

Abuela grins. She always wins.

Miguel pulls up with the kids about twenty minutes later, and we all go out to grab kids and bags from the car. I pull Miguel into a hug. "It's been too long," I tell him.

"It's easier for you to come to us," he mumbles gruffly. "It's hard to get all the kids out of the house."

I realize he's right as I grab two-year-old Fia out of the back seat. I need to do better. "Hey, baby girl," I coo to my favorite child in the world, covering her chubby face with kisses.

Dad unbuckles Nathan—who's a big boy now, at five whole years old—and helps him get out of the car on his own. "You've gotten at least an inch taller since I saw you last month, little man! Did you start kindergarten?"

Nathan's head bounces enthusiastically. "I get to ride the bus every day like a big person," he says proudly.

"Like a big boy!" Dad winks at Nathan and takes his hand. "Why don't we big boys go ahead of the ladies and see what's in the house. I heard abuela made some food for everyone!"

I shake my head in amusement, and a twinge of sadness, at how wonderful dad is with Olivia and Miguel's kids. I'd love to have kids someday—but unless I find a woman younger than me... My biological clock is starting to tick. I'm only twenty-eight, but I haven't found anyone I want to spend the rest of my life with, much less someone I'd want to raise a family with. I squeeze Fia tight and give her a light raspberry on the cheek.

She bursts into giggles. *"¿Dónde 'tá Talia?"* she babbles.

I point to the other side of the car, where abuela is getting Talia, Fia's twin sister, out of her car seat. "She's over there. See her?"

Fia, silly child that she is, waves at her sister, and Talia waves back excitedly from abuela's arms.

"Down." Talia wiggles her way out of abuela's arms.

"Natalia, hold on to abuela's hand, please." Olivia gives her a firm look. "Or mine. You can choose." She grabs two bags from the car and starts to herd everyone toward the door.

Talia grabs abuela's hand and drags her toward the house. "We play outside?"

Abuela taps her on the nose with a grin. "As long as it's okay with your mom and dad. You know the rules—you need at least two adults outside with you." Talia tugs at her hand again, but abuela shakes her head. "I have to cook dinner, so it's your mom, dad, Tía Carmen, or your granpápi."

We have a swing set, a slide, and a sandbox in the backyard that have been there since I was a kid. I didn't play out here very much, but dad kept them—in the hopes of having something to entice grandchildren with, I suppose. It's one of the reasons that Miguel and Olivia come over as often as they do.

I know I should visit them at their place more often, but once they're here, it's a lot easier on everyone. They live in a townhouse, and while they have enough living space, they don't have a safe place to play. There's a playground in their complex, but it's hard to keep track of three kids, even with two sets of eyes on them—especially when other kids are around.

Dad's in the sandbox building castles with Nathan, and Olivia and I are pushing the girls on the swings, when my phone rings. That's odd, at seven o'clock on a Friday night. It's not like I have a huge group of friends. There are a few women I see periodically, but they would all text before calling.

I pull my phone out of my back pocket. It's Michael Johnson, my PR Specialist at work. Very few things would require a call to the CEO of the company on a Friday night. I turn to Olivia. "I need to take this." Swiping to answer the call, I walk a few feet away from them.

"It's Carmen," I answer simply. "What's going on, Mike?"

"Chump's back. You're his next target."

Fuck.

3

SARAH

I open the door and poke my head into my boss's office. "Bob said you wanted to see me right away, sir?"

"Sarah, come in. Close the door."

I close the door behind me and look at Richard Tomsen curiously. His forehead is furrowed. Not good.

"Sit down, Sarah." He glances at me and sighs.

I frown, complying, but keep my mouth shut. I study him for a long minute.

He opens his mouth and takes a breath to speak, but then closes it, shaking his head.

"What's wrong, sir?" I ask, trying to keep my heart from racing. I can't think of anything that I screwed up on. I'm good at my job. When he doesn't answer right away, I ask, "Did I do something wrong?"

He chuckles quietly, shaking his head. "No. You're fine, Sarah. It's nothing like that." He rubs his hand over his face.

"Sir?" He's making me nervous. He never makes me nervous. *What is this about?*

He looks up at me and meets my gaze. "Sarah, you've worked with me for nearly a decade. It's Richard."

I nod in agreement. Most of the men in the office call him Richard. Most of the women call him Mr. Tomsen. Even in a work environment where women make up half the staff and are well-respected, it still feels like there's a line we shouldn't cross—for some unspoken reason. It's been like that everywhere I've ever worked. "Then, *Richard.*" I enunciate his name deliberately with a hint of amusement. "What is it? Something's wrong."

He shakes his head. "Nothing's wrong. I just wanted to ask a favor of you." He sighs heavily. "Feel free to say no. It won't reflect badly on you."

I look at him curiously, my forehead creased. "I rarely say no. I don't think I've ever told you no. Whatever it is, just ask." I'm not sure if I'm more exasperated or more worried.

He nods curtly. "Delmont's Architecture Gala is Friday night. I wondered if you'd like to come with me." He holds his hand up and inhales deeply. "It would be a wonderful opportunity for you. You know most of the who's-who in the architectural scene around here, but there'll be a number of regional and national faces there this year. I thought it would be a good opportunity for you to meet some new people."

I tilt my head to study him. "This would be in a purely professional capacity?"

He nods. "Of course. Technically, you would be my plus-one, but I would consider it a professional courtesy, nothing more." He steeples his fingers, letting out a long breath. He leans forward on his desk, his chin in his palms. "That's why I was reluctant to ask you," he says sheepishly. "I just think it would be beneficial for you, that's all."

I raise an eyebrow at him, biting the inside of my cheek thoughtfully. "Actually, I would love to go, but my normal sitter is out of town for the weekend. I don't know if I could find someone to watch my daughter." Beth and her family will be out of town this weekend, and I don't know who else I could ask with such short notice that I'd be comfortable leaving her with.

"How old is she? She's in middle school now, right?" he asks thoughtfully.

"She's twelve. She's old enough to be home by herself for short periods of time, but not for a whole evening—especially not once it gets dark."

He groans. "The next eight or ten years are going to be the hardest years of your life."

I laugh softly. "She's a good kid, for the most part."

He nods, a faraway look in his eyes. "I'm sure she is," he says softly. His gaze focuses on me again, an idea popping into his head. "My daughter, Carmen. I bet she's free for the evening. She offered to come with me if you don't want to go. I bet she would much rather spend time with your daughter than at some stuffy old gala with me." A grin spreads across his face. "Have you met her yet? Her firm is the one that commissioned the cultural center."

"Carmen? I've emailed her a few times. I think I've talked to her on the phone once or twice. Haven't met her yet, though."

He nods, satisfied. "If she can watch your daughter for the evening, would you like to come? Like I said earlier, the offer is open, but it won't reflect badly on you if you prefer not to. I almost didn't ask you because I don't want you to feel uncomfortable. But that would be pretty sexist of me, wouldn't it?" He gives me a sheepish smile.

"You've never been anything but a gentleman, and I know that neither of us would jeopardize our working relationship. I'm not worried about it." I don't add that he's not my type. It doesn't seem relevant.

He blows out a long breath and his shoulders relax. "Thank you. I'll run it by Carmen and have her give you a call to touch base, okay?"

"Sure. Is the gala black-tie?" I ask.

"Yes. Dinner is at seven, then mingling and drinks. I'll pick you up if you're planning to drink."

I nod amenably. "I probably won't drink much, but I might have one or two. Sounds like a plan."

I glance at the phone ringing on my desk. It's been a busy day, and it's almost time to finish up for the day. I don't recognize the number on the caller ID. "Sarah Reynolds, Tomsen Designs," I answer.

"Hi, Sarah. This is Carmen Tomsen from Tomsen Media. Ugh. Just Carmen, Richard's daughter."

A laugh bubbles out of my throat. "Carmen. Hi. What can I do for you?"

She giggles. "Sorry, the work spiel comes out of my mouth without me thinking about it when I'm in the office. Dad said if I watch your daughter Friday night, I'm off the hook for his boring gala."

I roll my eyes, smiling. "It might be boring to you, but it'll be a wonderful opportunity for me to network with some bigger fish in the industry. You seriously don't mind hanging out with my daughter for a few hours on a weekend?"

"My choices are between your kid and my dad. Your kid wins." Her laugh is infectious, and I grin. "How old is she?"

"She's twelve—in middle school. She's easy to handle." I sigh softly. "Well, she'll be easy for *you* to handle. Sometimes she's a pain in my ass, but that's par for the course with her age."

"Oh, yeah. Twelve is fun times," she murmurs, her voice far away. She inhales deeply and lets out the breath. "I was thinking we could meet some night this week. Nothing big, just so I can meet you both before your big date with my dad."

I swallow thickly, suddenly uncomfortable. "Purely professional," I say drily.

"Of course. He just hasn't gone out at all in more than fifteen years, so I tease him. That's all," she tries to backtrack.

"Maybe I shouldn't go," I say to myself, second-guessing my decision. Richard has never given me any indication that he'd be interested in me beyond a professional relationship, but I don't want to encourage him.

Carmen sighs. "Don't pass up a wonderful opportunity, Sarah. He hasn't shown any interest in anyone since my mom died. It's been a long time. He's okay, but I can't see him ever getting involved with anyone else."

I frown thoughtfully. I didn't know he was a widower. "How long has it been?" I ask quietly.

"Almost sixteen years," she says softly. "He's okay, though." She pauses for a moment, and I can hear her swallow. She clears her throat. "Now. How about sometime this week so I can meet the two of you before you leave your precious treasure in my hands Friday?"

"Sure. You want to come over for dinner tomorrow or Thursday? Lily's got ballet tonight and Wednesday. We normally eat out after. Nothing fancy, but it's hard to cook when we don't get home until after six-thirty."

She lets out a full-throated laugh. "A girl after my own heart. Exercise, then undo it all with fast food!"

I smile. "Nah. It's usually Subway or Panera Bread—something marginally healthy. We save the sinful stuff for the weekend. We usually have Saturday afternoons and evenings for just the two of us. Mother-daughter time. That's when we splurge."

"Sounds beautiful," she says softly. I can hear a wisp of a sad smile in her voice, then it's gone. "Tomorrow for dinner sounds great. Can I bring anything?"

"Just yourself. Do you have any food restrictions or preferences?" I ask. I would hate to make dinner for someone and then find out they couldn't eat it.

"Nope. I'll eat just about anything. Don't go to any extra trouble for me, Sarah. I just want to meet you and Lily. I can come by after dinner if it's easier for you."

"You're coming to my house and I'm feeding you. End of discussion," I tell her firmly. "Now give me your personal number, and I'll text you my address. We eat at six-thirty."

4

SARAH

"Where are you going on a Friday night?" Lily asks me as she sets the table.

"There's a big party for architects—and since I'm an architect, I'm going to go."

"Is it going to be fancy?" she asks. When I nod, she presses further. "You haven't been on a date in forever. Is this like a date?"

I snort. "Definitely not a date. I'm going with my boss, but only as a work thing." I rub the lemon over the grater to add a little extra zing to the salmon and dill we're having for dinner, then stick it in the oven.

The doorbell rings, and Lily jumps up in excitement. She runs to the intercom and pushes the button. "Who is it?"

"My name is Carmen. I'm here to see Lily and Sarah." She has a playful smile in her voice.

"You're in the right place. We're on the fourth floor. Number 403. Do you want me to come down and get you? There's an elevator so you don't need to climb all the stairs."

"Lily," I call out to her. "She's a big girl. She can handle it. You can meet her at the elevator if you want to," I suggest.

Lily pushes the button again. "Mom says I can meet you at the elevator." She pushes the button to buzz Carmen into the building, then runs out the door into the hallway to meet our esteemed guest.

I hear their laughter in the hall a minute later and I smile. Richard is an upstanding guy, so of course his daughter would be fine. It's still a relief to hear the two of them laughing together so quickly.

"Mom." Lily's voice cuts through my thoughts. "She brought you flowers. Pretty flowers." She reaches into the cabinet where we keep the flower vases. "She's pretty, too. You should be going out with her instead of her dad."

"I'm not going out with her dad, Lily. I'm going to a work function. It's not a date," I remind her.

Carmen comes into the kitchen and extends a hand to me. "Carmen Tomsen. Nice to finally meet you." She's dressed in a casual yellow floral dress with cap sleeves, the skirt ending right above her knees, and strappy sandals. Her eyes are a dark chocolate brown, and her dark hair is straight, halfway down her back. She has the legs of a runner—all muscle.

I pull my eyes away from her toned legs. "Sarah Reynolds. It's weird that we haven't met yet, right? I'm the lead PM on your project." I shake her hand, and she clasps mine between hers. "You didn't need to dress up." I motion toward her dress.

She laughs lightly. Her hands are warm and soft, and she holds mine for a long moment before letting go. "I just came from work." She shrugs. "I brought you flowers."

I smile bigger than I intend. She has an easy energy about her. "You didn't need to bring anything." I take them from her, bringing them to my nose before fixing the beautiful arrangement in the vase. "They smell divine. I love the smell of fresh flowers." I turn to my daughter. "Lilybug, do you know what kind of flowers these are?"

"Yep." She bounces her head up and down. "They're lilies, like me. I think she brought them for me, mom. I'm the one who has to put up with her, not you. You'll be off on your *date.*" She singsongs the last word.

"Hey, *Lilybug,*" Carmen says, emphasizing her nickname. "Your mom said it's not a date. It's not a date. Drop it, please." Her tone is friendly but firm.

"Yeah, yeah. He's not her type, anyway," she answers flippantly.

"Bug, can you put the flowers on the table for me?" I hand her the vase and nudge her out of the kitchen.

"Not your type, eh?" Carmen laughs lightly, raising an amused eyebrow at me. There's a hint of curiosity in her voice.

Lily comes back into the kitchen. "She doesn't date boys," she says firmly. "Or men. Do you want a tour of the apartment? I can show you around."

I don't date, period. Well, almost never, anyways. "Dinner will be ready in fifteen or twenty," I tell them. "Bug, you can show her around if you want." I turn to Carmen. "Would you like some chardonnay with dinner? We're having salmon."

"It's one of mom's specialties," Lily chimes in. She's not usually this chatty with new people.

"The chardonnay or the salmon?" Carmen teases Lily. She turns to me. "Sure, I'd love a glass. Stop me at one, though."

"The salmon, of course," Lily cuts back in. "She didn't make the chardonnay. Doesn't your hair get in your way all the time? Mine is getting too long, and yours is longer than mine."

Carmen shrugs. "I keep it in a braid if it gets in my way." She pokes Lily playfully. "What do you do with yours?"

I hear their voices trail through the apartment. It's not a big place—just the living room and dining room, plus our bedrooms. Carmen asks Lily about her ballet lessons, and Lily turns on the music for *Swan Lake.*

Is she going to dance for her? I slip into the living room. "Whoa there, Missy. We need to move the coffee table if you're going to dance in here." I pull it out of the way so Lily can show off her moves. Missy—the cat—comes hopping out from behind the couch. I pick her up to give her some snuggles and nod Carmen toward the couch. Prima ballerina time.

Lily bends down and kisses Missy's head in my arms before taking her position to dance.

"Don't you want to get your slippers on?" I ask her curiously. If she wants to really show off what she's capable of, she needs her ballet shoes on. "Go on. We can wait a minute."

Lily runs off to her room to grab them, and I turn to Carmen. "She's actually really good. It'll be harder to see in jeans in the living room, but trust me."

Carmen nods amenably. She reaches her hand out to Missy, who sniffs at Carmen and proceeds to butt her head against her. "I was going to ask if I could pet her, but... She seems friendly."

"You want to hold her? She loves anyone who'll give her cuddles." At Carmen's nod, I drop Missy into her lap.

Carmen leans down and gives her a kiss between her ears. Missy wiggles around in Carmen's lap to get comfortable, and she rubs a hand along her back. "She's precious." Carmen's smile turns into a frown when she notices Missy's missing leg.

"She was in an accident when she was a kitten. She's basically lived all her life without it," I explain with a shrug. "She's no ballet dancer, but she gets around better than that old man." I point my chin to Oliver in the cat bed on the other side of the couch.

Carmen lets out a happy sigh. "I've always wanted a cat. My dad's allergic," she explains.

"You live with him?" I ask, surprised. She's old enough I'd think she'd be out on her own by now. She owns her own business. I'm sure she could afford it.

"Him and my abuela—my grandmother on my mom's side. I could get my own place, but they like having me around." She shrugs. "They give me my freedom, and it's kind of nice to have someone to come home to."

"You don't think I need to worry about him Friday, do you?" Every time she brings up the fact that he's single, the fleeting thought goes through my mind that I should cancel Friday night.

She shakes her head. "No. I can't imagine he would even think about an employee like that. But even if he *did* try to start something, just tell him to back off. He'd respect you one hundred percent for being straight with him." She searches my face for a long, probing moment. "Are you really worried?"

I shake my head. "No, not really. But I'm not interested—in him or anyone at work—and I don't want things to get awkward."

She laughs good-naturedly. "He's not a bad guy. You could do a lot worse." She shrugs.

Lily pops back into the living room and sits down next to me to put her ballet shoes on. "Mom doesn't like guys. He could be the best man in the world, and she still wouldn't want to date him." She ties up the ribbons on her slippers. "It's not his business who she wants to date anyway."

Carmen looks at me with raised eyebrows. It always seems so much easier for young people to come out. They don't have to worry about discrimination at work, about losing their job. I don't think it would come to that, not at Tomsen Designs, but there's no reason to test the waters either—not at the moment, anyway. "I'm sure he wouldn't have a problem with that," Carmen says softly.

Lily takes the center of the floor and gets into position to dance. "Ready." She nods at me to start the song from the beginning. I hit the play button and watch her start to move, mesmerized. When I watch my daughter dance, I see brilliance—an athlete with musicality, poise, control, and elegance. Her movements, even partially hidden under jeans and a loose T-shirt, are those of an accomplished dancer. She's ninety-five pounds and five-foot-two-inches of muscle and grace. She takes my breath away every time. The last note fades and Lily hits her final pose.

"Wow," Carmen breathes.

"Told you she's good." I chuckle, winking at her. "Some of it's a mom's pride and joy," I admit, "but she's honestly one of the best dancers in the area. Her form is the best in the whole state of Illinois."

"Probably the whole Midwest," Lily corrects me, sitting down to free her feet from their confines. "At least that's what Madame Grace says." She shrugs.

Carmen turns to Lily, mouth agape. "Did you seriously just do eight Italian fouettés in freaking jeans?"

Lily shrugs. "Sure."

I hear the timer in the kitchen and excuse myself, amused at the shock on Carmen's face. I pour two glasses of chardonnay and a glass of strawberry-lemon-infused water for Lily. I stick them on the table before pulling the salmon and veggies out of the oven.

"That smells divine," Carmen says, coming into the kitchen and inhaling deeply. "Can I help with anything?"

"Nope. Both of you sit down," I insist, plating the salmon and filling the plates with roasted vegetables. I breathe in the aroma. It really does smell good.

"I wish you hadn't gone to such trouble for me, especially on a weekday," Carmen says quietly. "I didn't mean to make extra work for you."

"Nonsense," I tell her, putting a plate in front of her, and another in front of Lily.

"We have to eat anyway," Lily points out before she digs in, laughing.

5

CARMEN

"Are you looking forward to the gala tomorrow?" I ask dad Thursday night at dinner. "You haven't gone the last few years." I leave my question unasked. He'll talk if he wants to talk.

He takes a bite of his chicken and chews it slowly. "Honestly, I probably wouldn't go, but a few nationally-known architects are supposed to be there. I thought it would be good for Sarah to go. Ella and Alexi will be there, too. I'd like to introduce them."

"So you *do* want to take her out," I accuse him with a shit-eating grin on my face. "I knew it."

He does a poor job of hiding his smile. "It'll be nice to go out again. I haven't been to a high-end gala like this in a long time." He shrugs a shoulder, trying to act nonchalant about it.

"This woman's beautiful." Abuela grins knowingly with her crooked smile. "I can tell by the way you've been humming all week, *mijo.*"

"She's my employee." He lowers his eyes to his plate and takes another bite. Shaking his head, he sighs softly. "It would be inappropriate. Plus, she made a point of asking if it was in a—" He clears his throat. "—a professional capacity."

"She *is* beautiful." I wink at abuela.

"Put your feelers out, *mijo,*" abuela says tenderly. "A little touch here, a little touch there. Her arm, her lower back. You never know—she might be receptive."

For a seventy-two-year-old, my abuela is something else. She moved here to the States after mom died—to help dad take care of me. I honestly don't know what we would have done without her. My dad is like a son to her, and she's told me many times that she'd be thrilled to see him find love again.

Dad sighs again, a wisp of sadness escaping his throat. "We'll see. I don't want to make her uncomfortable."

Abuela and I are cleaning up after dinner, and dad's disappeared into his reading room. I put my hand on her arm. "Don't encourage him, abuela. Not this one."

She studies me for a long minute, a furrow in her brow. "It's the first time I've seen a woman bring a smile to his face, Carmencita. She might make him happy."

I shake my head. "She's almost fifteen years younger than him. She works for him. That's not a cool look these days. What happens to her job if they try to make something work and it doesn't?" I ask. " She has a kid to take care of. She's not the type to risk her job over a man."

"Even one as good-looking as your papá?" She laughs, sitting down on the couch next to me. Her eyes roam over my face. "He gave all his perfect genes to you, you know."

I burst out laughing. As good-looking as my dad may be, I did not get my looks from him. I look exactly like my abuela and my mom, just a shade lighter. Sometimes I look at old pictures of my mom when she was my age, and I swear it's a picture of me. That's how much I look like her.

Abuela must see the cloud of memory cross my face because she reaches out to give me a quick hug. "So she's pretty, is she?" she teases.

I roll my eyes. "I have to say that dad has good taste in women. She's a good cook, too."

Coming through the living room, dad overhears me. "If you ever move out of here, you'll need to find someone who can cook for you," he teases.

"If you manage to catch Sarah, I'm taking abuela with me when I move out," I laugh. "But we'd come over for dinner every night anyway. Sarah can cook, we'll clean up."

"I'll make sure she knows what she's signing up for." He laughs whole-heartedly—but his laughter trails off. He shakes his head soberly. "I shouldn't even be joking about it. She works for me." Walking into the kitchen, he pours himself a finger of rum and throws it back. He pours another two fingers, letting out a long breath.

I look at abuela, eyebrow raised, before looking back at him. "We're just teasing, papi," I say gently.

He nods, his eyes meeting mine. "I know, *cariño*. I know. But there's something special about her. There always has been."

I join him in the kitchen. "Both her and her daughter," I murmur, squeezing his forearm. "Did you know that her daughter Lily dances? She's really good."

"Maybe I'll get to watch her sometime," he murmurs.

"Papi?" I say softly, trying to catch his gaze.

"What, *cariño?*"

"Be careful with her. You're going to have to see her every day at work."

He nods thoughtfully. "For better or worse, right?" He looks into my eyes. "Would you be okay with me dating again?"

I snort loudly. "Is *that* what you're worried about? Papi, please go out and find yourself a woman to make you happy." I shove his shoulder gently. "It's probably safer to find someone you don't work with, but hey—whatever floats your boat—as long as it floats hers, too."

6

SARAH

"Come on in," I call to Carmen as Lily lets her in Friday after-noon. "You didn't have to come so early. He's not picking me up for another hour."

"Lily said we need to help you get all dressed up for the special occasion." Carmen laughs.

I glance at her in jeans and a button-down short-sleeved bright pink shirt with a cream tank underneath. "Hey." I smile, forcing myself to look at her face. "That pink is perfect with your skin tone," I compliment her. "Party in my room, if you must. Lily was just keeping me company."

"Do you want me to do your makeup for you? I'm pretty good with face and hair," she offers. She suddenly takes a step back. "Sorry. I just waltz in here behind your daughter and invade your space. I can wait in the living room until you're done."

I shrug my shoulders. "Please. Feel free. I'd love someone to do my hair and makeup. I'm usually all about practical. It's been a long time since I've gotten dressed up. I open the closet door and pull my dress out, holding it up against my body. "This is what we're working with. What do you think?"

She just stares at me for a long moment before letting out a long breath. "You're going to a gala. You need to look sexy." She takes the dress from my hands. She puts it up against my body again, first holding it at the shoulders, then the waist, her hands on my hips. My breath catches at the contact, and she glances up at me, her eyes widening. She pulls away from me.

Nodding to herself, she hangs the dress back in the closet for now. "Hair up or down?"

I frown slightly. "Is it that bad?" I ask her.

The corner of her mouth twitches. "My dad is a lucky man tonight," she says softly, biting her lower lip. She gives herself a little shake. "With this dress, I think we should do the hair up. Show off your neck a little."

I reach out and put my hand on her forearm. "This is not a date," I remind her quietly. I'm torn, because I want to look good tonight, but I don't want Richard to misread my intentions, either. It's not him I'm dressing for. It's for myself—and if I'm being honest, I want to stand out, because it means people will remember me. That's what networking is all about. Meeting people and making an impression. *Fuck.* If having boobs is going to work in my favor, then I'll use that fact to my advantage. It doesn't mean I'm going home with anyone, though.

Carmen puts her hand over mine. "I know, Sarah." She purses her lips together, studying me for a long moment before she slowly pulls away from me. "Makeup," she says. "Do you want to blend in or stand out?"

I chuckle. "I want to stand out, but not in a sexy way. Just—" I sigh. "I want to make an impression. I want them to remember me tomorrow."

"Okay." She nods firmly. "In here or in the bathroom?" There's a mirror by my dresser, but that side of my room isn't well-lit.

"Everything's in the bathroom. There's enough room for everyone if Lily sits on the throne or the side of the tub."

Thirty minutes later, Carmen has me looking like a movie star. "I've never felt so beautiful." I smile gratefully.

"You're always beautiful, mom," Lily laughs. "This is extra-special beautiful, though."

"Will you help me get the dress on without messing up my face?" I ask Carmen. Her hands have been all over my face and hair, and I've gotten surprisingly comfortable with her in the past hour. Especially for how much her touch on my skin lights up every nerve ending in my body. I start to backtrack. "I'm sorry. If you're not comfortable with that, Lily can help," I murmur, realizing that I'll be in my underwear in front of her.

Lily has already mentioned a few times in front of her that I'm not into men, and I really don't want her to be weirded out if she's figured out that I like women. It makes a lot of women uncomfortable.

Shrugging, Carmen laughs. She pulls the dress out of the closet. "Sarah, relax. I've seen boobs and undies before. Every time I look in the mirror." She unzips the dress and puts the hanger back in the closet. "Lily, come here. Give your mom a shoulder to balance on."

Carmen holds the dress open for me to step into, my hand on Lily's shoulder keeping me steady. I wriggle the dress over my hips and reach my arms into the three-quarter-length sleeves. I push the form-fitting black dress over my shoulders and turn around so Carmen can zip me up. She does so slowly, as if savoring the experience. Her finger traces my skin along the neckline, and I inhale unsteadily.

"Can I take pictures, Mom? I need to get my camera. You look so fancy." Lily looks at me like she's never seen me before. She runs off to her room to grab her phone.

I turn around and look at Carmen, my heart beating too fast. Is she doing this deliberately? I'm sure it's just because she's helping me get ready. Right?

"Very beautiful." Carmen smiles, her eyes soft. "Hold still," she murmurs, reaching up and tucking a strand of loose hair back into place. "You'll make an impression. Everyone you meet tonight will remember you."

"Thanks to you." I laugh, pulling away from her. Not because I'm uncomfortable with her touch. Just the opposite—I want to lean into her, into the electricity I feel when our skin meets. I swallow nervously. She's a client. She's probably straight as an arrow. She's also my boss's daughter. I can't go there.

I need to stop. She's just freer with personal space than I'm used to. It doesn't mean anything.

Richard is dressed to the nines in a bespoke navy suit and professional tie. He looks really good. It's weird to think that this man is the same nervous guy who pulled me into his office Monday morning. He pulls the chair out for me to sit down at our table.

"Thanks," I murmur softly as he sits down at the chair next to me.

With a nod, he motions to the nametags on the table across from us. "Did you see who's at our table?" He seems so much more relaxed than when we're at the office.

"The legendary Bill Harrison," I breathe in awe. "He designed the D.C. Cultural Center. We based a lot of design ideas off his work—it was genius. Is he really here tonight?"

"In the flesh." An older gentleman smiles, sitting down across from me. He's only a handful of years older than Richard, but he looks like he's got more than a decade on him. He has a five o'clock shadow and a playful grin on his face. "Who do I have the pleasure of meeting?" His eyes graze over my body, stopping a little longer than necessary on my chest.

"Sarah Reynolds, with Tomsen Designs." I reach across the table to take his hand. He holds it for a beat too long. *Not* the impression I wanted to be making tonight. "Pleasure to meet such an accomplished artist." I smile tightly, pulling my hand back.

"Richard Tomsen," Richard adds next to me, reaching across to shake Bill's hand firmly. When he lets go, he casually rests his arm across the back of my chair, squeezing my shoulder possessively.

I let out a slow breath, thankful for his keen eye and quick thinking. I shouldn't need a man to protect me from unwanted advances. Bill glances between Richard and me, giving us a slightly disappointed nod.

"I've heard you guys are working on the new cultural center here in town," Bill inquires.

Richard nods. "Sarah's the lead architect and manages the project. It's coming along nicely. It should be ready to open in about six months." He takes a sip of his water, leaning back in his chair. "She's in competition for Lead Architect at the firm." He smiles softly at me, his eyes twinkling.

I laugh lightly, looking at Bill. "We actually looked at your D.C. Center for inspiration, especially in regard to the environmental footprint. Ours will run completely on green energy, and we're planning a green roof to grow vegetables for the underserved in the community. We'll harvest rainwater for the garden."

He nods approvingly. "I've seen the general design online. It looks like an impressive feat. Even bigger than the one in D.C." I notice he doesn't call it *his,* and I wonder if I judged him too harshly, too quickly. As long as he's not hitting on me, I really like him—he's very personable. "We wanted to harvest rainwater in D.C., but local regulations wouldn't allow it."

After dinner, Mr. Harrison leaves us to mingle, and Richard turns to me. "I'm sorry if I made you uncomfortable putting my arm over your shoulder. I got the impression his extra attention wasn't welcome."

"Honestly, I appreciate it," I acknowledge quietly.

"He has quite the reputation as a lady's man." Richard chuckles, standing up. He offers me his hand.

"I've heard that, too." I take his offered hand. "I just wasn't expecting him to come on to me. He didn't, really—but he was definitely checking me out. At least he backed off when he realized I wasn't interested."

Richard nods. "He seems like a great guy. Sometimes I think people like him—people who make their career their life—end up regretting that choice when they get older."

We meander toward the open bar where people are starting to gather. His comment makes me look at him in a different light. "Speaking from experience?" I ask softly.

He chuckles, shaking his head. "I have a beautiful family. Even when my wife was alive, family was always a priority for me. Still is, even though my daughter's been off apron strings for a while now."

"How long has she been gone?" I ask curiously. Carmen has mentioned her mom once or twice, but only vaguely.

"Almost sixteen years. Literally a lifetime ago." His smile is soft, reminiscent of long-ago memories. "Carmencita was only twelve. I don't know which of us was more heartbroken," he says softly.

"It must've been hard to raise her on your own." I know I'm raising Lily on my own, too, but it's different. Everything in my life is stable now, and even though I'm on my own, we have an amazing support network around us, our own found family.

He shakes his head. "Sofia's mom moved in with us after the accident—Carmen's abuela. Her grandmother," he clarifies. "Carmen was hurt pretty badly in the accident. She needed multiple surgeries and lots of physical therapy." He shrugs indifferently. "She's okay now, but I don't know what I would have done without Isabela's help." He puts his hand gently on my upper back, guiding me toward the bar. "Drink? Then I have someone else I'd like to introduce you to."

I nod agreeably. I don't think much about his hand on my back. It feels like a safe place. He seems more protective than anything. Part of me wishes Carmen hadn't dressed me to the nines, but another part of me is grateful. People are definitely taking notice. I wonder how much his being touchy-feely has to do with his offhand comment about Lead Architect. Bob and I have been unofficially competing for the title for years. Until recently, Richard has seemed content to have two lead architects, but he's given me both of the firm's biggest projects in the past year.

I bring my Moscato d'Asti to my nose and breathe in the aroma, the sweet, luscious notes of peach and apricot layered over orange blossom and honeysuckle. I take a sip and roll it around my tongue, sighing happily. I need to come to fancy galas more often.

Richard leads me to a couple near the center of the room. "Alexi, Ella." Richard shakes Alexi's hand, then gives Ella a quick hug. *Weird. Does he know them personally?* "This is Sarah Reynolds. She's designing and building the Carmen's Cultural Center."

I shake Alexi's hand, and Ella pulls me into a hug. *Aha. A hugger.* Ella gives me a huge smile. "I've heard about you. You're pretty young to be designing such big projects, aren't you?"

Richard laughs. "She's the best—age has nothing to do with it. She has innovative ideas and creates designs that are good for the community *and* good for the environment. Plus, she always comes in under budget."

Ella laughs, her eyes slowly appraising me. "To smart, beautiful women," she winks, toasting me.

Richard's hand moves to my lower back, and he takes a step closer to me.

I look at the couple, searching my mental repository. Alexander and Eleanor. Greene. That's it! "Are you guys the ones who designed the Wave Convention Center in the middle of the desert? And the Bloom Campus up near the Twin Cities?"

The Wave Convention Center is a huge project completely off-grid in the middle of the desert, partway between LA and Las Vegas. There's literally a city of housing and other businesses popping up around it, all utilizing the same tech as The Wave.

The Bloom is an extensive campus in the middle of rural Minnesota, decked out to stay off-grid and self-sufficient, even through the area's brutal winters. Thinking outside the box is an understatement. While their work is highly unconventional, it could very well be the basis of the future.

"Yep, that's us!" Ella bounces. "How long have you been working with Rich?" she asks me.

I glance at Richard, curious how much he knows them beyond a professional capacity. I turn back to Ella. "About ten years."

"I hired her when Carmen was just finishing high school," Richard adds. "I remember moving her interview around because of graduation." He chuckles good-naturedly. "I could tell from the beginning she was something special." His hand slides across my back, landing on my hip.

Is he serious? Is he testing to see how far he can go? I try to lean away from his touch without being obvious about it, and he drops his hand, clasping them behind his back without missing a beat. "What are you guys working on these days?" he asks Alexi.

Ella puts her hand on my arm. "Walk with me," she says quietly as Alexi and Richard get into a discussion about their new project.

I smile wide, following her away from the men. I like her energy. Her hand lingers on my arm for a beat longer than appropriate, and I raise an eyebrow at her. "Top secret project I can't know about?" I tease her.

She shrugs playfully, finally letting her hand fall from my arm, only to put it on my lower back to guide me to the women's restroom. "We're keeping it quiet for now, but Richard and Alexi go back more than thirty years, so he's allowed in on our secrets." She opens the door to the restroom for me, then quickly glances across the bottom of the stalls before locking the door behind us.

Raising an amused eyebrow, the corner of my mouth twitches up. "You worried about company?" I ask, my breath catching.

"Did I read you wrong?" she asks, taking a step closer to me.

I bite my lower lip, shaking my head. "No, but I've never—"

She takes a step closer to me and I forget whatever I was going to say. "Can I kiss you?" she asks softly, looking up into my eyes.

"Your husband..." I murmur softly, with a slight shake of my head.

She reaches up, running a thumb across my bottom lip, and I close my eyes. "He doesn't mind," she whispers. Her hand curls around my neck, pulling me closer. I can feel her breath on my lips.

There's a quiet knock on the door, and Ella groans. She closes the gap between us, brushing her lips softly across mine.

A quiet moan escapes my throat, and my hands find her hips. I pull her closer to me.

The knock is louder this time, and she pulls away from me, sighing reluctantly. "I'll be out in a minute," she calls through the door. She slowly traces her finger down my arm, igniting all the nerves in my body before stepping back and unlocking the door. A tall brunette in a slinky emerald dress rushes in with apologies and something about her stomach.

Ella giggles, leading me back out to the dwindling crowd of people. "Do you want to find someplace to disappear to for a few minutes before finding Rich and Alexi?"

I close my eyes and let out a long breath. A quickie with a beautiful woman or going back to my handsy boss? "As much as I'd like to—" I give her a small smile, because I really would like to. "I should probably get back. It seems like people are starting to clear out pretty quickly, and I don't want Richard to wonder where I've gone."

Her laughter is music. "Oh. Alexi would let him know not to worry."

She must see my eyes widen because her brow furrows. "He doesn't know? You seemed kind of cozy, I just thought..."

"Oh, God no. No one at work knows—and we're not cozy. Not even a little bit," I stammer.

"That's not what he seems to think," she murmurs, meeting my eyes.

I sigh loudly. "Yeah, I noticed that, too. This was supposed to be a professional event. I thought we discussed that."

"You should tell him you're not interested." She pokes me. "He's a big boy. He can handle it."

I nod, rolling my eyes. "He put his arm around me at dinner, to get Harrison to back off. Then he made a comment about me being in the running for Lead Architect. I somehow don't think he's going to be happy hearing 'no' from me."

"Just tell him you're not into men. Be honest with him," she suggests.

I shake my head. "I'm not willing to risk my job. I don't really have the best track record when it comes to people accepting me for who I am."

"Sarah." She turns to face me, a hand coming up to cup my cheek. "He's not like that." She punctuates each word, holding my gaze. "Trust me. He probably just said that to get Harrison to back off. Besides—I don't think I've seen him with a woman since his wife died, and that was forever ago." She slowly rubs her thumb against my jawline before letting her hand drop.

I nod, pulling away from her. It's been so long since I've had a woman touch me.

"Sorry," she murmurs into my ear. Then she's laughing, grabbing my arm, and dragging me back to the men. "Hey. Do you want my number, just in case we're ever in the same place at the same time?"

7

CARMEN

"What do you want to do tonight with your mom gone, kiddo?" I ask Lily as we watch Sarah float out the door.

"She's really pretty, isn't she?" Lily says softly. "I wish she could find someone who makes her happy."

"She's not happy?" I'm surprised to hear the concern in her voice. This kid seems pretty mature for a middle schooler.

Lily shrugs. "She's happy enough with work, but it would be nice if she had other things in life to enjoy, too."

"She enjoys your ballet," I chide her gently. "How long have you been dancing? You're really good."

She shrugs again. God, this kid and her indifference. "I started lessons when I was four, but mom taught me before that. She was better than me for a long time. Then she got old." She flops down on the couch and picks up the remote.

I burst out laughing. "Your mom is not old."

"She's almost forty, and she's out on a date with an old man who has a grown-up kid," she challenges me.

"It's not a date, remember? Don't call it that when she's around, or you'll upset her. Although maybe he could make her happy?" I suggest to her gently.

She snorts, shaking her head dismissively. "Are we going to get food or just scrounge? I can make something if you don't know how to cook."

I gasp, dramatically placing my hand over my heart. "You wound me," I say, not entirely feigned. I really can't cook to save my life. "I can't make much, other than basic Colombian dishes. You probably don't have the ingredients, and you don't need that many carbs if you're dancing tomorrow. How often do you have classes?"

Tossing the remote on the coffee table, she heads into the kitchen. I follow her. "Just Monday and Wednesday after school. Then I have a private lesson on Saturday for a few hours," she adds mildly.

"Do you like it? It seems like a lot of pressure for a kid your age." I did ballet when I was her age, too, although I was nowhere near the caliber she is.

She shrugs. Again. "I don't compete. There is no pressure," she punctuates. "I only do it for fun and for a challenge. Sometimes I do recitals with the other girls, but I don't stress about it." She pulls out a box of whole wheat pasta, two thawed chicken breasts, and some cream, garlic, parsley, and a lemon.

"What do you want me to do?" I ask her.

She shrugs. Again. "Just sit and keep me company. Or if you're bored, you could play Candy Crush or something. Whatever you old people like to do to kill time." She smirks at me. "I can make chicken and pasta." Her voice softens. "It's actually one of my favorites, and mom rarely makes it because it's too simple. So when it's my night to cook, I'm the boss. And I'm the boss tonight." She throws her shoulders back and watches me to gauge my reaction.

I roll my eyes at her. I can see what Sarah was saying about her trying to be difficult. "Okay. You're the boss," I grant her. "Tell me if I can help. But FYI, I don't play Candy Crush, and I'm not old."

She's quiet for a moment, heating up the pot of water for the pasta. "Did you dance when you were younger?" she asks me.

"What?" That came out of nowhere.

"You know what an Italian fouetté is." She laughs. "People don't know what that is unless they're into ballet."

Right. That slipped out of my mouth the other night after she surprised me with her beautiful dancing. "I danced when I was younger," I say softly, my eyes clouding over at the memory.

"Why'd you stop?" she asks.

I swallow. "I—" *Oh, come on Carmen. It was sixteen years ago. It's not a secret.* "I was in an accident. I hurt my leg pretty badly."

"It looks okay now," she points out, her glance naturally falling to my legs. "Did you ever go back to it? Dancing?"

I look down at my hands. I did go back to it, once I was able to walk again.

"You don't have to talk about it if you don't want to." She shrugs again. "I just can't imagine giving it up."

"I did go back to it, but it took a lot of work." I manage a weak smile. "It took me more than a year after the accident to be able to walk again, then it took me a few years to be able to do even basic dance moves. A few years, and a God-awful amount of hard work."

"Everything in ballet is hard work, if you're doing it right." She chuckles softly. "That must have sucked, though." She pulls the pasta off the stove and drains it.

"I still dance sometimes," I say quietly. I don't know why I'm telling her this. Not many people besides dad and abuela know. After the accident, dad had one of the rooms in the basement transformed into a dance room, with a barre and mirrors. Once I could tentatively walk again, he paid for private lessons. I couldn't face the other girls when I couldn't even do a proper plié. "I have a mini dance studio in the basement."

Her eyes widen in surprise. "Wait. Are you serious? Like at your house?" She pulls the chicken off the stove and starts to heat the garlic before splashing some cream into the pan. She looks over at me.

I nod, pleased with myself for getting a reaction—any kind of reaction—out of her. "It's not big, maybe the size of your bedroom, but it's big enough to practice." I grin. "It's not really my house—it's my dad's. But I live there, so I guess it's mine, too."

She finishes the sauce, then plates the chicken and pasta. I get up to help her with the plates, but she shoos me back to my seat. "You're a guest. I've got it." She puts a plate in front of me, the other across from me. "What do you want to drink? We have chardonnay or sauvignon blanc—or water, milk, juice..."

"I'll take some sauvignon blanc. But I'll get it. I don't want you handling alcohol."

She laughs, filling up a glass of water and dropping a few ice cubes into it. "Knock yourself out. Mom wouldn't care, though. She lets me have a little sometimes."

"Your mom lets you drink wine? Isn't that illegal?" I ask in surprise.

She bursts out laughing. "You going to turn us in?" She shakes her head. "It's only illegal to buy it for me or sell it to me. I think." She shrugs, pulling a glass out of the cabinet and passing it to me. "Me having a sip of wine in the comfort of my own home in a safe environment isn't going to hurt anyone."

"Fair point." Chuckling, I put the bottle of wine back in the fridge and sit down next to her. "This smells delicious."

"Tastes good, too." She winks at me. We eat in silence for a few minutes before she glances at me. "You still dance? Since you have a studio at home?"

"Well, it's not a full studio—it's just a small room." I raise an eyebrow at her in amusement. "I don't dance as much as I used to. I think of it more as a workout. I still need to stretch a lot so my leg doesn't tighten up. If I don't, I start walking funny."

She finishes chewing a bite of chicken and frowns. "So it's more like physical therapy then."

I shrug dismissively. "I prefer to think of it as stretching and dancing. Sucks less in my head that way."

"How come you still live with your dad? Is it because of money? Mom always says it's hard to afford things with only one working adult."

I huff out an incredulous laugh. There's no way Sarah has trouble paying bills. I don't know what dad pays her, but she's probably the highest paid employee in the company, after him. Maybe Lily's ballet is more expensive than I thought. "Your mom doesn't have trouble paying the bills, does she?"

Lily giggles. "No, but that's because she works her ass off all the time and does everything her boss asks her to do." She scrunches her nose a little. "Even go out on a date with him."

I chew on that for a long minute. Does dad pressure her to do things that she's not comfortable with? She's made a couple comments to me over the past few days that she wasn't sure about going with him tonight. My ass was too busy trying to get out of the gala to really pay much attention to it.

My stomach drops.

Abuela said he's been humming for the past week, and he even asked me last night how I'd feel about him dating again. I groan inwardly. I hope he has enough grace to be subtle if he tries to make a move on her. Would she let him, because she feels like she needs to?

I feel sick.

Lily brings my thoughts back to the here and now. "Do you have a bad job? Is that why you live with your dad?" she asks curiously.

I manage a chuckle. "No. I have a good job. I'm actually the boss." I purse my lips in amusement. "Not here—you're obviously the boss here. But I'm the boss at my work."

"So you just live with your dad cuz he has a dance studio at his house," she announces. You've got to love twelve-year-old logic. "Not a dance studio, just a room," she corrects herself knowingly.

"My abuela is there, too. She lives with us."

"Your grandma?" she asks, looking for clarification.

I nod. "My mom was Colombian. That's where my abuela is from, too. They speak Spanish there."

She laughs. "I know that. I'm taking Spanish in school."

I raise an eyebrow in curiosity. "I didn't know you could start a language in middle school. Do you like it?"

She nods, standing up and taking her dishes to the sink. "I started Spanish and band this year," she tells me.

I bring my dishes into the kitchen, too. While she fills the sink, I grab the washcloth and wipe the table off. "Is it hard to learn a language?" I ask curiously. I grew up with two, but I never tried to learn a new one. It seems like most people have a hard time with it.

"It's close enough to French. We don't really do much besides grammar worksheets and vocab lists, though." She sounds disappointed.

"You speak French?" That surprises me. "You could always find a friend who speaks Spanish. It's more fun to learn a language that way anyways."

"I learned from Madame Grace. My ballet teacher. Mom got me a French nanny for a few years when I was little. Mostly because I asked Madame Grace too many French questions during ballet class." She shrugs again. "Weirdly enough, there aren't any kids that speak Spanish in my grade. Ukrainian, Arabic, French, Korean. But no Spanish."

"Well, you've got me if you want to practice it."

"You'd talk to me when you're not watching me?"

I laugh. "As long as your mom is okay with it, sure." I take the last dish from her and dry it before sticking it back in the cabinet. "What's next, boss?" I tease her. "Game night? Movie? Binge *The Great British Bake Off* on Netflix?"

"I'm kind of tired. Can we just watch a movie?"

"You're the boss. What movie are we going to watch?"

"Can we watch Frozen 2?" she asks hesitantly. "It's my favorite—and I'm going to be stressing for mom until she gets home, so I need to curl up with my fur babies and try to relax."

"Sounds like a perfect plan." I sigh softly. "Do you worry about your mom every time she goes out without you?"

She shakes her head, frowning. "Just when she's out on a date."

"Does she go out often?" I ask curiously. I'm fairly sure she's gay, but if she goes out a lot, I would know her socially—if not personally, I'd at least know *of* her.

She snorts. "No. Never." She grabs Missy—the cat missing a leg—from beside the couch and sits down. She drops a kiss on her head and picks up the remote.

Lily falls asleep curled up with Missy in her lap and the older tabby cat curled up against her hip. I pull a throw blanket over her and turn off the TV. I always assumed apartments were noisy, but it's quiet here tonight.

I walk over to the bookshelf and look at the titles Sarah has. *Succeeding as a Woman in a Man's World. Accepting Yourself.*

Four Disciplines of Execution. Letting Go of Toxic Relationships. Deep Work. Atomic Habits. Does this woman have any interests outside of work?

The door opens quietly, and I glance at the hallway. She doesn't see me as she silently shuts the door, lets out a long deflating breath, and leans her forehead against the door. I take a noiseless step into the living room—out of view of the hallway—to give her a little space. This is her home, and I don't want to witness whatever's going on in her head. I quickly sit down at the end of the couch and pull my phone out, feigning distraction.

She quietly comes into the living room. "She fell asleep?" She looks lovingly at Lily. "Let me guess. Frozen 2? Or Moana?"

I chuckle. She still looks beautiful, even after what seems like a less than stellar evening. "Frozen 2." I smile. In a softer voice, I ask her, "Did you have a good time?"

"I met quite a few new people—including a really fascinating couple who are nationally known, even outside professional circles. It was a productive night." She's an expert at evading questions she doesn't want to answer.

"Did my dad behave himself?" I ask good-naturedly.

Her face drops in surprise, for just a split second before her bright smile is back. "He was a gentleman." She gives me a small smile. "Apparently he's thinking of me for Lead Architect, which was a surprise to me." Her voice is careful, flat.

"That's exciting," I say neutrally, "isn't it?" Lily's earlier words about her mom doing anything her boss asks of her come back to me, and I watch her.

She slips off her shoes, and her shoulders suddenly slump. "It's what I've been working towards for ten years, so yes?" She sounds small and defeated.

"Do you want me to pour you a glass of wine? You look like you could use one," I offer. Not that it's mine to offer, but hell.

"Would you? That would be amazing." She sighs softly. Walking over to the couch, she pulls the blanket off Lily. She runs her fingers through the front of her daughter's hair. "Bug, let's crawl in bed." She picks Missy up and pulls Lily gently off the couch. "Come on, Bug. Bedtime."

"Did he try to kiss you, Momma?" she murmurs sleepily. *What the hell?*

"No, baby. Not yet, at least." Sarah sighs, resigned.

"Good," Lily answers. "Carmen already made me brush my teeth when I changed into my jammies," she mumbles as they disappear into her room. I hear Sarah tuck her in and tell her goodnight.

When she comes back out, I hand her a glass of wine. She sets it down on the counter. "Will you unzip me first? I need to get out of this slinky shit."

I raise an eyebrow. "That slinky shit looks sexy on you, momma." I hold her gaze for a beat before she looks away.

"A little too sexy." She sighs in exasperation. She turns toward her room, and I follow her.

"Unzip me?" she asks, turning her back to me.

I unzip her dress down to the waist, and push the fabric over her shoulders, my hands grazing her bare skin. My fingers must linger a moment too long because her whole body freezes, tensing. She lets the dress drop to the floor.

I pull my hands away, and take two steps back, trying to act natural. Her skin is so soft, and I feel a spark when I touch her. I feel my face flush. *No, Carmen. She's going out with your dad. She's off limits.*

She steps out of the puddle of dress on the floor and walks slowly to the dresser, grabbing a pair of sweats and a Delmont Dance Studios T-shirt. I watch her, transfixed by her muscles and her curves. Thank God she doesn't turn around until she's pulled her clothes on. I watch her take a deep fortifying breath before turning back to me. "So much better," she says with a weak smile. "You want to have a drink with me before you take off?"

I shrug a shoulder. "You want the company?" I don't have anywhere else I need to be—not even anywhere else I want to be, really—but I don't want to be an imposition, either.

"Sure? Unless you have a hot date waiting for you." She laughs lightly.

"Nah, I'm in the middle of a dry spell—maybe because everything is ramping up with the cultural center." I stop myself. "Sorry. You probably don't want to talk about work anymore."

She grabs another glass from the cabinet and pulls out the bottle of wine. She pours me some, handing it to me before sticking the bottle back in the fridge.

She shrugs, picking up her own from the counter. "I don't mind that. It's just when men think that—just because you look nice, you want in their pants. Can't a woman just be good at her job without needing to ride a dick to get to the top?" She motions toward the couch.

I follow her into the living room, slack-jawed. "Are you talking about my dad? Did he do something inappropriate? Because I'll have his balls if he as much as touches you without your consent."

She chuckles rawly. "Your dad was the gentleman who needed to rescue me from three separate assholes who undressed me with their eyes then tried to lay their hands on me."

"You shouldn't need to be rescued," I point out. "But I'm glad he was there to fend them off," I add softly. *I shouldn't be looking at her lips.* "Hold still," I whisper, "your lipstick is smudged." I lean toward her, slowly wiping it from the side of her lip. I smile playfully. "He's not a bad guy, you know."

She lets out a long sigh. "I know. He's actually sweet and funny and smart." She shakes her head. "He's also fifteen years older than me, and he's not really my type."

"You don't go for older men?" I ask, fishing for confirmation of my suspicion.

"I haven't really dated anyone since I had Lily. I've been focused on my career and raising her."

"She's a good kid," I nod. "Sweet. Smart. I can see how she might be a pain in the ass sometimes, though." I chuckle. "She called me old and told me she was the boss tonight."

Sarah laughs. "She's at that stage where she tries to assert her independence one minute, then acts like a five-year-old the next."

"By the way," I say, "I told her she could have my phone number, as long as it's okay with you. I have a little dance studio at home. She wanted to come and see it sometime." I give her a half-smile. "It's not really a dance studio, just a room with a barre and some mirrors, but she seemed pretty excited about it."

"You dance?"

I roll my eyes. "I wouldn't call it that. I stretch and move around a little. I'm well past my dancing prime."

She laughs. "You're still young." She waves a hand through the air dismissively. "You want to watch a movie before you head home?"

8

SARAH

I glance around the rooftop terrace, impressed. I've been to plenty of upscale eateries, but this tops them all. "I'm meeting with Carmen Tomsen, Tomsen Media," I tell the hostess.

She nods, motioning for me to follow her. She takes me to a small table on the periphery, along the glass wall. We can see all of downtown from our table. Before meeting Carmen last week because of the Gala, this was supposed to be our first in-person meeting to discuss the progress on the Cultural Center. I nod my thanks to the hostess as she seats me.

Carmen gives me a bright smile, reaching over the table to shake my hand. "Nice to see you again."

"Ms. Tomsen. How are you today?" It feels a little strange being so formal with her, but this is business, and she is the client for my biggest project.

"Carmen, please. I was cuddled up on your couch with your three-legged cat last Friday night while you were out with my dad. I think you can call me by my first name." She winks.

"Carmen, then." I fight a sigh. "I was hoping that our marketing coordinator could join us today, but something else came up. It's early enough in the build that it shouldn't cause a problem."

Carmen nods. "Of course."

The waiter approaches. "Can I get you ladies started with drinks? An appetizer?"

"Can we get salmon tartare to start with? Then I'd like the seared sea bass. I'll take a glass of chardonnay and ice water with that, please." Carmen nods at me.

"I'll take the grilled vegetable salad with balsamic glaze, and a Sérénité Sunset." I close my menu and place it at the end of the table with Carmen's.

"Before you tell me about the project," Carmen says warmly after the waiter leaves, "tell me how Lily is." She puts her chin in her hand, leaning on the table.

I chuckle softly. "She's been talking about you constantly. You made quite the impression on her."

"I'm not that impressive." She fights a grin. "What kind of nonsense is she telling you about me?"

I huff out a laugh. "Nothing spectacularly interesting. Just that you used to dance. You still do. She wants to come see your dance studio and watch you dance."

The waiter comes back with our drinks and salmon tartare. I take a bite of the appetizer and close my eyes, savoring the burst of citrus, salmon and cucumber on my tongue. I let out a moan of pleasure. "Can you take me out for lunch more often? It's not often I eat this good."

"If you keep making noises like that, I'll take you out to lunch every day," she murmurs, almost too quietly for me to hear.

She clears her throat. "You'll get plenty of lunches out of me before this project is officially complete." She smiles sweetly, returning to our interrupted conversation. "Lily's welcome to come over and see my dance room if she wants to. You too, of course. I'll be around most of the weekend. Just give me a call. Seriously."

I shake my head. "I've got plans tonight. Maybe tomorrow or Sunday? She'll be at Beth and Sophie's tonight."

"Sophie?" She frowns at me.

"Sophie is her friend that lives down the hall. My friend Beth's daughter. She goes there after school most days, until I get home from work."

A shadow crosses her face. "Sorry. My mom's name was Sofia." She shakes off the memories. "What are you doing tonight? Lily said you don't normally go out much." She tries to shift the conversation.

I stare at her for a long minute. Does she seriously not know? I had the impression that she and Richard were close. Why wouldn't he mention it to her? "Just having dinner with a friend." I shrug nonchalantly.

"Just a friend?" she teases me. "Anyone I know?"

I stifle a groan. "Yes, just a friend—and yes, I'm fairly sure you know him pretty well."

Her forehead creases. "My dad?" she asks in disbelief.

I raise an eyebrow in amusement. "You seriously didn't know?" I sit back and take a drink of my cocktail. "I had the impression you two were close."

She purses her lips together thoughtfully. "We are. But when we disagree on something, we generally agree to disagree and leave it alone."

Interesting. "So you disagree about him eating dinner with a friend?" I ask curiously.

She shakes her head. "No. We disagree about him pursuing you." She sits back in her chair to study my reaction.

I school my face, but my stomach turns sour. "Is that what he's doing?"

She takes a sip of her drink, and I watch her swallow. "He's feeling you out, trying not to push you into anything. He thinks as long as he's respecting you, he can pursue you, gauge your interest. Like him being your boss doesn't factor into it at all." She doesn't take her eyes off my face.

"And you disagree?" I ask lightly.

"Fuck, yes," she spits vehemently. She sighs loudly. "It's one thing if you're legitimately interested. But if you're not, it puts you in a position where you have to make a decision whether to accept his advances when you don't want to, or risk the fallout at work. It's not a fair situation to put someone in."

"You'd never put one of your employees in that position?" I ask, trying to pivot the conversation away from me.

"Hell no. I'm not sure if it would be worse with the woman being the boss or the man being the boss. Either way, it puts someone at an unfair advantage. There's a reason it's against the rules in so many companies."

I give her a noncommittal nod and half a shrug. She has a valid point. I really can't argue with her.

"Are you interested in exploring a relationship with him?" she asks softly.

I tilt my head and study her. "I don't know him well enough to judge that yet," I say, dropping my eyes to my drink, wrapping my hands around it.

The waiter arrives with our meal. "Can I get anything else for you ladies at the moment? More drinks?"

Carmen nods to him. "We'll take another round. Thanks."

After he goes, I'm quiet for a few minutes, pushing my salad around while Carmen eats.

She glances at me. "You're good at avoiding things you don't want to talk about, Sarah."

Sitting up, I square my shoulders and start eating. "We're here to talk about your project, not my personal life." I laugh lightly, trying to dispel the awkwardness.

She nods, giving me a small smile. She's not going to let it go that easily, but at least she lets it go for now. "Yes, the Cultural Center. We have a bit of a PR nightmare brewing. But first tell me about your end of the project. How is the build going?"

I frown slightly. "A PR nightmare?" It's not my domain, and it doesn't affect the architectural side of things, but that doesn't sound good.

"The build first," she insists. "Where are we at?"

I nod. "The exterior of the building is complete. Rough-in plumbing, HVAC, and electrical are in. We have a team working on landscaping and exterior work. We're on schedule to be done in six months—probably eight by the time testing and inspections are fully approved. We're looking at April or May. You should be able to have the ribbon-cutting ceremony in June as planned."

Her face breaks into a real smile. "I'm so excited for this thing to open, to get these programs running for the kids."

"A lot of the programs are already running in other locations, right?"

She bobs her head in affirmation. "Yes, but most of them are in cramped quarters. Most of the programs are underfunded and don't have enough volunteers or space to handle all the kids in the community that should be benefitting from them."

"It'll be open just in time for summer break. I've seen some of the plans you have for the center. They're pretty ambitious—amazing, but ambitious."

The corner of her mouth curls up. "Ambitious is my middle name." She bites her lower lip, giving me a strangely hungry look, then sighs. "I grew up with everything I could ever need, and most of what I ever wanted. There were never any obstacles in my way. Not financial, anyways." A cloud passes over her face, but she pushes it away. She takes a deep breath. "I was luckier than most kids."

I would argue with that, knowing that she lost her mom when she was twelve, but that's not what she needs to hear right now. Something Lily said the other day keeps playing in my mind, too.

She was hurt in the accident. It took her a year to be able to walk again. She still has to do therapy for her leg. "And now you want to give back," I finish.

"I want to level the playing field for everyone," she corrects.

"Fair point. So what's the PR nightmare that you mentioned?" I ask, pivoting away from getting too personal. I'm not sure why the two of us are constantly drawn into conversations about our personal lives. This isn't normally how I deal with business relationships.

She pushes her nearly empty plate away and wipes the table with a napkin. Reaching into her bag, she pulls out an iPad and swipes it on. "We've had a little chatter from trolls about the project. It's not unusual to see minimal backlash in a community, especially from," she pauses, choosing her words carefully, "less open-minded individuals."

"Isn't it kind of early for that kind of thing? We're not looking to open the doors for another nine months. It's barely been mentioned yet in the community." I'm not an expert at public relations, but a project of this magnitude, especially when it's funded by individuals, isn't touted until things are much closer to completion.

She nods thoughtfully. "I have my team monitoring for chatter. It's standard for all our clients, of course. It's good to get ahead of these things before they grow roots. Most of the time it passes rapidly, anyway. Trolls usually move on to other targets quickly."

"You don't think that's the case with this one, though," I surmise by the shift in her tone.

She shakes her head. "No. I've had Michael monitoring this particular threat for the past month. Michael Johnson is my PR Specialist, monitoring and watching these types of threats—for the Media company. I have two employees that work under the philanthropic umbrella full-time, but neither of them is an expert in dealing with this type of thing."

My pulse quickens. *Threats?* "What kind of threats? Do I need to increase security at the building site?"

She chews the inside of her cheek, thinking. "No. Not yet. But tell your site super and construction manager to be on alert, and to make sure all workers are cleared to be on premises. When we see him ramp up his game, we'll have to ramp up security. We normally use Sentinel Services when we need security, but we can use your choice of companies if your people are more comfortable with that."

"When, not if?" I ask, concerned. "You anticipate he'll escalate?"

She nods. "It's rare for this type of thing to go past the internet. Most trolls are just bitter losers who have nothing to do but spew nonsense anonymously from behind a screen."

"This guy is different?"

She taps a file on the iPad and pulls up the profile of an older man, maybe in his 60s. "Meet Charles Montgomery. Retired business tycoon, sixty-seven years old. Background in finance. Built his empire by exploiting immigrants, poor peeps, and marginalized communities. There are over five hundred current cases against him in the courts right now for not paying workers what they're owed. Contractors, employees, many who claimed they worked for him under the table and he owes them years of wages."

"Shady business practices, sure. Not to dismiss his behavior, of course, but what makes you think he would escalate to physical violence?"

She taps on a section of his profile and pulls up a list of big NGOs and charities, plus a number of smaller ones I've never heard of. "He's fought hard against a lot of these organizations. Some of them, big names. Many of them, he got shut down. They didn't have the resources to fight him."

I look at the list. "All Shades? Queer Acceptance? Women in STEM? These are all huge organizations. They all run off donations, don't they?" I don't recognize any of the other names here.

She swallows thickly. "We worked for all three of those pro bono. We mostly shut him down, but he's relentless. He has deep pockets, and he's very vocal. He guests a lot on right-wing podcasts and TV shows. There are a lot of sheep that listen to what he says."

"You think you're his next target."

She meets my eyes. "We are his next target. The people of Delmont. This isn't about me, Sarah. It's about the hundreds of thousands of people in this city who need us to level the playing field so they have the chance to play a fair game."

9

SARAH

It's just dinner. He's not expecting anything from me but conversation. Getting to know each other as colleagues, nothing more.

Right.

I decide on black jeans and an emerald green blouse, a simple silver necklace and stud earrings, and minimal makeup. Now that I think about it, it's remarkably similar to how I dress at work—but with my hair down, and jeans instead of a skirt.

Lily is at Beth's with their family for dinner. She told me I need to be home by nine because they have plans tonight—which is just as well, because I don't want to be out with my boss that late. Casual dinner is one thing, but that late is veering into date territory for sure.

When he picks me up, he opens the door for me. When we get to the restaurant, he opens the door for me and offers me his hand. I try to relax, to smile politely.

He must notice my nerves because he puts his hand on my arm. "Sarah, relax. It's just dinner between friends. Okay?"

I nod and exhale slowly.

"We don't have to do this, you know," he says quietly. "Do you want to just go home?"

I chuckle nervously. "We're here. We may as well eat, right?" I kick myself as soon as the words are out of my mouth. That was my opportunity to get out of this without it being awkward. Now he thinks I'm interested—or at least open to the idea.

"Come on," he laughs. "Let's find some food. This is one of my favorite places. They have some of the best Indian and Asian food in the city."

His laugh relaxes me, a little. He puts his hand on my lower back, guiding me toward the restaurant. I fight the urge to shake it off. "Tell me about Lily. Carmen says she's a ballet dancer?"

That, I laugh at. "Lily would say that she dances, but she wouldn't call herself a ballet dancer—some rebellious independent streak that she doesn't want to be labeled. Ask anyone who sees her dance, and they'll tell you she's a dancer. A damn good one, too." I punctuate my words with a nod.

Richard opens the door for me. The hostess catches Richard's eye and leads us directly back to a quiet alcove off the side of the main room. He pulls out my chair for me before sitting across from me at the small private table.

The waitress hands us menus. "Can I start you out with drinks? Appetizers?"

Richard puts his menu down. "I'll have a Kingfisher beer and onion bhaji to start, please."

The waitress turns to me. "I'll have a mango lassi, please, and the vegetable samosas to start." She nods before disappearing.

"So," Richard continues, "why does Lily not consider herself a dancer?"

I chuckle softly. "She was six or seven when Madame Grace—that's her ballet teacher—was pushing her to do something that would help her in a competition. She crossed her arms and said she didn't do ballet for the competition, she did it for fun. We talked about it a few times over the course of the next few weeks, and we decided not to do any more competitions."

Richard laughed. "Strong-willed child."

I shrug in acquiescence. "She loves ballet. She loves the challenge of it. She's one of the best dancers in the Midwest. We've had colleges sending out scouts the past year. Madame Grace says they're just keeping an eye out, but they normally only go to competitions. We've hosted a few at the dance studio, though."

"Does she like to perform?" he asks curiously.

"She loves to perform for small groups. Not on stage, though." I roll my eyes. "Although it wouldn't surprise me if she changes her mind when she gets older. Life has a way of changing the way we see things."

"I get the feeling that it's hard to change the mind of a Reynolds," he teases.

"Damn near impossible," I tell him through laughter.

The waitress interrupts us with our drinks and appetizers. "Have you decided what you'd like to order?"

Richard nods. "I'd like the lamb rogan josh curry please, with some basmati rice on the side."

"I'll take the chicken tikka masala with some garlic naan. Thanks."

She takes our menus. "Enjoy."

"What about you?" I ask him, sure that he's tired of hearing about Lily's ballet. "Do you ever think about kicking Carmen out? There are days I can't wait until Lily is eighteen so I can threaten her with that."

"Honestly, there were a few years when I considered it." He shakes his head slowly. "She still has complications from the accident sometimes. It's not anything serious, but it's nice for her to have me and Isabela around to help when she has a rough day. Plus, she can't cook to save her life."

I chuckle. "Are you serious? Lily said she made dinner last Friday, and Carmen just sat at the table and kept her company." Which is very Lily. She loves to be in charge—until she gets tired of it and wants someone else to do the work.

He laughs. "Maybe if we make dinner a regular thing, Lily can teach Carmen how to cook."

I give a half-shrug. She could also learn from YouTube or Netflix without me going on uncomfortable dates with my boss, but I don't say that out loud. I'm actually enjoying myself, as long as he keeps it in the friend zone. I decide to change topics. "What complications does she have from the accident? I didn't realize she was in a bad accident."

He huffs quietly. "It was the accident that killed Sofia. Carmen almost lost the ability to walk. Her leg was crushed. It took her over a year to be able to walk again."

"Wow," I breathe softly. "I would never know by looking at her. Does she walk with a limp? I didn't notice when I met her." I reach for one of my samosas and take a small bite. My teeth sink into the crispy pastry, and I let out an involuntary moan. These are so good.

He shakes his head. "No. As long as she does her stretches every day, she walks okay. But when she misses them, her gait shifts within a day or two. That's how quickly the muscles start contracting." He reaches for an onion fritter. When he takes a bite, the crunch is loud enough that we both look at each other and burst out laughing.

We talk a little about architecture until our food comes. It's comfortable conversation. Things we like—and don't—about our industry and the recent trend toward a zero-carbon footprint, his favorite projects over the years, other architects we admire.

After our food arrives, he brings up Alexi and Ella, the couple I met at the gala last week.

"Ella said that you and Alexi go way back," I say curiously.

He nods. "We were roommates our freshman year in college, more than thirty years ago. Thirty-four, in fact." He started college the same year I started kindergarten. That blows my mind.

"They're very innovative in their approach to new—" My phone rings in my purse. "Sorry. I want to make sure everything's okay at home," I apologize. "It's Lily. Let me take this really quick?"

He nods, and I stand up to take the phone call in the hallway. "Hello? Bug? Is everything okay?" I glance over at our table and notice him pulling his phone out, too.

"Mom? Are you having fun on your *date?*" Lily asks sweetly.

"Bug, you did not call me to ask me about my dinner. What's wrong?" But already, my racing heart is slowing down. She wouldn't be teasing me if there was really something wrong.

"Beth and Sophie are going to leave soon, but I was wondering if Carmen could pick me up and show me her dance studio. She only lives about fifteen minutes away from here. She says she's a safe driver, and she'll bring me home once you're home. Or if you and *Richard,*" she singsongs his name, "come to their house after dinner, we can go home together. Please? Pretty please??"

"Is Beth there? Can I talk to her?"

Lily hands the phone to Beth. "Sarah? I talked to Carmen. She said she's met you and Lily, and you know her dad. Otherwise, I would have flat-out told her no."

I laugh softly. "Carmen is okay. I trust her. She hung out with Bug last week when you guys were gone Friday night—when I went to the gala."

"Okay. I thought she sounded familiar. You're okay with her going over there for a little bit?"

"Sure. Send me a text once she gets picked up, please. Just so I know." I'm paranoid about always knowing who she's with. I don't always need to know where she is, as long as she's with someone I trust—but she's still my little baby. "Pass me back to her."

"Of course. Here she is."

"Can I go, Mom? Please?" Lily's whine comes through the phone again.

"Yes. Text me when you leave and when you get there, and wear your seatbelt. Be good for Carmen."

"I will, Mom. Thank you!" she squeals.

"Have fun," I tell her, ending the call.

I head back to our table. Richard has an amused look on his face.

"Let me guess." I laugh. "That was Carmen checking if she could bring a friend home for a dance party."

He nods, his eyes twinkling. "What did you say? Will you let her?"

"Yes, but I expect texts when she leaves Beth's, and again when they get to your house. I hope you don't mind if I keep my phone out. It's our normal system. I need to know where she is or who she's with."

He nods. "Do you leave her home alone yet? It's a hard transition age—for her and for you." He picks up his fork to continue with dinner.

"A little here and a little there. Sometimes she'll stay at home by herself when she knows Beth and Sophie are down the hall." I take a bite of my chicken. "Was it a hard age for you? Giving Carmen more freedom?"

He's silent for a long beat, his eyes on his plate. "It was different for us. Carmen was twelve when her mom died." He swallows thickly. "Even besides that—after the accident, she couldn't do much of anything by herself for a long time."

"I'm sorry," I murmur, not knowing what else to say.

He lifts a shoulder in a half-shrug. "It was a long time ago. She's okay now." He straightens his shoulders. "We're all okay now." His voice is stronger this time. He gives me a small smile. "Would you like dessert?" he asks as he sees the waitress heading our way.

"I don't know if I have any room left," I admit, my stomach full.

"You should try the mango kulfi," the waitress says with a smile. "It pairs well with your drink," she nods toward me. "I can get you a small bowl to share."

Richard nods. "That would be lovely, thank you." After she leaves, he turns to me. "I'm sorry. I should have asked if you mind sharing. I shouldn't have presumed."

I laugh, more relaxed than I've been all night. "It's fine. It's just ice cream." I almost make a joke that as long as he doesn't try to take me home, we'll be fine. But then I remember that he *is* taking me home to his house—because my daughter is there. That's as safe a way to end the evening as any, I think gratefully.

"Can I ask you a question, Sarah?" Richard's voice is soft but serious.

I take a quiet breath and pray this whole thing doesn't blow up in my face. I nod. "What is it?" I ask him, meeting his eyes.

"Whatever this is between us—whether it ends up being just friends, or more than that," he starts. He puts his hands up. "Seriously, either way. Honestly, I'd love to get to know you better and see if this goes anywhere, but if it's just friends, I'm one hundred percent okay with that. There's no expectations and no pressure."

No pressure on him. The corner of my mouth curls up. "I'm good with keeping things as friends." I think I've told him this a dozen different times in a dozen different ways in the past few weeks, but I don't want to point that out. "Was there a question in there somewhere?"

He laughs. "I was getting to that." He takes a long breath. "I want to prepare you to take the Lead Architect position for the company."

I raise an eyebrow. "What about Bob? He has more experience and seniority than I do."

"You're a better architect. You're more forward-thinking. You're more resourceful. You're more focused." He studies me for a long beat. "Bob is very good at his job. But as a leader for the company, and potentially someone who can take over the company when I retire, you have that potential. He doesn't."

I nod slowly, trying to think. Of course he waits to bring this up until after I've had two cocktails and my reaction time is slowed. "This has nothing to do with the fact that you want to get into my pants?" I ask, as shocked as he is at the words that come out of my mouth.

The waitress clears her throat as she approaches with our mango ice cream. "Another round of drinks?" she asks, feigning that she didn't overhear that last piece of the conversation.

Richard chuckles, but his face reddens. "No, thank you. We'll take the check though." He smiles at her.

Smirking at him, I raise an eyebrow, waiting for an answer to my question.

He clears his throat uncomfortably. He didn't plan to be called out like that. To be fair, I hadn't planned on it either, but he's the one who brought it up.

"If I'm sleeping with the boss, that's the only reason I got the position," I point out.

"Sarah, everyone knows you're the best person in the office for the position." He closes his eyes and shakes his head. "But I was serious. It's not contingent on seeing you outside of the office."

"It has nothing to do with you wanting to get into my pants." I drop my gaze to study the bowl of ice cream between us. I take a small bite and close my eyes. *Damn, this shit is good.*

He shakes his head. "One has nothing to do with the other," he mumbles.

I nod. "You should have some of this ice cream. It's really good." I meet his gaze. "I'm happy to be friends, Richard. I actually enjoyed myself tonight, to be honest. I just don't think a romantic relationship in the workplace would be a smart idea for either of us."

He nods, then takes a bite of the ice cream between us. "Mm, that is good," he murmurs. "Are we okay?" he asks quietly.

I nod. "Of course." *As long as I can do my job without unreasonable expectations.*

We pull into the driveway at Richard and Carmen's house, and he comes around to open the door for me. His phone dings, and he pulls it out to look at it.

"It's Carmen. She says Lily's downstairs dancing. She's in the office watching. Come on," he says with a smile, putting his hand on my back to guide me. I hide my frustration with an inaudible sigh.

He unlocks the front door and leads me through the main living room. A huge fireplace sits nestled into one wall. Opposite that, huge front windows light up the whole room. He knocks quietly on the office door and pushes it open. There's a huge seventy-inch screen TV against the far wall. My daughter's on it, almost life-size. Richard guides me to the open space in front of the screen next to Carmen.

"Good to see you again," Carmen says, hugging me tightly before her eyes turn back to Lily's image. Richard steps closer to me, his arm across my back, his hand resting on my hip.

I hear a slight shuffle and glance toward the door. An older woman, Carmen in thirty or forty years—or at least what I imagine she'll look like then—puts her finger to her lips and nods toward my daughter dancing on-screen.

Carmen sits down on the sofa and grabs my hand, pulling me down next to her. "She's really amazing," Carmen says. I think she's talking to Richard. I'm not sure how much he knows about dancing—if he can understand half of what Lily's doing, lost in her own little world. She looks so happy, so free.

Carmen's grandmother comes into the room, quietly standing next to Richard.

"Abuela," Carmen says, finally noticing her. "That's Sarah's daughter Lily. I told you what a beautiful dancer she is. *¿Recuerdas?*"

"*Claro, es increíble,*" her grandmother murmurs. She's incredible. "*Mijo,* come with me a minute," she whispers, pulling him out of the room.

"How long has she been dancing?" I ask Carmen, pulling my leg under me. "You guys can't have been home very long."

She shakes her head, shifting so our shoulders are leaning against each other. "Maybe fifteen minutes? Not long. She grabbed her ballet shoes before we left. I connected her to the Wi-Fi here so she could turn some music on. There's a whole collection of classical stuff attached to the computer down there."

"So this is your little dance studio, eh?" I ask her playfully. "It's not really that little."

Carmen looks up at Richard, standing in the doorway. He gives us a sad smile. "She's a beautiful dancer," he says to me.

"Pápi, occurió algo?" Carmen asks him something I don't understand.

"Nada, solo que tonto soy." He chuckles, shaking his head. "I'll be back in a minute."

I glance at Carmen. "What was that about?" I ask her.

The corner of her mouth curls up in amusement. She shakes her head. "He just realized why he's been friendzoned." She raises an eyebrow at me, waiting for me to understand.

My body stiffens against hers. I start to pull away, but she grabs my hand and pulls me against her warmth.

"Relax," she whispers. "He's fine. He just feels like an idiot. He'll get over it."

10

CARMEN

It's Sunday, and Sarah and Lily are over for the afternoon. They've been coming over often on Sundays so Lily can dance in her own little studio. She loves it. Olivia and Miguel were going to bring the little ones over today, too, but Fia and Talia have a cold—most likely something that Nathan brought home from school.

Sarah and I are sitting outside in the backyard, relaxing. Lily is dancing. I'm not sure where dad and abuela are, but the house is quiet. It's nice like this.

Sarah glances at me. "You miss the little ones?"

I shrug my shoulder. "A little, when it's quiet like this."

"You ever think of having your own?" she prods curiously.

"Thought about it," I say softly. For a long time, I was so sure I wanted to be a mom. But with my twenty-ninth birthday next week, I'm starting to wonder if my time is running out—or if it's really what I want anymore. While I've always wanted to be a mom, I don't want to be a single mother. I've seen how much work the kids are for Olivia and Miguel, and I can't imagine choosing to do it on my own.

She gently bumps her knee against mine. "Penny for your thoughts," she murmurs.

We've become friends over the past few weeks. More because of Lily than anything, I think. It's nice to have someone to talk to. I have a lot of business associates and acquaintances, but few real friends. "I don't know," I answer honestly. "I always wanted to be a mom. I love kids. I love Lily. Nathan and the twins. But my clock is ticking." I chuckle softly.

She scoffs. "You're still so young. How old are you?" She pokes me in the ribs with her elbow.

I close my eyes, breathing in her scent. She smells of peaches and cinnamon. Sometimes I wish she wouldn't sit so close to me. It brings back the memories of her soft skin that night I unzipped her dress after the gala, how she casually walked, naked except for her black silk bra and panties, across the room in front of me. I pull away from her, putting a few inches between us, and push away the fire in my belly. "I'll be twenty-nine next week," I tell her.

She rolls her eyes, laughing. "You have years left before your clock runs out, Carmen." She lets out a long breath. "Can I ask you something?"

I frown at her. "Of course. What is it?"

"It's personal. You don't have to answer if you don't want to," she says nervously.

"Okay... Whatever it is, just ask. We're friends, right?"

She nods. "Why do you pull away from me every time we get close? I do my best to respect your space, not to do anything to make you uncomfortable. But it seems like you are, anyway."

I look at her curiously. "You think I'm uncomfortable with you?" I sigh quietly, shaking my head.

"I know you are, Carmen. Every time I get close to you, you pull away from me."

"I'll answer your question, if you really want to know," I say reluctantly. "Can I ask you something first, though?"

"Of course." She nods. "What is it?"

"The night of the gala last month," I say with a pause. "Who smudged your lipstick?" Her eyes widen, her hand covering her mouth. She reddens, and I laugh. "I'm assuming it wasn't my dad."

She shakes her head. "Do you know Alexi and Ella Greene? Friends of your dad's, apparently?"

I nod. "Sure. We've known them for years. Dad went to college with him, and they've been buddies ever since. We don't see them a lot because they're rarely in the area, but yes. Why?"

She chuckles. "Ella saw your dad trying to move in on me and rescued me. I followed her to the bathroom, and she locked the door behind us."

"You didn't!" I snicker loudly. "She's almost as old as my dad!"

"You realize I'm almost forty. Ten years really isn't that big of a difference. Besides, she looks good." She grins. "That, and she had me pinned against the bathroom door."

I smack her shoulder and lean back, crossing my arms over my chest. "I didn't take you for the type that goes for a quickie in a public bathroom." Maybe I need to reconsider my view of her.

She shakes her head. "I'm not. I've never done that before." She bites her lip thoughtfully. "It was just a kiss. If that woman hadn't interrupted us with her insistent digestive distress, I might have made an exception for her. It *was* a nice bathroom." She chuckles.

"Did dad notice?" I ask, fighting back laughter.

"I don't think so. He was too busy trying to play it cool and get his hands all over me without my noticing." She rolls her eyes. "Okay, I answered your question. Will you answer mine?"

I close my eyes and take a deep breath before I look at her. "Because when you're close to me—close enough for me to smell you, close enough to feel the heat of your body—I'm afraid I'm going to touch you in a way you don't want me to." I swallow thickly. I lean away from her. "I don't want to make you uncomfortable like he did."

She reaches over and takes my hand, tracing her finger down my arm. She turns my hand over in hers, her thumb gently rubbing along the inside of my wrist. "Not even remotely the same thing," she whispers, her eyes meeting mine. Her eyes drop to my lips, and she swallows.

"Mom!" Lily comes barreling through the doorway, breaking our trance. "Oh." She stops suddenly, staring at us. She looks at us curiously for a minute and laughs. "God, it's about time you guys figured it out. Never mind, it can wait." She turns around and heads back into the house.

Sarah laughs like a schoolgirl. "Carmen." Her voice is low, her eyes on my lips.

"Wait a minute, Sarah." I close my eyes, struggling to find my voice. "We can't do this. We work together."

"It's not the same," she whispers.

"Girls!" Dad hollers through the door before barreling through.

Sarah turns my hand over and gently kisses my palm. "Raincheck," she softly whispers into my palm before letting go.

"What is it, Dad?" I try to regulate my voice. I'm not frustrated with him; I'm frustrated with the circumstances. *No, I'm frustrated with him.*

He sighs loudly. "Sorry to interrupt." He gives us a small nod of acknowledgement before continuing. "Remember your troll friend, Chump Change?"

"Charles Montgomery," I correct him wryly. I turn to Sarah. "The guy I told you about at lunch a few weeks ago."

"I had Ethan create some monitoring alerts. We got some hits," he says excitedly.

"Dad, settle down. Have him send stuff to Mike in the office tomorrow. Actually, we should probably have them coordinate. Ethan can probably learn about better monitoring techniques from him." I give him a hard look. When he doesn't get it, I widen my eyes in exasperation. "Can you go please?"

He looks back and forth between me and Sarah, his eyes growing wide in understanding. "Oh, sorry," he whispers in a hushed voice. He shuffles back into the house.

Sarah groans, covering her face with her hands. "Fuck," she breathes, somewhere between horror and laughter. "I'm almost forty years old, and I don't think I've ever been so mortified to be caught by a girl's dad before in my life."

"He'll get over it," I laugh, wiping the tear from a corner of her eye.

"Wait," she says suddenly, pulling my hand away from her face. She kisses my palm and lets go. "I thought he figured that out a few weeks ago, that night you first let Lily come dance in your studio."

I roll my eyes with a chuckle. "I seriously have no clue. We haven't talked about it. I told you. We don't agree on the way he approached that whole thing, so I stay out of it."

She leans back suddenly and closes her eyes, groaning. Her face pales.

"Sarah? What's wrong?" She looks like she's going to be sick.

She shakes her head, trying to clear her thoughts. When her eyes open and she looks at me, she's frightened. "What if he fires me?" She swallows thickly, glancing around us.

"What do you mean? Why would he fire you? You're his best architect."

"Carmen, a lot of rich white guys like to keep the status quo. He might be homophobic."

I just stare at her for a long minute. A very long minute.

She swallows again. "I've lost a lot of things in my life because there are people who don't agree with my lifestyle."

I shake my head, slack-jawed. I honestly don't even know what to say. I pull my phone out of my pocket and text Lily. *Come out here and bring my dad please, asap.* I put my phone down on the table next to us. "You honestly believe that." It's not a question. I can tell by her ashen face and the fear in her eyes that she believes it.

Lily sticks her head out the door and looks at me.

"Come here, sweetie. Is my dad behind you?"

Lily nods, pulling my reluctant dad through the doorway.

As soon as he sees Sarah's ashen face and my wet eyes, he rushes over to us. "What's wrong?"

"Mom? What is it?" Lily sits next to Sarah, and Sarah pulls her into her lap.

Dad looks at me. "Carmen? What is it?"

I bite the inside of my cheek. "Sarah's afraid you're homophobic and she might lose her job." I try to choke back my tears. I see Sarah's arms tighten around Lily as she hides her face in her hair.

Dad's face drops in shock as he looks at Sarah and Lily. Lily eyes him curiously, almost defiantly. "*Mija,*" he says to me softly without taking his eyes off Sarah, "can you take Bug in the house? *Porfa?*" He looks at Lily. "She'll be okay. I promise."

Lily turns to look her mom in the eye. An entire conversation takes place between them without a word—there's so much said between the two of them that no one else hears. After a long moment, Sarah nods, and Lily takes her mom's face in her hands.

She kisses her mom's forehead and squeezes her tightly before hopping off her lap. She grabs my hand and pulls me back into the house.

SARAH

Richard studies me for a long minute once Carmen and Lily disappear. He sits down next to me and gently takes my hand, like I'm fragile.

"You realize my daughter's gay, right?" His voice is quiet.

I nod. Like he didn't just walk in on us about to kiss.

He sighs, shaking his head. "Sarah, I may be the blindest fool in history, but who you love..." He squeezes my hand. "If you're lucky enough to find love in this crazy world, I'm going to be happy for you no matter who it's with. The same with Carmen. Why should it matter to me who you love?"

I bite my lip, fighting back tears. I let out a choked sigh of relief. "I'm sorry."

He shakes his head with a dumbfounded chuckle. "No, Sarah. I'm sorry. I should have realized at the gala you weren't interested. I shouldn't have even invited you out for dinner."

I shake my head. "You never pushed me. I always agreed to it." My voice shakes.

"Carmen was right, though. I put you in a position where you felt like your promotion, or even your job, could be compromised if you didn't go along with it. No matter how many times I told you it was your choice."

I don't know what to say to that, so I just look down in my lap, wringing my hands.

"Hey. Look at me," he says gently. I look up to meet his eyes. "Your job is safe. Okay?"

I nod, breathing a little easier.

"You know there are other gay people in our office, right?" he says suddenly.

I frown at him in surprise.

"It's none of my business, though." He shrugs a little. He bites his lip and studies me for a beat. "I don't know who's hurt you in the past," he says quietly, "but I'm sorry, for whatever they did to you."

11

SARAH

"Sarah, I told you. Justin and JJ are out until at least eight, and Avery is at a movie with Kayla. Her mom is picking them up after. I made lasagna for dinner, and we need extra mouths to eat it, so get your asses over here." Beth isn't going to let this go.

"Fine. We'll be home in a few minutes, okay?" I click the call off and shrug to Lily.

"We're being forced into *lasagna-tude* tonight, aren't we?" She laughs. "Sophie told me that Avery and Kayla were going out to see that new movie, and JJ has a game tonight, so I figured. Plus, I think Beth wants to grill you about Carmen," she says smugly.

"There's nothing to grill about Carmen. We're just friends," I point out.

She rolls her eyes. "Mom, the tension between you two is so thick I could cut it with a knife. You seriously just need to give in to it. You'll be happier when you do."

"I am happy," I argue, laughing.

"I said happier, Mom. That means more happy than you are now. Try it. I dare you to prove me wrong." She giggles, pulling out her phone. "Have you at least talked to her?"

"Since when are you an expert on relationships? Do you have your eye on someone?" I try to turn the tables on her.

"I'm twelve, mom. Nice try." I notice she doesn't answer my question, though. "Is Mr. Tomsen treating you okay at work?" she asks, pivoting topics.

I park the car, and we each grab a dance bag before heading for the elevator. "He's been fine. We talked. I haven't had any problems with him or anyone else."

We walk into the empty elevator, and she pushes the button for the fourth floor. "I told you that not everyone is like grandma and grandpa," she says quietly, wrapping her arm around my waist.

I know it's nobody's business who I choose to love, but it was drilled into me for so long that what I am, *who* I am, is wrong and broken. It's hard to completely let go of all that negativity my parents tried to instill in me. "I know, baby." I kiss her gently on the top of her head as the door opens on our floor.

After we drop Lily's dance things off at our apartment and I slip my shoes off, we head down the hall to Beth and Sophie's. Lily knocks on their door before simply walking in. "We're here," she calls loud enough for everyone to hear.

Sophie silently motions to Lily, and they head straight for Sophie and Avery's room.

Beth puts a sheet of garlic bread in the oven, then pulls me into a hug. "I want to hear all about this woman."

"You met her a few weeks ago," I remind her. "She picked Bug up to go see the dance studio at her house."

"Yesss, that was when you were dating-slash-not-dating her dad," she reminds me. "You want some wine?" At my nod, she pulls two glasses out of the cabinet. She pours the cheap wine and hands me one. Pulling out a chair, she sinks into it with a tired sigh.

I sit across from her and take a sip of wine. "He eventually realized that I wasn't interested in a romantic relationship and let it go." I shrug nonchalantly. "He apologized the other day for putting me in an awkward position. We sat down and had a long talk to clear the air between us. We're both past it."

"And Carmen?" she asks, drawing out her name.

I sigh softly. "We're friends, but that's all there is to it." I bring the wine to my nose and close my eyes, inhaling the scent. It's not very effective. Beth and Justin have mediocre taste in wine. At best.

Beth laughs. "This is cheap wine, Sarah. You can't do that and think it exempts you from the question."

I give her a guilty smile. "I like her, but it's complicated. There's not really anything to tell, to be honest."

She tilts her head and looks at me. "Complicated how? Because she's a lesbian and you're afraid to get involved with someone who can make you happy?"

Nail, meet hammer.

I shake my head. "No. I mean, not really." I let out a strangled laugh. "I like her, Beth. I really like her. But she's ten years younger than me. Her dad is my boss."

"Her dad was trying to get in your pants a month ago," she reminds me.

I wave that off. He and I have talked about it and moved on. "She's my client. The project I'm working on is for her company."

"So she's tangentially related to the company who's paying for your current project. That's not a big deal, Sarah."

I shake my head. "She's the fucking CEO, and it's her pet project." It's more complicated than that, especially for Carmen, but Beth doesn't need the details. "She is literally paying my bills right now."

She nods. "Okay, that complicates things a little. But you don't actually work with her much, do you?"

I take a long breath. "It's not even that. I think we could work around that, but she feels like she's putting me in the same position as her dad put me in."

"But—" Beth stops to think about that, and her voice drops. "Oh." Because if Carmen tries to pursue something with me, it is—literally—the exact same situation Richard put me in a few weeks ago. "But you like her," she argues.

"Yes. We were going to talk about it the other day, but then something else distracted us. I haven't had a chance to talk to her since then. She's texted me a few times, but I haven't answered yet."

The timer rings for the garlic bread, and she gets up to pull it out of the oven. "Are you avoiding her?"

I sigh, shaking my head. "Not really, no. She's the one who said we need to back off, and I'll try to respect that. I still want to talk to her about it, but I don't really know what to say."

"You'll *try* to respect that? What does that mean?" She turns and catches my eye. Stares me down, is more like it.

I swallow. "I *will* respect it," I say. "The project will be done in a few months. The grand opening is in June. So maybe I bide my time. If we're both still interested, then we can see where things go."

"You should still talk to her," Beth points out. She puts the lasagna on the table and tosses a piece of garlic bread on each of the four plates.

"I will," I promise. I wonder if Lily orchestrated this whole lasagna-fest just to get me to talk to Beth about Carmen.

"Sophie, Lily." Beth barely raises her voice, but rings the bell on the kitchen counter. "Dinner's ready."

We're almost finished eating when my phone rings. We don't have a hard and fast rule, but we normally ignore phones while we're eating.

"You should get that, Mom," Lily says placidly. She looks at Beth.

I look at my daughter curiously and grab my phone from my pocket. Carmen. Lily raises an eyebrow at me and nods at my phone.

"I thought we should talk," Carmen says when I meet her at the elevator.

"You mean Lily thinks we should talk," I say drily.

Carmen laughs. "Come on, Sarah. Great minds think alike, right? She just wants you to be okay. So does my dad. So do I." Her voice softens.

I swallow, the emotion rising in my throat, and I nod. I open the door and let her in. "I didn't know there was much to talk about," I say quietly. "It sounded like you already made up your mind." I look at her for a long moment. "You want some wine? Lily's next door, but she'll be back soon. She has ballet early."

"Yes to the wine, and yes to Lily coming home whenever she comes home. I'm not planning to lay you out and ravish you tonight," she teases, laughing.

I bite my lip and glance at her. I pour us both a glass of wine, handing her one. "That's a bummer." I fight a smile.

The corner of her mouth twitches up, and she raises an eyebrow at me. "You're not going to make this easy for me, are you?" she asks playfully.

"If you're not interested, all you have to do is tell me that." I sit down at the table and motion for her to take a seat.

She sits across the small table from me, her hands fiddling with the glass of wine. She takes a slow deep breath. "Is my dad treating you okay at work? Is he giving you a hard time?"

"Everything's fine at work, Carmen. Everything is fine with your dad. Better than fine, actually. We talked." I shrug my shoulder. "You didn't drive all the way to my place to talk to me about your dad."

"You're right," she says, watching me.

"Can you just say what you want to say and get it over with?" I know I sound irritable. I don't mean to, not really, but this is driving me crazy.

She reaches across the table and puts a hand over mine. "Tell me how this is any different from what my dad was doing a few weeks ago." Her voice is soft.

"I don't work for you, Carmen. This project—it's just for a few months. It's short term."

She chuckles softly. "*That* is the difference?" She trails a finger along the back of my hand, and I feel a shiver course through me.

I pull my hand away from her. "Now you're just fucking with me." I sigh softly. "Seriously, just tell me you're not interested, and I'll let it all go. It's just... A few days ago, I could have sworn you wanted to kiss me."

I push my chair back from the table and stand. "Look. It's fine. Let's just keep everything professional. If Lily wants to go to your house to dance, that's fine." I walk toward the big window in the living room, trying to steady myself.

This is why I don't want to talk. For the first time in fifteen years, I wonder if I can finally accept myself for who I am, to let myself explore the possibility of being happy. Apparently not.

Carmen comes up behind me. I can see a weak reflection of her in the window. She reaches out to touch my shoulder, but pulls her hand back at the last minute. "Sarah," she chokes softly. "We should wait until the project is done." Her voice is barely a whisper.

I shake my head. "I can't." I take a step away from her and turn to face her. "I can't *want* you like this for the next six or eight months and not touch you." I step closer to her, into her personal space.

She lifts her face and looks into my eyes, searching. For what, I honestly don't know. She can read everything in the heavy cadence of my breath. Her gaze drops to my lips. Her tongue slowly traces her bottom lip.

My breath catches. I shift my gaze, raising my head and looking over her shoulder. I can't look at her. I can't breathe when I look into her eyes.

She raises her hand, her fingers almost brushing my cheek, before she makes a tight fist instead, her breath ragged. She blows out a long breath, letting her finger ghost over the hollow of my throat. Then her warm breath is on my neck, her soft lips, the nip of her teeth.

I swallow unsteadily, my throat bobbing under her hungry lips. I close my eyes and step away from her. "You can't have it both ways." I struggle to find my voice. "Maybe you can do that with other women, but I can't." She's still standing close to me, and I want so badly to reach out and touch her. I don't move, but she must feel me stiffen.

She steps back, giving me some space. "Are we okay?" she asks quietly, her voice desperate.

"We're fine," I tell her, resigned. "Like I said, if Lily wants to go over to your place to dance, it's fine. I just think we need to keep some distance between us when we're not working."

12

CARMEN

I look up at the knock on my office door. "Michael? What is it?" It's my PR Specialist. He's got his game face on.

"We need to call a meeting with your dad's team. Montgomery is escalating again."

I groan loudly. "Can you call Ethan—" I shake my head, thinking. "No, we need everyone on this if we're going to stop him. You. Emily for socials. Lucas for the creative side." I click my pen a few times, contemplating. "I want all three of you ready to go in thirty minutes. Can you let them know for me, please?"

"Yes, ma'am." He grins. He loves this shit. I swear he gets off on it.

"Michael?" I call after him before he pulls the door shut behind him. He glances at me expectantly. "Don't *ma'am* me."

He laughs. "Right. I'm on it, boss."

I pick up the phone. For a brief moment, I debate calling dad instead of Sarah, but that's just me being a chickenshit. We've emailed a handful of times over the past few weeks. Lily has come over to dance a few times, but I haven't really talked to Sarah since the night she shut me down. After I tasted the soft skin of her neck.

I clear my head of the unwanted memories. *Correction.* They're not unwanted, but they're unwelcome at the moment. I dial her number. For a minute, I wonder if she's going to answer.

She picks up on the third ring. "Sarah Reynolds," she says softly. She knows it's me.

"Sarah." I swallow, pushing away my feelings. I don't have time to deal with that right now. "It's Carmen Tomsen, from Tomsen Media," I say, like she doesn't know exactly who she's talking to. "Carmen."

"I know," she says wryly.

"Sorry. Look—" I sigh. "Let's do this awkward shit another day, okay? We have a problem with the Charles Montgomery situation. Is your Construction Manager in the office today? David, right?"

"Yes, he's here. I think everyone on your project is in the office today. Do you want me to get everyone on a conference call?" she asks.

I shake my head. "No. I've already got half my team prepping for a field trip to your office. You think your boss will let us borrow a conference room for an hour? There are four of us coming—plus your Con Man, and anyone else you want in the loop. Socials, marketing. I want Ethan Mitchell there, too. He and Michael will need to coordinate some things."

"David hates being called a con man. Don't let him hear you call him that." Her construction manager. She laughs at my shortening of his title. "When will you be here?" she asks seriously.

"We'll be on the road in half an hour. So forty-five minutes, maybe. An hour tops, depending on traffic and how long it takes Emily and Lucas to get ready."

"We'll be waiting. Did you talk to Richard yet?" she asks.

"No. Can you fill him in? I'm not sure if he wants to get involved or not. Besides being in the loop, I'm not sure how much help he can actually be. His skill sets are elsewhere."

"I'll fill him in. He can decide what he wants to do with the information."

I look around the room at the other eight people around the conference table. I reach my hand across the table to the one woman I don't know. "Jennifer, right?"

The petite blonde nods. "Marketing coordinator."

I shake her hand warmly and give her a quick smile. "Carmen Tomsen. Nice to meet you." I look around at everyone milling about. "All right. If you can all take a seat, please."

Everyone sits down around the table, Sarah's people on the left side, my people on the right. "We have a public relations nightmare on the horizon. Name is Charles Montgomery. He's coming for us." I pull up a picture on the tablet and cast it to the screen beside me. "He's more affectionately known by my team as Chump Change. Rich bigot who likes to make life difficult for anyone who believes in equal rights, equal protections, and equal opportunities for people who aren't straight rich old white men." I glance at my dad. "No offense, Mr. Tomsen."

"None taken." He chuckles, putting his hands up in a motion of surrender. It occurs to me that this is the first time I've held a meeting of this magnitude with my dad in the room. I briefly wonder how he feels about me taking charge, but then I dismiss the thought. This is my playing field. This guy has been my nemesis off and on for years, and I'm the best person to bring the fight to him.

I look at Sarah's team. David Sanchez, Construction Manager. Jennifer Turner, Marketing Coordinator. Ethan Mitchell, the online Public Relations Manager that's been working with Michael to monitor these early signs. "You guys," I nod towards Sarah's team, "are going to think we're overreacting. I want you to hear me out before you make any judgments." I make eye contact with each member of her team. Dad gives me a slight nod. Sarah's shoulders drop when I catch her eye.

Motioning to Michael, I pass him the tablet. He stays in his seat as he brings up some tweets. His tone brooks no nonsense. He doesn't need to be in front of the room to command it. "Montgomery's been lurking on social media. He started on Truth Social about six months ago, when we first broke ground on the building. He wasn't getting a lot of traction for a long time. Delmont isn't big enough to garner national attention."

He flips through a couple pages of nasty messages. "He targets any and all groups that aim to equalize the playing field for minorities. People of color, LGBT, economically disadvantaged. The guy's an asshole."

I open my mouth to reprimand him. In our office, that's acceptable—largely because it's the truth. However, we're not on home turf, and that language isn't appropriate.

But Dad's faster than I am. "It sounds like it," he says quietly.

I nod to Michael to continue. "We monitor this type of chatter all the time, for a variety of different clients across diverse industries. Normally, this type of talk is just that. Assholes exercising their right to free speech."

He flips to the next screen. "This is a list of the NGOs and groups he's targeted in the past."

"Besides the three big groups, I've never heard of the rest of them," Jennifer points out.

Michael nods in acknowledgement. "That's because they didn't have the resources or community involvement to fight him. He essentially shut them down."

"This guy has a lot of money," I say. "He built a financial empire on shady business practices, taking advantage of the groups of people he's trying to keep at a disadvantage. Trust me," I tell them, "when I say this guy is bad news. We've dealt with him enough that we know how he works."

Michael laughs darkly. "He's picked the wrong fight. We know how he operates, and we know how to counter him."

I give him a hard look. "Don't get cocky." I look around the rest of the room. "We worked with Queer Acceptance and All Shades and essentially shut him down. We worked with a PR firm out of New York against him when he went after Women in STEM. It wasn't easy, and it wasn't cheap."

"It was pro bono," Emily points out. "It was free for the organizations."

"It wasn't free for us," I remind her. "It was worth every penny to keep the organizations up and running, for the services they provide, but it was *not* free." My voice is an angry growl, and Emily puts her hands up, nodding in acquiescence.

"Yes, ma'am," she says quietly.

"Don't *ma'am* me," I say sheepishly as Michael echoes me. "Don't *ma'am* her."

Sarah snorts softly, and my dad's mouth turns up at the corner.

"Sorry, Emms. You know how this guy gets under my skin. Still, that's not an excuse to talk to you like that." She gives me a curt nod, and I turn back to Sarah's team. "I just want to give you a little history on this guy. We're not dealing with a random internet troll that's going to go away. He's escalated."

Michael takes over again, flipping to the next screen. "This is when we know shit's going to get real with this guy," he says, pointing to a screenshot of a public thread on exterminating the gays. "This kind of language trips the monitoring. This has traditionally been the tipping point where he and his people have started trying to infiltrate locations. Building sites are especially easy to gain access to."

"With what aim, exactly?" David Sanchez, the construction manager, asks.

I turn to address him directly. "In the past, it's been as workers for electric and HVAC systems—at least the ones we've found out about. I suspect we didn't discover all of them."

"We can require everyone on-premises to wear badges and get cleared in—" he says.

"But you can't guarantee he hasn't already infiltrated the companies in the past few months with his own people." I finish, reading his thought process.

"I'll talk to my liaisons at the companies doing work for us. There are legal issues with disclosing that type of information to us, but given the circumstances, I might be able to request they only give us people who've worked for the company for at least a year. We've worked with both the electric and HVAC companies for years and have good working relationships with them. The HVAC company does our plumbing systems, too."

I nod. "Good thinking. Maybe you can also let the leads of each crew know what's going on and to be on the lookout for anything suspicious. I'd prefer not to tip our hand if we can avoid it. He might escalate faster if he realizes we're onto him."

Michael grins. "He doesn't know that he's up against us, and that we've beaten him at his own game before."

I give Michael another hard stare. "This isn't a game, Michael." I admire his enthusiasm, but this isn't the time or the place for it.

"I know, boss," he says, chastened.

I look around the room. My dad is running his fingers through his hair in anticipation of the unknown. Sarah appears concerned, but poised for battle. Ethan and my people look determined; Jennifer looks pensive, like she's chewing on something new and she hasn't decided what it is yet. David looks like he's ready to get to work securing the build site.

"That's really all I've got right now. Ethan, Emily, and Michael are working on the social media and internet side of things. The only thing we currently need on your end is securing and monitoring the build site. But it's important that you know what's coming. We have a fight ahead of us."

Sarah speaks up. "Do you think it's necessary to pull in extra security for the build site?"

I shake my head. "It wouldn't hurt, to be honest. But at this point, it's an extra expense that I don't think is warranted. Yet."

Dad speaks up. "Do we need to be concerned about physical violence? At the build site or against any of our employees?"

I sigh deeply, hedging for a long moment. "Not yet." I feel all eyes in the room turn toward me. "Montgomery and his people have never crossed that line. However," I punctuate, "the people he riles up have. He hasn't gotten to that stage yet. Once he starts organizing groups for protesting, actually getting bodies to come out and show up, then we'll need to have that conversation. That's also when we'll need to get law enforcement involved."

"You mean *if*," Dad counters firmly.

"I mean when." I look at him for a long moment. "Delmont is his town as much as it is ours, and there's no chance either of us will go down without a fight."

13

CARMEN

"Did you have a good day?" I ask dad when he comes home from work.

He chuckles. "Besides an impromptu meeting with some of my favorite people?" He winks at me. "Besides that, everything was fine. Sarah seemed upset after you left, though," he mentions thoughtfully.

I shrug indifferently. "Not surprising, considering the threat we're up against. But there's really not much she needs to worry about besides ramping up security. It sounds like David has that pretty well under control. We'll cover any additional costs incurred. Maybe I should have mentioned that to her."

"*Mija.*" His tone stops me.

I glance at him curiously. He rarely uses my Spanish nickname. Abuela uses it sometimes, but it was something that mom always called me, and it's always been a bit sacred in a weird, sentimental way.

"It wasn't about that. It was about you. It was seeing you again." His voice is gentle.

I know he's expecting some response from me, but I don't have one. It's painful to think about her. The fact that I need to stay away from her until this project is finished hurts. I saw first-hand what it did to her when he was chasing her, and I won't do that to someone I'm in business with. It's not fair to anyone.

"Carmen, you should talk to her." He's gentle but persistent.

"And what, Dad?" I sigh angrily. "I saw what it did to her when you were chasing her, even being subtle and respectful. I won't do that to her," I spit out.

He sits down like I slapped him.

"I had no idea I was causing her so much distress." He wipes his hand across his face. "If I had any clue she likes women—"

I raise an eyebrow at him, daring him to complete that thought. "So if she likes dick, it's okay to put her in that position?" I ask him, disgusted. That's not being fair, but I don't really care right now.

I grab a bottle of wine out of the fridge and storm upstairs. He knows better than to follow me. I close the door behind me—gently, because I don't want abuela to hear me. I don't want to listen to her defend him.

I just want Sarah. I need Sarah. Like I need air.

I just can't get it out of my head, how frustrated and hopeless she looked that night when she came home from the gala. Her blasé nonchalance at lunch when she said she was going out with my dad again for dinner. As friends.

I pull a long swig from the wine bottle and collapse onto the couch in my sitting room. It's different though, isn't it—this thing between Sarah and me? It's mutual. I'm fairly sure it is, anyway. I frown to myself.

The adult thing would be to talk to her about it. Not flirting. Not sending mixed signals. Not fucking inhaling the softness of the skin at her throat. *God.* I don't think I've been that wet for someone since I was a teenager. I wanted her so bad.

I want her so bad. Present tense. Seeing her today just reminded me of what I've been avoiding for the past couple weeks. I down the rest of the bottle of wine, my throat burning pleasantly. I just need to talk to her.

I pick up my phone and text her. *Hey, you okay? Dad said you seemed upset at work today.* I send it before I give myself a chance to back out.

A minute later, my phone dings. *fine*

I sigh despondently. *C'mon Sarah. This is me reaching out. Can we talk?*

The thread shows that the message was read, then nothing. A minute later, three bouncing bubbles. Then nothing.

I give her two more minutes before I bury my head in my hands. Grumbling, I grab my phone again. *I get it. I'll leave you alone. If you change your mind, I'm here.* Send.

I toss my phone on the couch and pull my knees up to my chest, wrapping my arms around them. I rest my chin on them, rocking myself gently. I miss her.

My phone chimes loudly, startling me. Maybe I shouldn't have drunk that wine so fast. I grab my phone.

she's making dinner. chill the fk out. this is Lily. and you millennials complain about us kids having no patience?

Watch your language, I reply before thinking about it.

that part was from mom. she says you can come for dinner if you want

I can't drive. I'm drunk.

she says you can call her later

Then, a minute later, a text from Lily's number. *you don't want to know what *I* have to say*

I chuckle. *Actually, yes I do. Lay it on me.*

do you actually like her? for real?

I swallow. That's the question, isn't it? It occurs to me that a twelve-year-old is grilling me over text. *I do, for real. I don't want to make work awkward, though.*

yeah well. you kissing her and then ghosting her for weeks doesn't make anything awkward at all. not even a little bit

I bite my lip and sigh. *Fair point.*

look, I like you, but don't fuck with my mom. she's fragile. either make a legit effort or let her go

Fair enough. Thanks Bug. Can I ask a question?

you can ask

is she okay?

no

I bite my lip, frowning. The three bubbles tell me she's not done.

she acts like it for everyone else. but i'm the only one who hears her cry herself to sleep at night

An hour later, my phone dings. It's Sarah. *did you want to talk?*

can I call?

My phone rings. So I guess that's a yes to the phone call. "Hey," I say softly.

"Hey," she replies hesitantly.

There's an awkward silence. "Are you okay?" I ask quietly.

She lets out a long sigh. "Not really," she mutters, her voice shaky. "But what doesn't kill you makes you stronger."

I close my eyes and shake my head. "Look. I—" I sigh audibly. "Will you listen to me for a minute? Please?"

"I think that's why I called, isn't it?" she asks drily.

I groan silently. "Okay, I deserved that." I take a deep breath. "I think this would be better in person, but I'm drunk because of you so I can't come to you. And it would be really awkward for you to come here, with Lily and my dad around. Plus, this way you can hang up on me if you decide to. But please don't. Decide to hang up on me, I mean."

"Carmen? Just say it. I won't hang up on you."

"Look. I like you a lot. More than I've liked anyone, ever. Well, maybe except Alisha Brouwer in ninth grade, but that was just puppy love. It doesn't count."

"Carmen." Her voice holds a warning.

"Right. Sorry. That night you came home from the gala after being out with my dad—I was looking at your bookshelf when you came in. I saw you come in the house, close the door, and basically melt with relief that the night was over... Frustration that you had to put up with all the unwanted attention... I heard the worry in your voice when you mentioned a promotion in the same breath as your boss putting his arm around you. The way you resigned yourself to dating him because you didn't know if it would affect your job. I saw all that, Sarah."

She's quiet, but she makes a small, choked sound in her throat. She's listening.

"I know my dad. I know he was just interested, doing his best to show that in a respectful way without being pushy. He would never have made things awkward if you turned him down."

"I friendzoned him nine times, Carmen. Nine times, I told him I was happy to get to know him as a friend."

"I want to hit him for you," I say quietly, seething.

"Let it go, Carmen. He was always respectful."

I shake my head vehemently. "Nine times is not respectful, Sarah." I suddenly drop my anger. It hurts too much. "Look. I'm the boss, and I can't imagine *ever* making one of my people feel like that. It makes me sick just thinking about it."

"I understand," she says softly.

"It's why I'm fighting this so hard, this thing with you." I implore her to understand.

"I get it, Carmen." Her voice is harder. She's shutting me down.

I swallow thickly. "I think our situation is different, though. I'm not your boss. We don't even work for the same company."

"True," she says cautiously.

"If I asked you out on a real date, would you be interested?" God. I've never felt so unsure of myself asking a girl out in my life.

"That depends," she murmurs.

"On?" I hold my breath, waiting for her answer.

"Are you going to kiss my neck like you did that night?" Every nerve in my body feels how much she wants that.

14

SARAH

I take Lily's face in my hands. "You're sure you're okay with me going on a date." I need to know she's okay with this.

She wriggles out of my hands. "Mom, you're going to dinner with her. You're not marrying her. At least not yet." She wiggles her eyebrows at me. "You two need to grow up and learn how to communicate, though. You both suck at it."

I chuckle. She's not wrong.

"Isn't it going to be weird to just go out for dinner?" she asks curiously. "How is it going to be different from a business lunch with her?"

I shrug. "It just is, because it's a date. We'll come back here after dinner. You can come home then, if you want."

"Beth said I can stay the night. I guess Avery is staying at Kayla's, so I can sleep there."

I shake my head. "Nope. You're coming home. We're not kicking you out of your own house. Me and you, we come as a package deal. If she doesn't like that, it's her loss," I say firmly. "I'll let you and Beth know when we get home. I expect you home by eleven at the latest. Got it?"

Carmen gets here before I'm ready. Although, to be fair, I don't think I'll ever be ready. It's been forever since I've gone on a bona fide date, at least with someone I wanted to go out with. I don't even know what dating etiquette is these days.

Lily lets her in and sticks her head in my room. "Mom, she's here. She has flowers for you."

I look at myself in the mirror one last time, suddenly wondering if this is a good idea. She said to dress casually, so I just have jeans and a low-cut green blouse on.

"You look fine, Mom," Lily says softly. "Just be yourself. If she's right for you, that's all you need." She comes in and gently pushes me toward the door. "And if she's not, then I'll kick her ass. Just go have fun."

I chuckle, ready to reprimand her for her language, but Carmen beats me to it.

"You know the walls are thin here, Bug." Carmen laughs. "You can defend your mom's honor, but do it without swearing, please."

"There'll be worse than that if you hurt her." Lily shrugs noncommittally. She reaches into the cabinet, pulling out a vase for the flowers, and partially fills it with water.

Carmen hands me a dozen roses with a cheeky smile. "These are for you," she tells me, holding my gaze. "Beautiful flowers for a beautiful woman." Judging by the grin on her face, she's having way too much fun with this.

Lily groans loudly. "You're so gross. I'll be down the hall. Don't text me until after you're done making out." She makes a shuddering face and mimics vomiting before running out the door. Carmen laughs.

I busy myself putting the flowers in the vase. "Thank you. They're beautiful." I smile nervously at her.

"Her acting like that—is she for this thing with us or against it?" she asks curiously.

I avoid her eyes, arranging the flowers and putting them on the table. "It's complicated," I say quietly, "but I think she's mostly okay with it. She's just at that age." I shrug.

"That point where they think kissing is gross to thinking it may be interesting?" Laughing, she looks at me. She takes in my jeans, my blouse, my hair down around my face. "You do look beautiful," she says appreciatively.

I laugh, biting my lower lip. My eyes follow the low-cut yellow blouse that hugs her curves, down to her ass, accentuated by her tight black jeans. "You look good enough to eat." I cover my mouth, horrified. *I did not just say that out loud.* I avert my eyes.

"You're blushing." She grins, taking a step toward me.

I shrug my shoulder, embarrassed. "I can't believe I said that out loud." I groan. "I'm sorry. It's been so long since I've been on a date that I have no idea what I'm doing. I'm making a fool of myself."

Laughing, she takes a step back to give me some space. "Just relax, Sarah. If you want something, tell me. If I'm pushing you into something you're not comfortable with, tell me. Just be yourself."

I take a deep breath and nod. "Okay."

"So tell me what you want. We have dinner reservations at Mama Rosie's downtown in an hour. But we can change that if you want."

"Will you..." My voice trails off, my insides quivering. I want her mouth on my throat again. Just once. "You said..."

She can see me struggling, and the corner of her mouth twists up in amusement. "You want to cash in on that kiss already?"

I nod, swallowing nervously. It's been so long since I've wanted the touch of a woman. That's not true, not exactly. I've been wanting a repeat of that touch since it happened, almost three weeks ago. Even just thinking of her touch now, my breath is shallow and rapid.

"Come here," she murmurs. She meets me halfway as we erase the distance between us. She looks up at me, raising a hand to trace the hollow of my throat with her fingertip. My breath catches as she leans closer to me. I can feel her breath on my neck. But she holds back.

"Carmen." My breath is guttural, heavy with needing her.

"What do you want, Sarah?" I hear the teasing smile in her voice, her lips tickling my skin.

"If you want to take me to dinner," I remind her, my voice throaty, "you owe me a kiss."

She brushes her lips against my skin, too briefly, and pulls back. "Like that?" She raises her eyebrow playfully.

"You're going to have to try harder than that," I tease her. *"Ma'am."*

She growls, but doesn't reprimand me for the moniker. Instead, she leans forward and kisses the hollow of my neck, oh so softly. Her hot breath tickles my skin, and my head falls back with a quiet moan. She moves along my collarbone, her tongue tasting and her teeth nipping.

My hands find her hips, pulling her body into mine. "My God, Carmen," I whisper softly. I swallow, my breath unsteady.

She presses her body against mine for a brief moment before pulling away, leaving my body yearning for more. She laughs softly. She can hear what she does to me. My breathing gives it away. *"Now* will you come to dinner with me?" she asks with feigned exasperation.

I look at her and pretend to consider. "What's in it for me?" I tap my chin thoughtfully.

"Food?" She laughs. "If things go well, maybe I'll brave another kiss—although I don't know. You have a pretty fierce guardian, and I'm not sure I want to cross her." She takes me by the elbow. "Should we walk or drive? It's only about a ten-minute walk from here," she tells me. "If you can walk after that kiss," she teases.

I ignore her innuendo. "It'll probably be easier to walk. Parking downtown on a Friday night is not for the faint of heart."

She nods. "Then I can have a drink, too."

"Speaking of..." I start, once we're walking down Walnut Street toward the restaurant.

She glances at me. "What were we speaking of?" She licks her lower lip and takes it between her teeth.

"You, drinking," I tease her. "What was up the other night? What had you so wound up? You don't seem like the type to drink alone." At least, up until Tuesday night, I hadn't thought she'd be. She seems responsible, and her behavior the other night felt like anything but.

She lets out a long sigh.

"If you don't want to talk about it, it's okay. But it seemed like the catalyst for you calling me. I'm just trying to figure all of this out," I tell her.

She nods. "It's a fair question. Although, FYI, I don't mind having a drink alone. But I don't get drunk alone. I don't get drunk, ever. That's the first time in..." Her voice trails off. "A long time," she finishes quietly.

"Is it because that Montgomery guy is coming after your project?" I ask her curiously.

She snorts derisively, shaking her head. "I have a great team of people to fight that. It's a headache, but not worth losing sleep over. Definitely not worth getting drunk over." I nod silently, giving her space to go on. "When dad came home, he mentioned that you weren't really yourself after my team and I left. After that meeting."

Fair enough. "I'm a big girl, Carmen. I like you, but if all this makes you uncomfortable, I can let it go."

"But?" she asks, sensing that I have more to say.

"But you can't fucking kiss me like that if you want me to leave you alone." I sigh in frustration.

She stops, grabbing my arm and turning me around to face her. She cups my cheek with one hand, her thumb tracing my jawline. "I haven't even kissed you yet, Sarah," she murmurs, staring into my eyes. I bite my lower lip as she slowly drops her hand and continues walking.

"That sure as hell isn't the message my body received upstairs," I point out.

She nods. "You're right. I'm sorry." She's quiet for a moment. "And I'm sorry I ghosted you after the other night when we talked. It took a middle-schooler to call me out on my shit to realize how childish I was being, not talking to you."

We get to Mama Rosie's, and she opens the door for me.

"Ms. Tomsen." The hostess gives Carmen a welcoming smile. "Your table is in the back. You'll have a more private dining experience there. Follow me."

"Thanks, Tina. We appreciate it." Carmen smiles, and we follow her to a small booth in a quiet corner at the back of the diner.

After we're seated, I look at Carmen. "What do you mean? Did Lily say something to you?"

She raises an eyebrow in amusement. "She texts me all the time, not just when she wants to dance."

I hold back a laugh. "I hope she doesn't say anything inappropriate. She talks to Beth a lot, too. Sometimes I wonder if I'm doing such a bad job raising her that she needs to look for other adults besides me to talk to."

Carmen shakes her head, chuckling. "She knows more swear words than I'd expect from a kid her age, but nothing worrisome. It's healthy for her to have other adults she feels safe talking to."

I glance at Carmen curiously. "She has a potty mouth. She probably gets that from me, but she usually watches what she says around adults. As long as she knows when to filter herself,

I'm not worried about it." I frown. "Why was she talking to you about me, though?"

She shrugs, embarrassed. "Just to encourage me to talk to you. She was worried about you," she mumbles. "But when my dad started pushing me about you the other day, I kind of lost my shit with him." She shrugs, picking up her menu and nodding toward mine.

I laugh. "I come here all the time. I know what I want."

She puts her menu back down as the waiter approaches to take our order. After he leaves, she looks up at me, her gaze gentle. She swallows hard. "That's why I was drinking. He was pushing me to talk to you, encouraging me to explore things with you."

"Is that why you're here?" I bristle uncomfortably. I'm such a fool. I look past her, avoiding her gaze.

"God no." She scoffs. "Look at me, Sarah." She's quiet until I meet her eyes, then she sighs. "Didn't that kiss show you that I want you? God, Sarah. I haven't wanted anyone so badly for a long time."

The waiter approaches with our drinks and appetizers. Bruschetta topped with fresh tomatoes, basil, and balsamic glaze for me, and stuffed mushrooms for Carmen.

She waits until we're alone again and stuffs a mushroom in her mouth. "These are so good. You have to try one." She nods at her plate, pushing it toward the middle of the table so we can share.

"Everything here is good." I laugh, pushing my bruschetta next to her plate and nodding an invitation.

She takes a bite of bruschetta and lets out a happy sigh. "Anyway, dad said something that pissed me off. Don't get me wrong.

He's generally a great guy, but he stuck his foot in his mouth in the worst fucking way." She shakes her head. "It wasn't about you," she assures me. "But between what he and Lily said, it made me think about us. It's not the same thing as you and dad."

I watch her, studying her body language. "No, not even close. And please don't put your dad and me together as a unit like that. Your dad and I are colleagues, nothing more. There was never a 'me and him,' not ever."

She nods, acceding my point. "I just don't want to put any pressure on you. But that's not any different from anyone else I'd want to go out with, honestly."

"Fair enough. You don't think working together will be weird?" I ask her.

"Assuming we're both interested in seeing where this goes, it seems like it would be weirder to fight it. *Are* you interested in seeing where this goes?" she asks me.

I look down at my hands, my fingers wrapped around my drink.

She groans. "It's okay if you're not," she says, her shoulders falling.

I look up at her. "Do you automatically assume the worst when someone doesn't give you the answer you want right away?" She did that on the phone the other day when I was making dinner, too.

"Sorry. You looked like you were going to shoot me down."

I shake my head. "I was going to say yes, but..."

She opens her mouth to say something, but then closes it, nodding for me to continue.

"But it's been a long time since I've been with anyone, and I don't know what I'm doing," I finish.

She snickers. "It's like riding a bike, Sarah." She winks at me, and my face goes hot.

I roll my eyes at her. "I meant dating, being in a relationship. I have no idea how to do it anymore, especially since I have a kid."

"And she comes before anyone else," Carmen finishes for me.

15

CARMEN

I sneak into the ladies' room for a minute before we leave. I pull up the text thread with Lily. *We'll be home in about 15m. I think your mom would be happy if you were back sooner rather than later. She misses you.*

Sarah seems alternately giddy and nervous on our walk home, so I try to give her space. I've never been with a woman who has kids, so this dynamic is new for me, too. She seems hesitant for other reasons, though, and I haven't quite figured her out yet.

"Thank you for dinner," she murmurs on our way up the elevator. We're alone. She takes my hand in hers, turning it over and tracing the inside of my wrist.

"It was my pleasure," I say, laughing. *Oh, how I want to kiss this woman.* Part of me prays that Lily will be back soon—because if she's not, I'm afraid neither of us will be able to keep our hands off each other.

"I don't want you to read into this, but do you want to come in and hang out for a while? Sex is off the table tonight. Lily will be back soon. But I'd like if you came in for a while."

I hold back a snicker. "I wasn't planning to do it on the table tonight anyway." I wink at her. "Our first time will have to be in a bed, unless it's in a public bathroom at some fancy ball. That works, too."

She bursts out laughing. "I have honestly never done that. Have you?" She studies me curiously. "I can see it. You seem a little more adventurous than I am in the sex department."

"Is that a good thing or a bad thing?" I ask her as the elevator reaches the fourth floor and we get off.

She chuckles nervously when I don't confirm or deny her supposition. "Neither. Just an observation."

She follows me into the apartment and closes the door behind her. I spin around, facing her, a foot or two between us—not enough to make her feel trapped, but enough for her to feel cornered. "Does it bother you?" I ask her quietly.

Most of the women I've been with in the past decade, besides Vicky, have been casual. Since Vicky, no one has mattered. Warm bodies, human touch, fingers, lips, tongues. But this thing with Sarah, whatever it is—or has the potential to be—is different.

She licks her lower lip and chews on it, thinking, before she answers me. "No, it doesn't bother me. Except..."

"Except what?" I ask softly.

"Except I don't want to disappoint you, that's all."

I laugh softly and grab her hand, pulling her all the way into the apartment before letting go. "Not a chance in hell of that happening." I put my purse down on the counter and walk into the living room, motioning for her to follow me. I sit down on the couch. She sits opposite me at a comfortable distance.

"You know there are no expectations here, right? I don't expect anything from you. You don't even owe me a goodnight kiss. I don't expect sex. Now or later. Lily or no Lily. You don't need to use her as an excuse to tell me no."

She nods, looking slightly chastised.

"I won't complain if you decide you want to kiss me later, though." I raise an eyebrow at her. She doesn't say anything for a long moment, and I wonder if I said something wrong. She seems so hesitant. I can read her well enough to know that she really likes it when I kiss her neck—there's no way she was faking that—but I can also see that a part of her wants to shut this down. "Penny for your thoughts?" I ask her gently.

She's quiet for a moment, then straightens her shoulders, laughing. "Don't worry, I'll give you a kiss or two before you leave," she teases. "Do you want a drink? Wine, or something non-alcoholic if you prefer?"

"I'll have some wine." It'll give me an excuse to stay longer.

We're in the kitchen when the door opens. "Is it safe for me to come home?" Lily yells from the hall.

Sarah looks at me and grins. "It's always safe for you to come home," she tells Lily, sticking her head through the kitchen doorway.

Lily comes all the way in, then looks between me and her mom. "I didn't want to walk in on you doing something gross."

"Well, I was going to kiss her, but I can wait until later. Do you want a drink? Or a snack?" Sarah asks Lily.

"Hey!" I object animatedly. "Kissing isn't gross—not if you find the right person." I turn to Lily, laughing. "Is there anyone at school that you think would be fun to kiss?"

She avoids looking at me, and her face turns bright red. She looks at her mom. "Can you make some popcorn? Maybe we can watch a movie? Or should I go read in my room or something?"

Sarah raises an eyebrow at me, then tousles Lily's hair. "I'll make popcorn, and we can watch a movie. But I get to sit by Carmen, okay?"

I glance at Sarah and hide a chuckle. "How about Bug and I find a movie, and you make the popcorn. I'll save you a spot." I wink at her.

Lily and I head into the living room, and I pick up the remote. "I wanted to sit by you," she says, crossing her arms.

I tilt my head and look at her. "I can sit in the middle, then you can both sit by me. How does that sound?"

She nods. "Can I pick out the movie?"

I nod, then park myself in the middle of the couch. I pat the cushion on my right. She sits next to me and pulls up Disney Plus. As she's scrolling through the movies, I lean over and whisper in her ear. "The person at school that might be fun to kiss—boy or girl?" I elbow her.

She turns her head to study me for a moment. "Promise not to tell mom?"

I frown and glance over at Sarah, still in the kitchen. "Is there a reason you don't want her to know?" I ask curiously. "I can keep your secrets, but," I wait until she meets my eyes, "if I ever feel like you're in danger or it's something your mom should know, deal's off. Fair enough?"

She lets out a long breath and nods. "It's a boy," she whispers into my ear, blushing.

"He must be cute." I wink at her. "What's he like?"

She turns back to the TV and picks Moana from the list of movies on the screen. She puts the remote on the coffee table until the popcorn gets here. "He's smart. He's nice, but he got in a fight this week at school."

I frown. Lily doesn't seem like the type who would go for bad boys. "What did he get in a fight about?" I ask her.

She shrugs. "Two girls were holding hands at lunch, and Chuck M. was being mean to them. Aiden told him to shut up, and when he didn't, he clocked him one."

"You like him because he did that?" I ask her curiously.

She shakes her head. "No. I like him 'cause he's smart and nice. When he's not punching people for being asshats." She shrugs again. "Plus, he's cute."

I ruffle her hair, laughing. "Fair enough." I lower my voice. "Why don't you want your mom to know?"

She shrugs again, this time with a snort. "She's not exactly the best role model with relationships."

I act offended, widening my eyes. "Are you saying I'm not a good choice?"

She rolls her eyes. "You two wouldn't even be talking if I hadn't pushed you to talk to her, and she'd still be crying herself to sleep at night."

Sarah walks into the living room as Lily says that. She stops in her tracks.

Oh, fuck.

"Oh, fuck," Lily breathes quietly. She looks from Sarah to me, then sighs. She meets her mom's eyes. "It's true, mom. She hurt you. You guys needed to talk and figure shit out."

Sarah looks at Lily for a long moment. She lets out a long breath and nods. "Fair enough," she says quietly. She puts the bowl of popcorn on the coffee table in front of Lily and looks at both of us. The air goes out of her lungs before she turns around and retreats back to the kitchen.

Lily bites the inside of her cheek. "Well, it's true," she says softly, standing up. She glares at me. "You. Don't leave." She heads into the kitchen after her mom.

I glance around the living room, then turn the TV off. So Lily wasn't shitting me when she said that, judging by Sarah's reaction. I wasn't sure how much of her texts were real and how much was exaggerated.

I think about leaving, but Lily's right. Sarah and I need to talk. It seems like neither of us are very good at that.

Lily comes back a few minutes later. "Please don't leave without talking to her," she says quietly, her watery eyes searching mine. I nod. She sits down next to me. "Do you really like her?"

I nod. "Yes, I do, Bug. But you know how her boss made her uncomfortable by taking her out for dinner?"

She nods. "But he never touched her. Not really," she adds quickly. "At least that's what she says."

"But she felt like she had to do things she didn't want to, because he was her boss. Like going to dinner, right?" She nods, and I continue. "In some ways, I'm like her boss, too. Until summertime, when the project she's working on is finished. Did she tell you about that?"

Lily shakes her head. "It's different, though. She likes you."

I notice Sarah out of the corner of my eye, standing in the kitchen doorway, but I turn my focus back to Lily. "I like her, too." I fight a smile, but she sees it anyway, and I laugh. "I like her a lot. But because of work, we have to be careful. I don't want your mom to feel like she owes me anything, or that she needs to do anything for me that she doesn't want to do. Does that make sense?"

Lily nods. "Like if she doesn't go to dinner with you, she might not get the promotion. Or if she doesn't kiss you, she might lose her job."

I look up at Sarah, aghast. "Did he...?"

Sarah shakes her head. "It wasn't your dad, Carmen. Relax."

I bite my tongue. That means it was someone, either in my dad's office or before that. I turn back to Lily. "A little bit like that, yes. But your mom and I, we're going to try to make something work between us because we both want to." A small smile spreads across Lily's face, but I stop her. "Will you promise me something?"

"Does it involve killing anyone?" she asks, raising an eyebrow. Sarah snickers from the doorway.

I shake my head with a chuckle. "I certainly hope not." I meet her eyes. "You have my number. If you ever feel like your mom doesn't want me around anymore, I want you to tell me, okay?"

Lily huffs out a laugh. "Oh, trust me. If I think you're not treating her right, you'll hear about it."

I reach over and pull her into a hug. "Your mom is lucky she has you looking out for her."

Lily shrugs. "Sometimes she thinks I'm a pain in the ass." She glances at her mom, then laughs. "She's not wrong." She stands up and grabs the bowl of popcorn. "I'm going to go listen to music. With my earbuds turned up all the way. So I don't hear whatever goes on out here."

Sarah laughs, and Lily gives her a hug before disappearing into her bedroom. She stands there, watching me for a long moment. "That's not how I pictured our first date ending." She gives me a small smile.

I stand up and walk to her. "It's not over." I search her face for some idea of what she's feeling. "Don't be mad at her. She just cares about you." I take a step closer, into her personal space. "Are you okay? I want to hug you," I tell her softly.

She chuckles. "Yes, I'm okay. She just surprised me, that's all."

"You didn't yell at her for saying fuck." I bite my lower lip.

"Neither did you," she volleys back at me with a grin. "If you want to hug me, you can. But if you do, I honestly don't know if it'll stop there." She opens her arms, stepping toward me. I meet her halfway, wrapping my arms around her back.

"You're okay, for real?" I tilt my head up to check with her. Her eyes are closed, her nose buried in my hair. "Wait. Are you getting off on my shampoo?" I stifle a grin.

"Just enjoying it." She moans softly. "It's been a long time since someone else got me off, Carmen. Your hair alone isn't going to get me there."

I loosen my arms and lace my fingers together, my hands falling to her lower back. I trace my lips lightly along the curve of her jaw. "That almost sounded like an invitation," I breathe into her soft skin.

She swallows, her breath hitching. I want to kiss her so badly, to feel her skin, to taste her heat.

"Sarah." I breathe her name, reluctantly pulling back from her. She loosens her hold on me, but her hands land on my hips, and I stay within her reach. I close my eyes and catch my breath.

"Hm?" she murmurs, her eyes lidded.

I pull her face to mine and rest my forehead against hers. "As much as I want to take you to bed and ravish you—" Her hands tighten on my hips, pulling my body against hers. "We should slow down."

"You really want to ravish me?" she teases, her breath heavy.

I nuzzle her neck, whispering into her ear. "You have no idea how much I want to fuck you right now." I feel her body shiver at my words.

I pull out of her arms, stepping back and putting some space between us. "We should probably talk, though—probably keep our clothes on for tonight. She's got to be up in the morning, right?" I nod vaguely toward Lily's room.

She groans softly. "You're not saying that because you don't want me, are you?" she murmurs softly.

I burst into laughter, shaking my head. "No. I would let you feel how wet I am for you, but I don't have that much self-control." I take her hand and pull her toward the couch to sit down. "Sarah, when's the last time you had sex in the house when your daughter was home?"

She closes her eyes, her face turning red. "Never." She shakes her head of that thought and tries to change the subject. "Can we go back to how wet you are?" She chuckles awkwardly.

"Oh, we will, but we need to slow down. For tonight at least." I close my eyes and lean my head against the back of the couch with a painful groan. "I haven't even properly kissed you, and all I want is to be between your legs."

She laughs. "You don't seem like the type to wait."

I blink, surprised. "When it's just some rando and it's just sex, I'm not. But you're not just anyone, Sarah. I've been waiting for you for months. Since you went to the gala with my dad."

"You've been waiting for me?" she asks skeptically.

I nod, not trusting my voice.

16

SARAH

I shake my head, confused. "What do you mean? You're the one who couldn't make up your mind what you wanted before."

She swallows thickly and looks away from me. "I don't want to put you in a position where you think I have any power over you. Over your job, I mean." She glances at me, then stares at the blank TV screen. She sighs, her shoulders falling. "I saw what it did to you, when my dad was chasing you."

I take her hand in mine, shaking my head. "Carmen, it's not the same thing. Besides, your dad never—"

"Stop already!" she growls, pulling her hand away from me. "I know he never pushed, Sarah. He's a good guy, and he didn't even realize the position he was putting you in. It would never even occur to him to let it affect your job. He's an idiot *because* it would seriously never occur to him."

I frown. "He's not an idiot, Carmen. That's not fair. He's one of the most intelligent men I know."

She drops her head into her hands, quiet for a long minute. "You're right. That wasn't fair of me. I'm sorry," she says quietly.

She turns to look up at me. "Can I ask you a question?" Her voice is tentative all of a sudden, subdued.

I study her deflated posture, not sure I want to deal with whatever demons she wants to bring up. But if I want any chance of a relationship with her to work, I guess we're going there. Wherever *there* is. I nod reluctantly. "What is it?"

"What Lily said. My dad didn't try to kiss you, did he?" She sounds almost fearful of my answer.

I chuckle. "No. The worst he ever did was put his hand on my back. On my hip, too—but no. He never crossed any lines like that. He didn't like the friend-zone thing." I stop for a moment, thoughtful. "It wasn't even that. He respected it, but he didn't want to accept it. I think he was trying to leave the door open for me to change my mind, like he wanted us to get to know each other better, and he thought I would change my mind if we did."

She nods slowly.

"I get what you mean though." I sigh softly. "He is kind of an idiot, because it never even occurred to him that I could feel threatened by it." She glances up at me, meeting my eyes, but I shake my head. "I never felt like my job was threatened, or even the promotion he was talking about. He'd be stupid to let me go somewhere else anyway. I could walk away from him in a heartbeat and have a dozen jobs lined up within a week. I'd come out of it in a better position than I'm in now."

She raises an eyebrow and sighs. "So he doesn't pay you a fair wage then." It's not a question, and I don't respond to it. I make enough for what Bug and I need and want—but I also know what Bob makes. He's the only other person technically at the same level as I am, and he makes thirty percent more than I do—which is a lot of fucking money, when it comes down to it. I swore Teresa to secrecy when she asked me about it last year. I don't want Bob knowing, either.

She groans and slowly straightens her leg in front of her, leaning over and stretching to wrap her palms around her foot with a small grunt.

"Does it hurt?" I ask, motioning toward her leg.

She shakes her head. "No, it just gets tight sometimes. Stress always makes it worse." She pulls both her legs up on the couch, wrapping her arms around her knees.

"I'm sorry."

"Don't," she stops me, holding my gaze. She regards me for a moment, biting the inside of her cheek. "One more question, and you don't need to answer if you don't want to." Her voice is flat, like she doesn't really care what my answer is.

"If you want to know how much your dad pays me, you'll have to talk to him. I'm not getting into that."

She huffs a light laugh. "I just might, seeing as my business is what's covering most of your paycheck right now." She shakes her head. "No, it's not about that." She takes a deep breath again. "What Lily was talking about, you having to kiss someone when you felt your job was threatened. Was that someone at my dad's company?"

I shake my head. "It was a long time ago, and no. It wasn't anyone at your dad's company. I really don't want to talk about it," I say coldly.

I turn to stand up, to shut her down, but something in her voice stops me. "Sarah."

"I don't want to talk about it, Carmen," I say through clenched teeth.

"You don't have to. I promise," she says softly. "I just had to make sure that kind of shit's not happening on his watch. Number one, because he would hate himself if he ever found out about something like that. And number two, I would never give my business to his company again." The venom in her voice surprises me.

I lean back against the couch, the air expelling from my lungs. "I've never heard of anything like that happening here. Breathe," I tell her gently. She's so tightly wrapped up around herself, closed off. I settle for resting my hand on her foot, the closest part of her to me.

"I need to tell you something." I can feel the dread in her voice, and the pain behind it.

"I'm listening." *So much for a fun first date.*

She swallows, closing her eyes for a long beat.

"Did you kill someone?" I ask after she's silent for too long.

She opens her eyes and stares at me, then chokes out a laugh. "I am not going to ask why you and Lily..." She shakes her head. "No. There's not a soul on earth who would be worth the consequences of murder."

I smother a laugh. "There are only consequences if you get caught." I squeeze her foot gently. "Whatever it is, Carmen, just talk to me. Whatever is in your past, I doubt it's going to change how I feel about you."

She nods, resting her chin on her knees. "About a year after I started Tomsen Media, I got involved with one of my employees. It was mutual. At least, at the time I thought it was. She was smart. Beautiful. She became my little protégé. I taught her everything I knew. She said she wanted to be partners. In life and in business. She wanted to be by my side as I ruled the world."

I raise an eyebrow. "Um. If it's your ambition to rule the world, that might be a dealbreaker for me," I deadpan. "I like my quiet life."

She snickers softly. "I'm spilling my guts here, and you're cracking jokes."

I shrug a shoulder. "Only halfway cracking jokes. I do like my quiet life." I reach over and put my hand on her arm. "Come sit by me. I want to hold you while you tell me the rest."

She bites her lip, and I see her eyes tear up as she wraps her arms tighter around herself.

"Carmen, I'm serious. This is obviously important enough for you to share with me, so please let me share it with you."

She reluctantly scoots over, and I tuck her into my shoulder, pulling her into me.

The fight leaves her body at the contact, and she relaxes into me. "No aspirations for world domination, I promise."

I lightly kiss the top of her head. "Politics?" I tease her.

"Hell no. But you know I fight for equal rights, and sometimes that draws attention." She's talking about Montgomery and his ilk.

"For that, I'll be standing with you. Now, tell me more about this evil ex of yours." I squeeze her shoulder gently.

"There's not much to tell, really. She was using me to learn everything she could. I proposed to her on Christmas Eve, and she fucking laughed in my face—literally laughed in my face. Then she took everything she learned from me and started her own company."

"Ouch," I murmur softly.

She huffs an ironic laugh. "She tried to use all of my contacts here, but it backfired on her spectacularly. Most of them were loyal to me and chose not to do business with her. She ended up moving to New York. She's building quite the company off of what she learned from me."

"She sounds like a bitch," I growl. I hate that word and rarely use it, but if the shoe fits...

Carmen turns to me and puts a finger over my lips. "Don't call her that." Her voice is barely a whisper. "It's true, but I'm the only one who can call her that."

"You still love her?" I ask gently, tucking a stray hair behind her ear.

She thinks for a long moment, her eyes glassy. "No, but the betrayal still hurts."

"It probably will for a long time," I tell her. "Sometimes love sucks."

She chuckles, then leans her head back against my shoulder. "Yeah." She reaches her hand up to mine on her shoulder, lacing her fingers with mine. "I had to tell you why the whole relationship thing at work gets under my skin so much. That's a huge part of it. Even when it's completely consensual, there are still power dynamics going on."

I squeeze her fingers. "I promise I'm not out for your job."

"I know," she says. "You know what I mean, though." When I nod, she continues. "That's half the reason I told you about Vicky."

Okay. I had pretty much figured that out as soon as she started the story. "What else?"

"I haven't gone out with anyone since her."

I frown, confused. "Oh. I had the impression that you—"

"God, no." She buries her face in her hand after stopping me. "It's been almost three years since she left. I'm not celibate," she hurries out like it's a horrible thing. "I just don't get attached to anyone. No one has been able to make me feel anything, not since her."

"Oh." I've been completely reading her wrong. For months. I loosen my arm around her shoulder. "Sorry. I thought—"

She tightens her fingers laced with mine. "Sarah. Stop talking for a minute."

I nod mutely, not sure how to react. I really thought she felt the same way.

"There are a few women I hook up with sometimes. Or did, anyway. But it was always just empty sex. None of them meant anything, other than getting my rocks off. You know what I mean?" When I don't answer her, she raises an eyebrow at me expectantly.

I sigh in frustration. "No, not really. I don't do empty hookups." Plus, honestly, it's a little frustrating that every time I try to push for more from her, she pulls back. Maybe it's better if she's not interested. She lets go of my hand.

Burying her head in her hands, she grumbles. "I don't know if I can do this." She's quiet for a long time. A minute. Maybe two. I feel her hiccup into her hands. She raises her head, her eyes wet. "I'm terrible at relationships, Sarah. I don't know how to communicate my feelings very well." She wipes tears off her nose. "Ask your daughter. She's called me on it a few times already." She lets out a choked sigh. "I really like you. More than I've liked anyone in ... a long time."

"Is that why you pull away from me when I want more from you?" I ask, not trying to mask my bitterness. "When you're fine just jumping into bed with other women?"

She scoffs, then turns to look at me—to really look at me. I see the realization dawn on her, and her face drops. "No, no, no." She takes my face in her hands, still wet with her tears. "When I touch you, I feel overwhelmed with—everything. Like I'm going to explode. Like if I kiss you, I'll never come up for air again, and I won't care. Because if I have you, I don't need air."

She gently brushes her lips over my forehead, and I close my eyes. "Carmen," I breathe her name in warning.

"—and if I kiss you, we're going to end up in bed. And I'm going to touch you and explore every inch of your body, make you squirm until you come on my—"

Lily's bedroom door opens, and Carmen freezes, her hands framing my face.

"If you're going to do all that, can you at least get a room and close the door, please?" Lily walks into the kitchen to get a glass of water. "And I want to get some earplugs. I'm going to order some on Amazon. I'll order them tonight so they'll be here tomorrow.

Is that okay, Mom?" She leans against the doorway and takes a drink of her water, watching us.

I close my eyes and fight back a chuckle. This child of mine.

I can feel Carmen's laughter, her body against mine. "Do you want my credit card?" she asks Lily, deadpan. She turns back to me. "Your daughter is way scarier than my dad."

I burst out laughing. Lily walks over to us to give me a good-night hug. "Use the card on my account. Get the soft earplugs that you can sleep with, okay?" I tell her.

"Get a package of them. They're not meant to be reused," Carmen adds.

Lily raises an eyebrow at her. "Are you planning to move in already?" The corner of her mouth twists up.

"I'm saving you from getting an ear infection, you brat." She laughs.

"Good night," Lily says pointedly, rolling her eyes before heading back to her room.

17

CARMEN

"Also, that." I nod toward Lily's door as it closes, leaning back against the couch with a chuckle.

"Sweet child of mine." Sarah shakes her head, closing her eyes.

"Something to navigate." I shrug. We'll figure it out. "But honestly, we need to talk about sex. Preferably before we're in bed naked together."

"If you're looking for my resume, it's pretty short." She laughs uncomfortably.

I shake my head. "Don't do that, Sarah." I look at her. "It's important to you, and I want to respect that."

"I'm not a prude." She folds her arms across her chest defensively.

"Sarah, don't put words into my mouth," I warn her. "I never said that. I didn't even imply that—besides, it's not a dirty word. However you feel about sex is valid."

She sighs, dropping her hands into her lap. "Sorry. It's not something I talk about a lot."

"Yet we've barely touched each other. I have yet to kiss you properly. And we're both ready to rip each other's clothes off.

Am I wrong?" I briefly wonder how much she's talked to Lily about sex, considering her age. I push the thought aside. This is about me and Sarah.

"Not generally my style," she smirks, "and any time I try to get close to you, you pull away from me. Like you don't want me."

I shake my head. "I pull away because I know if we get started without talking about this, we're going to end up fucking in like three minutes flat."

She raises an eyebrow, the corner of her mouth twitching. "You think it would take that long?" She bites her lower lip.

I inhale deeply, trying to find the right words. I roll my ankle in a circle, trying to work out the tightness in my calf.

She must see me wince because she reaches out. "What helps?" She nods toward my leg.

I shake my head. "Nothing, really. I need to get up and move around a little." I study her for a long moment. "I don't want to just jump you," I tell her softly. I swallow thickly. "Well, I do. But I really like you. I want to see if we can make something work."

"Even though we both suck at communicating?" She chuckles under her breath.

"Especially since we both suck at communicating," I point out. "But I need to know where your head is at. Both because of work—I'm sorry, but we have to work together for the next few months, and that matters—but also because I don't just want to fuck you." I take her hand in mine, gently kissing her palm. "Don't get me wrong, I do want to fuck you. But I want more than that."

She nods. "At least we're on the same page, then." She glances toward the bedrooms and sighs.

"You're anxious. How long has it been?" I tease her with an elbow to the ribs.

"Don't you need to stretch your leg?" she asks, pulling away from me. "Come on. Let's get a drink." She pulls me up off the couch.

I wrap my arms around her, pulling her body against mine. I kiss her neck, right below her ear. "How long since you last had an orgasm?" I whisper, my breath tickling her ear. I can feel her body quiver against me.

She walks me backward until I'm up against the wall, pressing her leg between mine, her thigh pressed hard against my core. She turns her head, meeting my eyes. "Last night, thinking about you. Imagining your face between my legs."

A flood of desire hits me deep in my core. I swallow; I can't breathe. "Next time you touch yourself," I murmur, pulling her bottom lip between my teeth, "call me so I can listen to you come."

She moans softly. Her hand slides around my neck, and her fingers twine through my hair, pulling me closer. "No. Next time you'll be there," she growls. Her mouth is on mine, wild and insistent. Her tongue traces my bottom lip. I let her in, my tongue finding hers, tasting her. A low moan escapes the back of my throat, and she rubs her thigh harder against me. Sliding my hands under her shirt, I splay them across her back.

"Carmen." She breathes my name into my mouth. She tastes of chardonnay and bruschetta, and I run my tongue across her teeth. I breathe in the scent of her, of peaches and cinnamon, and the unique scent of Sarah. I feel my core tightening in anticipation. I roll my hips to get more friction against her.

Her mouth is suddenly on my jawline, the softness of her lips and the light nip of her teeth. "How long has it been since *you* had an orgasm? Hmm?" She chuckles, her breath sending a shiver of pleasure through my whole body.

I lean my head back against the wall, giving her better access to my neck. "You keep doing that and I'd say five minutes from now," I tell her, my voice husky. If I let myself, I could probably get off right now, as hot as I am for her.

"Do you want to stay?" she asks quietly, pulling back to gaze into my eyes.

I consider her for a long moment, trying to steady my breath. "You're serious?"

She nods without hesitation. "Yes. I wouldn't ask if I wasn't." She pulls back from me, easing the pressure she had holding me against the wall.

I glance toward Lily's bedroom door. "I think whether I want to and whether I should are two different questions."

Sarah laughs. "She's not clueless, Carmen. If she hears anything, she'll put some music on. It wouldn't be the first time." She kisses me lightly before stepping away from me. "Come have a drink." She motions toward the kitchen.

I furrow my brow, following her into the kitchen. "I thought you said you haven't had anyone here—"

"I haven't." She snorts. "What else did I say?" She raises her eyes playfully. She pulls the pitcher of strawberry lemon water out of the fridge.

My eyes widen in surprise. "You make enough noise that she can hear you?" I fight back an embarrassed laugh. I would die if my dad heard me getting myself off.

"She hears me when I cry myself to sleep at night, too," she says softly. "You already know that, though."

I nod thoughtfully. "I don't ever want you to cry yourself to sleep again because of me," I tell her, wrapping my arms around her.

"Lily would probably tell on me," she says wistfully.

"Hey. Do you think she's still awake?" I ask.

She glances at the clock. It's only a little after ten. "Probably. You want to check with her if it's okay for you to stay?" There's no teasing in her voice. "Go ahead. You can if you want to."

"You're sure?" It's weird, to feel like I need her permission to stay—but I'm in her house, with her mom, and I know how precious they are to each other.

"Go ahead," she repeats. "Knock first—but if she doesn't answer, just poke your head in. She probably has music on loud enough not to hear you."

"I won't walk in on anything?" I ask, raising an eyebrow.

She bursts out laughing. "No. She's twelve, Carmen." She shakes her head in amusement. "She has a lock on her door if she needs that kind of privacy. She's not supposed to use it for anything else, though. The rule is that if she has the door shut,

I knock. But when she's listening to music, she doesn't hear it. Hence, keeping the door unlocked."

"You've talked to her about locking the door if she needs alone time?" I raise my eyebrow in amusement, surprised.

"Um, yes? I'd sure as hell rather she hear it from me than learn shit like that from kids at school. Plus, thin walls," she adds. "I talk to her about almost everything. I don't hide things from her. It's not like she's five."

Chuckling to myself, I tuck a stray hair behind her ear. "You really want me to stay?" I ask her again, now that we're not pawing at each other.

"As long as you're comfortable with it, yes. If you don't want to have sex, I can wait, but I want to be in your arms." She laughs. "I want more, but I'll respect your boundaries."

Seriously? If she gets me started, there aren't going to be any boundaries. "Hold that thought."

I knock on Lily's door, softly the first time. When she doesn't answer, I knock louder.

"I'm decent," she calls through the closed door.

I poke my head in. She looks up and notices me, momentarily startled.

"It's you. Sorry. I just expected mom. What's up?"

"Can I come in a minute and talk? Or are you busy?" I nod at her phone.

She shrugs. "Nothing that can't wait a few minutes. What is it?" She scoots over on her bed and motions for me to come in. "Is mom okay?"

I sit down next to her and nod. "She's fine. She said she talked to you about me staying the night."

She shrugs. "Yeah?"

"Are you okay with me staying the night?"

"You mean, am I okay with you having sex with my mom?" she asks bluntly. "You know I'm old enough to understand about sex."

I laugh. "Yes, you're old enough to know about sex. But Lily—whether I have sex with your mom or not, that isn't up to you. That's up to her. I'm asking *you* if you're okay with me staying the night."

She shrugs again. "You're a grown woman. Do what you want."

I turn toward her and pull my leg up under me to face her better. I wince as my calf spasms. "Bug, you should know me by now. I like your mom. A lot."

The corner of her mouth twitches up. "I noticed. I'm pretty sure the feeling is mutual."

I gently shove her shoulder, and she falls back against the bed laughing. "You know, if you're not okay with me staying, I'll go home. The two of you come as a package deal, and unless I know you're okay with me being here, I'm going to go home."

"Does she want you to stay?" she asks, sitting up.

"Yes."

"Do you want to stay?" she asks.

I nod. "As long as you're okay with it, yes."

She shrugs again. "Then I want you to stay, too. Just don't keep her up all night. We need to leave for ballet at eight."

I close my eyes and shake my head at this child. She surprises me by wrapping me in a big hug.

I'm halfway to the door when she calls softly to me. "Carmen?"

I turn around. "What, sweetie?"

"Your leg. Are you okay?"

I smile. "I'll live, I promise. I just need to stretch it a little."

18

SARAH

"I told you she's fine with you being here," I tell Carmen as I lock up and turn the lights off.

She nods. "I know, but like I told her. You guys are a package deal, so I needed to check with her, too."

"I'm glad you get along with her," I murmur softly, closing the bedroom door behind us.

She stands in the middle of the room, looking around. "Come here," her husky voice commands me.

I come to her and wrap my hand around the back of her neck. "Can I kiss you?" I lick my lower lip, and my eyes drop to her mouth. Her breath catches.

She puts her hand on my arm, gently pulling out of my grip. "Not yet," she swallows. "Turn around, Sarah."

I turn around, confused. What's she playing at?

She puts her hands on my shoulders and gently pushes my hair to the side. She kisses me softly on the back of my neck. "This is where it started that night." She traces her finger across the bare skin above my collar. "Do you know how much I wanted to touch you that night?" she breathes into my ear. Her soft warm lips trail down my neck.

I turn my head toward her. "I thought I imagined it."

She wraps her arms around me, her hands splayed across my stomach. "And you still stripped down to your panties and you walked away from me."

I laugh lightly. After the night I'd had at the gala, it would have been a bad idea, no matter how much I wanted her. I take her hands and pull them away from my body. Turning around, I kiss her lightly. "Before you get me going again," I glance at the bed, "I want to get this makeup off. Okay?"

She rolls her eyes. "Are you always so practical?"

"Yes." I grin at her. "Sorry to disappoint. But your face will be happier tomorrow if you treat it right."

"Oh, I'm pretty sure my face will be happy tomorrow either way."

I laugh. "There's an extra toothbrush if you want. Anything in the bathroom you want to use, you're welcome to it." She pouts playfully, and I smack her butt. "Carmen, I'm not going anywhere. I promise."

She walks out of the bathroom a few minutes later and studies me silently for a moment. I pull two t-shirts out of my drawer and stick them on top of the dresser. She walks over to me and wraps her arms around my waist. "Do you always have a toothbrush for a first date?" she asks playfully.

"I like to be prepared." I chuckle, trailing my finger along her collarbone. I undo the top button of her shirt, tracing my finger along her soft skin. "May I?" I ask her, swallowing my nerves away. It's been so long since I've touched a woman.

She doesn't answer right away, and I look up to meet her eyes. "Please?" I need to touch her.

"Please," she begs, nodding. "Do you always move this slow?" She moans softly as I unbutton the next one and lean down to kiss her beautiful skin.

"I want to savor you," I whisper against her skin, freeing another button. I pull her shirt open, just enough to drag my fingertip across the exposed top of her breast.

She pulls me toward the bed. "Savor me naked," she urges, unbuttoning my jeans.

"My, my. Aren't you impatient." I chuckle, my lips tracing the bare skin above her bra. I nip at her. Undoing the rest of the buttons, I push the shirt off her shoulders and trace a fingertip from the bare skin over her belly button up between her breasts.

Her breath catches. "Sarah." She reaches behind me and unbuttons my shirt, pulling it over my head. She grabs my hips and falls back on the bed, pulling me down on top of her. "Take these off." She pushes my jeans over my hips.

I wriggle out of them while she pulls her own off, tossing them on the floor. She pushes me back against the bed and straddles me in her matching pink bra and panties. Her hands cup my breasts as she leans forward to kiss me.

I pull her down next to me and take her face in my hands. "Carmen, slow down. Kiss me," I whisper into the hollow of her neck.

She humors me for about thirty seconds, but then pulls back, meeting my eyes. "Are you having second thoughts? Because if you are, we should stop now." Her breath is hard as she leans back against the pillow, her eyes searching the ceiling.

"No, but this isn't a race." I trail a finger across her bare stomach.

"Yes, it is, Sarah. I'm going to combust here. Seriously. You keep hitting the brakes."

I shake my head. "No, I just want this to last. If I only get one night with you, I want to take my time and enjoy it."

"It won't be only one night," she promises me. She leans over and kisses me, softly pulling my lower lip between her teeth. "I have a proposition for you," she breathes heavily.

The corner of my mouth turns up in amusement. "Sex on a first date is already moving fast for me. I'm not ready for a ring yet."

She shakes her head, and I can feel her body shaking with laughter against mine. "No, not that kind of proposition. I want you to fuck me. Now." She swallows. I can feel how tightly she's wound up. "Afterward, we can go as slow as you want. I promise. I want you so bad it hurts. Literally. And you're not even wet for me yet."

I raise an eyebrow in surprise, trying to hide a smirk. "That's pretty presumptuous of you." I take her hand, guiding it between my thighs, my heart racing. She feels my wetness through my panties, and I moan. "No, feel me," I growl desperately. I entwine my fingers with hers, guiding her hand under the thin fabric. Her middle finger sinks into my wet center. My muscles tighten around her.

"Oh, God," she groans loudly.

I buck up against her hand, needing more.

But she pulls away from me, suddenly sitting up. "No, no, no," she groans. She sounds annoyed and panicked.

"Carmen?" I sit up, searching her pained face. I knew this wasn't a good idea. I thought we were on the same page, or at least close enough, that we could both get some relief tonight.

"Not you," she manages through gritted teeth. She nods toward her leg, stiff as a board, every muscle in her body taut.

Oh, God. "What should I do?" I ask her frantically.

She takes a long deep breath, then speaks through clenched teeth. "Kill me."

"Ha, funny," I say drily, although her body language shows she's not joking. "What else?"

"Push on my foot," she chokes through the pain. Her body shudders. "Do you have a heating pad?"

I climb down to the foot of the bed, and push against her foot, pressing it to a ninety-degree angle. "Like this?"

She nods. "Harder. As hard as you can." She closes her eyes in pain and leans over to wrap her hands around the arch of her foot. She groans at the slight relief. "Do you have a heating pad?"

I nod. "In Lily's room." I knock on the wall three times. That's our way of getting each other's attention without hollering. She's more likely to hear it through her music. I wait a few seconds and knock again.

"Mom?" her voice through the wall is timid, unsure why I'd be calling her at the moment—especially given the circumstances.

"Lily," I holler, "bring the heating pad in here. Now, please."

A minute later, Lily knocks softly and sticks her head in. She looks between me and Carmen in our underwear.

"Come in. Plug it in next to the bed," I tell her. "Turn it on high, please."

She plugs it in and passes it to Carmen, who wriggles it under her left hamstring.

Lily glances between us. "Sex doesn't look like very much fun," she deadpans. She raises an eyebrow at Carmen. "Looks painful, actually."

"It's my leg, you brat," Carmen growls, tossing a pillow at her.

"No shit, Sherlock," she replies. "Can I help?"

Carmen takes a deep breath against the pain. "Do you ever get muscle rubdowns after ballet?"

"Sometimes. If I'm working on something new and end up really sore."

"If I turn over, can you do my left hamstring? As hard as you can." Carmen sighs. She's starting to breathe a little easier now.

"Mom's better at it. Her hands are stronger." She stops for a minute. "Can you guys put shirts on or something?" she says uncomfortably.

Oh my God. I'm such an idiot. "Come hold her foot, Bug." As soon as Lily has pressure on Carmen's foot, I grab the T-shirts off the dresser. When I put them there earlier, I was thinking about running into the kitchen in the middle of the night for water or something, not this. I pull one over my head and bring the other one over to Carmen.

She pulls it over her head before scooting down the bed so her foot hangs over the edge. She turns over onto her stomach. "The worst starts about two inches above my knee. There are two main muscles. Start with the outer muscle."

"Holy fuck," Lily whispers in awe. "You can see it moving. I can literally see the muscles rippling."

"Sarah." Carmen groans. "Please."

I wrap my hands around her leg and dig my thumbs into her lower hamstring. I run my thumbs up the length of the muscle, feeling for the worst spots. When I rub Lily's legs, I can usually feel where the knots are. Carmen's whole leg feels riddled with them, though.

"Start at the bottom." She grimaces. "Dig as hard as you can." I do, and she screams out in pain. She catches her breath, wincing. "Don't stop," she begs.

"I don't want to hurt you," I argue.

"Trust me, it's the best way to get it to back off." She inhales sharply as my thumbs dig into her muscles again. "Lily, go get my purse. It's on the counter. Some water, too."

I can already feel her muscles starting to slow down, to relax under my ministrations, by the time Lily comes back a minute later.

She fishes a bottle of pills from her purse and looks at them with a frown. She half turns her body to look up at me. "If I take three of these, are you okay with me staying in the morning after you guys leave? I shouldn't drive for at least twelve or fifteen hours. Or I can have my dad come pick me up in the morning." She chews on her cheek with a sigh. "Then I'd have to tell him I was here."

Lily snorts. "He doesn't already know?"

Carmen shrugs awkwardly. "He could probably guess, but half the time he doesn't even realize if I'm home or not for the night. I let my abuela know I wasn't coming home so they won't worry, but..."

"You can stay as long as you need to," I tell her, lessening the pressure on her leg a little as I feel the muscles relent beneath my fingers. "I can bring you home later if you want, too. Take whatever you need to feel better."

Carmen pops three pills in her mouth and washes them down with the water. She snorts. "I take no responsibility for what I say or do over the next twelve hours." She tosses the medicine bottle back in her purse, dropping her head onto her arms in surrender. "Don't worry if I sleep through the morning," she mumbles into her arms.

Lily sits on the bed next to her and puts a hand on her back. "Are you going to be okay?"

"I'll live, Bug. I promise. Sometimes this happens." She shakes her leg a little, and I let go as she rolls away from Lily, onto her back. "It's more scary for you, especially the first time you see it. I should have warned you that sometimes it happens. It hasn't been this bad in a long time, though." She adjusts the heating pad under her leg again, then reaches for a pillow and sticks it under her head.

"Why does it do that? It looks like it hurts really bad."

Carmen nods. "Have you ever woken up in the middle of the night with a leg cramp?" Lily nods, and Carmen continues. "It's like that, only more intense—mostly because it doesn't stop. Stretching and massage help a little, but I can't massage that deep myself, not at the right angle."

"What do you do if no one's around to help?"

Carmen shrugs. "It usually happens at home. My dad helps. One of the guys at work has helped me out a few times over the years." She yawns, her jaw cracking loudly.

"Why does it do that? Can't the doctors fix it?" Bug asks.

Carmen laughs distantly. "When I was your age, I was in a car crash. It ruined my leg. Really bad. They told me I would probably never walk again." Her voice is slowing down; she sounds like she's underwater. "They wanted to cut my leg off and give me a new one. They told my daddy I had a better chance of walking that way."

I gasp softly. I knew she still had some issues from the accident, but I had no idea the accident had been that bad.

"Your dad didn't let them, though." Lily points out the obvious.

"Nope." Carmen has a dopey smile on her face. "He fought for my leg. I lost my mom. I couldn't lose my leg, too." She closes her eyes as the medicine finally knocks her out.

19

Carmen

"Boss." Michael sticks his head into my office.

I look up and see the frown on his face. "Montgomery is escalating?" I guess by his expression.

He nods reluctantly. "Seems like he's getting ready to rile people up right before Christmas. He's using it to highlight what an abomination we all are to their precious religion."

I shake my head. "Not all religious people think like he does, Mike. Don't stoop to his level."

"Yes, ma'am." He has the sense to look chastened.

I give him a minute to sit with that. "Does he have any events planned? It seems like most people are too busy with the holidays this time of year—and it's cold."

"He's pushing to get a group together at the mall the day after Thanksgiving as"—he throws up his fingers in air quotes—"a peaceful statement about their opposition to our values." He grimaces in distaste.

I bite my cheek, thinking. "It's a high traffic area, even more so on Black Friday. This is a new one for him. Do you think it'll gain any traction?"

He purses his lips together. "Honestly? I don't know. We're watching whatever chatter we can find about it."

I shake my head slowly. "It doesn't make sense. It'll be a high traffic, high visibility spot, but people are going to be busy shopping. It's the beginning of the Christmas season." Plus it's private property. "Hey. Do we know who the mall property owners are?"

He gives me a perplexed look. "No? I'm sure I can find out, though. What are you thinking, boss?"

"The mall is private property. We can't even put the cops on watch, not in an official way. They couldn't come in unless someone called them."

"Debatable on that," he murmurs, "but they can't be hanging around waiting for something to happen—not like in public spaces. We can give them a heads-up though. That way they're on alert if things go sideways."

"Nothing is going sideways, not at the mall on Black Friday. We can also give mall security a heads up. Work with Ali to find out about the owner first, and whose side they'd be on. He might have picked the place deliberately."

"On it, boss."

I scratch my head. "Mike?" He stops, already halfway out the door. "Send Ali in for me, will you?"

"Dad?" My voice pulls him out of his thoughts. He's been quiet all of dinner tonight, quieter than usual.

He pulls himself out of whatever la-la land he was in. *"Mija?"* He takes a bite of his food.

"Have you ever dealt with the owners of the mall?" I ask curiously.

He swallows his food and takes a drink, giving himself time to think. "Not directly." He shakes his head. "It's one of those huge corporations that owns malls all over the country, though. Why do you ask?"

I chuckle. I always ask my dad seemingly random questions. He always knows there's something behind them. "Montgomery is escalating."

"At the mall?" he asks, surprise coloring his voice. "Seems like an odd place to go."

I shake my head. "At first glance. But if you think about it, the weather and the season put him in the limelight."

"I thought he never got physically involved at any of the protests," he says, a question in his tone.

I shake my head. "It's doubtful he'll be there, but he likes to rile people up." I sigh in exasperation. "This is a new tactic for him. I feel like my team is going into this blind."

He laughs. "Carmen, it'll be fine. You know what you're dealing with. I'll have Sarah get a hold of the security team we normally use and find out about whoever's in charge of security over there—if it would be to our benefit to warn them ahead of time or not." If they're not on our side, it would be better not to give them a heads up.

"I'll have my team get with our contracted security company and dig a little, too." I bite my lip. "About Sarah..." I start, unsure how to approach this.

The corner of my dad's mouth twists up in a smile. I didn't tell him about my leg cramping up on me so bad the other night, but I'm sure abuela told him that I was over at Sarah's all night. "How are things going with her?" he asks, trying to sound casual. I can tell he's happy that I've found someone I like, but there's the awkward factor that she works for him. It's not a problem, it's just weird. Especially since it wasn't that long ago he was trying to get in her pants.

"We're fine," I say, dismissing that line of thought. "This is actually work related."

"I'm listening." He nods for me to go on. It's not uncommon for us to talk about work sometimes, especially since his company is working for mine right now—and Sarah's in charge of my build.

"Who are your lead architects?" I ask him.

He furrows his brow. "Sarah and Bob. Why?"

"Who's better?" I ask him, trying to keep the emotion out of my voice.

"Sarah, by a long shot. That's why she's getting the promotion. But if you two want some time off..." He wiggles his eyebrows at me. "We could arrange that, after the cultural center is finished—probably mid-April. Everything is on track with the build side of things."

I roll my eyes and chuckle. "Yeah, let's not jump that gun yet, Dad." Strangely enough, the idea of spending my life with her *has* occurred to me, but it's way too soon to talk about that.

"Why do you ask, then?" He sounds genuinely curious.

"I'm going to ask a question, but I don't want you to answer me." Confusion crosses his face. "How much do they each make, and are they being fairly compensated for what they bring to your company?"

He frowns, his eyes darkening. "Is she using you to get a raise?"

I raise my eyebrows. "No. She didn't tell me anything. In fact, she told me it's none of my business." Which isn't one hundred percent true, seeing as my business is covering her salary right now, but I digress. "She would probably kill me if she even knew I asked." Although, to be fair, she did tell me to talk to him about it if I want to know. In all honesty, I don't want to know, because I'm sure it would piss me off.

"Then why are you asking?" The frown across his face deepens.

I shrug noncommittally. "She said something that made me wonder, that's all."

"Carmen." He's not angry, but by the tone of his voice, I know he's not going to let this go. Apparently, my question hit a nerve. "What did she say?"

I shake my head. "It doesn't matter, Dad. Just forget it."

"If you don't tell me, I'll ask her," he threatens.

"If you were paying her a comparable salary, you wouldn't even blink at my question. You realize that, don't you?" I am so disgusted by his blindness when it comes to how he treats the women in his company. "We were talking about something else, something that Lily brought up. It had nothing to do with you." I look up and meet his eyes.

He nods. "Go on," he says, somewhat pacified.

"I asked her if she ever felt like her job was threatened—when you were going after her." The idea makes me want to vomit. "She said no—that you'd be a stupid fucker to let her go. She could have a dozen jobs lined up in a week, making a lot more money than she does right now." He looks like I slapped him in the face. "My words, not hers," I clarify quickly.

"Carmen." Abuela's soft voice surprises me from across the table. I forgot she was here. "Don't talk to your papá like that." She reaches over, putting a frail hand over mine and squeezing it. I give her a short nod of acquiescence before she stands up and grabs our plates. She disappears into the kitchen.

"The conversation wasn't about you, Dad. I mean, that one comment was, because I asked her, but it was in the context of a different conversation that had nothing to do with you. I swear."

He reaches for his glass of water and takes a long swallow. "Okay."

I stand up, planning to go help abuela clean up in the kitchen, but he stops me.

"Mija?" He's not angry, but I can't read the expression on his face. "Don't let her come between us, okay?"

"She has nothing to do with it," I say sharply. "It's just that I'm starting to see a side of you I don't know if I like, or if I can respect. Don't put that on her, just because she didn't let you get in her pants."

I turn and storm into the kitchen.

Abuela puts her hand on my shoulder, wet from the sink full of dishes. "Carmencita," she says softly. "You shouldn't talk to him like that." Her voice is gentle, disapproving.

I look at her and frown. "If mom was still alive and she was working, would it be fair for her to work for sixty percent of what a man makes doing the same job?"

"Your mamá was one of the best lawyers in the county, cariño. She would be making more than all of them."

I shake my head. "No, she wouldn't, abuela. That's my point." I blink back an angry tear before it falls. I grab a washcloth off the counter, turning around and vigorously scrubbing the stovetop and the counters clean. It makes me so mad. I gulp a deep breath of air, trying to calm myself. After getting myself under some semblance of control, I turn around to help her finish the dishes.

Before I turn to go, she stops me. "Are you okay, cariño?"

I sigh softly. I'm not upset with her. It's not fair that she has to witness dad getting pissy when I throw his misogyny in his face. "I'll be fine," I say brusquely. "I'm going to Sarah's. Don't worry if I don't come home tonight."

"Text me when you know for sure, so I don't worry." She takes my head in her hands, pulling me close and giving me a light kiss on my forehead. "I love you."

I wrap my arms around her in a tight hug. "I know. Love you, too."

It's barely seven on a Wednesday night, and I don't even know if Sarah and Lily will be home yet. They usually stop for something to eat on the way home from ballet. When I pull into their parking lot, I look around for her car. I probably should've called before I came over.

We've talked quite a bit the past few days, over text and on the phone, but I haven't seen her since I left their house Saturday afternoon. After that stupid night I ended up passed out from painkillers and muscle relaxers in her bed.

I decide to text her. *Are you guys home?*

After a few minutes of no reply, I text Lily. *Is your mom driving?*

yep

If I call, can you put me on speaker so I can talk to her for a minute?

sure, but we'll be home in a minute

I call Lily's phone. Better to call before Sarah realizes I'm already here.

"What's up? Is everything okay?" she asks before I can say anything.

"Put me on speaker." I can hear the background noise almost immediately. "I'm fine, there's nothing wrong. Sarah, can you hear me?"

"Carmen. What's wrong? You wouldn't call Bug's phone to talk to me while I'm driving unless something was wrong."

I sigh. "I got into it with dad. I debated between drowning myself in a bottle of good wine or coming to hang out with you two for the night. I'll be quiet, and I won't keep anyone up past their bedtime," I promise ruefully.

"You can sleep on the couch," Lily says, her voice serious.

Sarah ignores her. "You can come over. We'll be home in a few minutes." She's quiet for a minute. "Are you okay, though?"

I see them pull into the parking lot. "How about I tell you when you get home." I chuckle under my breath. She pulls into the parking spot next to me. She doesn't notice until I get out of my car.

"Oh. Hi," she says through the phone, surprised.

"Bye," Lily singsongs before ending the call. I can see her rolling her eyes at me through the car window.

After we get upstairs with my bag and Lily's dance stuff, Sarah turns to me. "What happened?" She pulls a bottle of wine out of the fridge. "You want a glass?"

Lily heads off to her room to shower and change into her pajamas, so we're alone for a minute. I shrug. "Half a glass? Stop me after that."

She pours herself one, too, and passes me mine. "So, what did you guys fight about?" She glances between the table and the couch, a question in her eyes.

I head toward the couch and sit down in the far corner. Missy jumps into my lap and headbutts me. I pick her up, giving her a snuggle before plopping her in my lap, rubbing my hand across her back. "It wasn't really—" I stop myself. It wasn't really a fight, and I don't want Sarah to end up in the middle of things between me and my dad. Even though this thing is tangentially related to her, it's not about her at all.

"It was about me." She sits down on the other side of the couch, putting her bare feet up on the coffee table. When I don't respond, she studies me for a long minute and sighs. "Will I need to deal with it when I go to work in the morning?"

"He's always professional at the office, right? Since all this started between us?" When she nods, I shake my head. "I don't think he's going to bring anything up to you at work, no." I really can't imagine him saying anything to her.

"Does he have a problem with us?" she asks quietly. "With us being together? The few times it's come up in conversation, he's seemed okay with it."

I shake my head. "No, nothing like that. He was actually teasing me at dinner about going on a honeymoon."

Sarah groans. "God, we've barely kissed. I haven't even gotten into your pants yet."

I laugh. "Chill, Sarah. He knows I was here last weekend, and that I spent almost all day Saturday with you. That's all."

She shakes her head. "You were out cold, and I wouldn't let you drive until those meds wore off."

I chuckle softly. "All he knows is that I was here. I didn't tell him about my leg acting up. Anyway, he was just making assumptions. "I like you. A lot. Honestly, I could see us together in the future, but we're a long way from that. Please don't take that the wrong way."

She laughs. "Thank God." She picks up the remote and turns the TV on. "If you want to talk about it, I'm happy to listen. But I honestly don't want to get between you and your dad."

20

SARAH

"Boss wants to see you." Bob glances at me as I walk into the office. I drop my purse off at my desk and look up at the clock. I'm one minute late. If Carmen's going to stay over during the week, I'll need to adjust our morning routine. I sigh under my breath.

"You want to see me, sir?" I ask, poking my head in through Richard's half-open door.

"Come on in, Sarah. Close the door?" I close it gently before sitting down. He must notice me stiffen. "You can leave it open if you want."

I groan uncomfortably. "It's fine, sir. What did you want to see me about?"

He bites the inside of his cheek and slowly wipes his hand down his face. "Work stuff." *He feels the need to clarify that?* "Montgomery seems to be escalating." He sighs audibly, shaking his head. "Hold on a minute."

Wondering what's on his mind, I wait. For a very long minute. I tighten my hands into fists in my lap, around the fabric of my skirt.

"Look, Sarah. You're one of my best employees. I have no problem with you dating Carmen, but..." He shakes his head. "She likes you, and if you guys make each other happy, I'm all for it."

"Sir?" He stops and looks at me. It's almost like he forgot I was here while he tried to find the words for whatever he's trying to say.

He growls to himself. "I don't want to lose you to her, that's all." He shakes his head again. "That's not what I—." He puts his palms on the desk, his shoulders sagging. "I don't want what you and she have to get in the way of your job here."

I raise an eyebrow at him in surprise. "I didn't think it was, sir."

"You're not looking for other jobs?" he asks, honestly surprised.

What the hell? I cock my head and study him, my brow furrowed. "Do I need to be?" I would need to finish the projects I'm working on now. At least the cultural center, since it only has a few months to go. I suppose the bridge project is in early enough stages that it could be reassigned without too much trouble.

I swallow the anxiety in my chest and meet his eyes. "I have no idea what Carmen said to you, or what you said to her. But if there are issues with my job performance or my employment status, I'd appreciate it if you'd discuss it with me. Not my girlfriend." Technically, I don't think she's earned that title yet, but whatever. "Did you have something you wanted to discuss with *me* this morning?" I ask him stiffly.

He swallows visibly and nods. "Montgomery is escalating. Did Carmen or her team talk to you about it yet?"

I shake my head, not trusting my voice. I'm not sure if I want to scream or cry. I've never had my personal life affect my professional life before.

"He's planning a protest at the mall on Black Friday. Next week." He clears his throat uncomfortably.

"I'll talk to Carmen and Ethan." I pause, waiting for him to say something. When he doesn't, I study him for a beat. "Did you want to talk to me about my job performance, sir?" I ask icily, forcing myself *not* to just get up and walk away from him. Which I've never done in the 10 years I've worked for him.

He closes his eyes and inhales slowly. He's obviously frustrated with something. Whatever he and Carmen argued about last night, probably. "No, you're fine, Sarah. Let me know if you need anything."

I get up and head for the door. When I reach it, I turn back. "Look," I say quietly. "I like her. I also like working for you." If I didn't, I would have been gone years ago. He's not perfect, but he's generally a good guy to work for. "Whatever disagreements you two get into, I don't want to be part of it. I don't want to be in the middle of shit, and I don't want to be put in a position where I need to choose sides."

He gives me a small smile. "Good. Then we're on the same page. But if you have a problem, talk to me, okay?"

I raise an eyebrow, the corner of my mouth twitching. "You mean a work problem, I assume."

"Yes." He chuckles. "Work. Your job. Me. If you have an issue with me, talk to me. Not her."

"Fair enough." I nod, the knot of anxiety loosening just a little. "Sorry I was late this morning, sir. It won't happen again."

That draws a laugh out of him. "You were less than a minute late, Sarah. It's not a big deal."

I pick up my cell phone as soon as I'm back at my desk.

What the fuck did you say to him last night? I text Carmen. *Why the fuck do I feel like my job is on the line now?*

Richard comes out of his office wearing his jacket and glances at me. He knows I'm livid. He raises an eyebrow at me and nods toward the door, a question in his gaze. He tugs at his jacket and nods toward mine. He wants to talk to me, outside of the walls of this office.

I inhale slowly, trying to calm myself. I exhale slowly, calming the adrenaline down a bit, and nod.

Richard walks over to Bob's desk. "We should be back in an hour," he tells him quietly. Only a handful of people are in the office this early, and no one's paying attention to us. Bob nods absently as he pulls something up on his laptop.

Richard opens the door for me, and we take the elevator down to the ground floor in silence. Once we emerge on the main floor, nearly empty now, he turns to me. "Where's somewhere you'll be comfortable talking? Coffee, donuts, park. Bar. I don't care where."

"I don't think there are any bars open this early, and it's fucking cold outside," I bite out.

He turns to me, frustrated. "Look, Sarah. Things are more complicated now, with you seeing Carmen. That's okay, as long as it's what both of you want. But you're still on my team, and we need to find a way to make that work. Okay?"

I give him a small nod.

"Ten years. I've always had your back. That's not going to change, whatever happens between you and Carmen. Or between me and Carmen," he adds, suddenly sounding sad. "I just want to go to a place where you feel comfortable talking with me. I thought it would be better away from work because this is obviously about more than that. But if it would make you more comfortable, we can talk with HR present."

My phone buzzes in my pocket, but I ignore it. She can answer for herself later. I glance at Richard. He genuinely wants to set things right with me. I shake my head. "We don't need HR. Mezzo Coffee is around the corner. They're not usually busy this time of morning."

We're both quiet as we grab two coffees and head toward the back of the cafe. I sit down silently, waiting for him to start. Oddly, I have no qualms about where this conversation will go. He and I don't always agree on things, but he's always listened to me and respected whatever I had to say.

He takes a sip of his coffee, then looks up at me. "I'm sorry," he starts.

After a minute, I nod. He seems to expect a response. "Okay." I drag the word out, wondering what exactly he's sorry for.

He chuckles. "You aren't going to make this easy on me, are you?"

The corner of my mouth twitches. "I don't go easy on anyone. It's one reason why I'm good at my job—which you know." I relax into my seat. "I don't even know what this is all about, to be honest with you."

He ignores my unspoken question. "Are you looking for another job?" He asks the question softly.

I try to hide my surprise at his bluntness. I choose my next words carefully. "I'm not actively looking for a new job."

"So you are scoping out other opportunities." He sounds disappointed.

I raise an eyebrow. "I've been scoping out new opportunities since before you hired me, sir. But I'm still working for you." This is so frustrating. "It gives me an idea of what skills are needed at the next level. It gives me an idea of our competition. It gives me an idea what comparable positions offer."

"And you're still working for me," he repeats my words.

"Come on, Richard. When you hired me ten years ago, I was barely out of school. I had potential, but I was nowhere near reaching it. A lot of what I've learned, I learned from you. But you know I have a wider skill set than that now. How do you think that happened?" Sometimes it frustrates the shit out of me that I'm a better architect than my boss. Not that I would ever call him on it.

I let out a long breath. "What did she say to you that makes you think I'm going anywhere?" If he's not going to bring it up, I will. I'd like to hear his side of the story before I hear Carmen's, anyway. There are always two sides.

He takes a sip of his coffee, looking at his hands. Finally, he looks up at me. "She asked me how much money you make, and if I pay you what you're worth."

I swear under my breath. "Of course she did."

"She didn't want to know. She just wanted me to think about it."

That's a relief, anyways. "You thought I was using her to get a raise." It's not a question, but it's not an accusation, either.

He doesn't answer me. He studies me for a long minute. "Did you know, when she was looking into different firms for the cultural center, that she didn't automatically pick us?"

I shake my head, chuckling. "No, but it doesn't surprise me. She doesn't do anything by halves. She only accepts the best of the best."

"She chose Tomsen Designs because of you. Of all the architects in the area, she picked you—because you're the best."

I had no idea. She and I rarely talk about work stuff, except when we're at work. "That's flattering," I say drily, "but I still don't understand why you think I'm going to bail on you. I suppose if things work out with me and Carmen in the long term, the three of us would need to sit down and talk about things, but we're not planning our honeymoon yet."

That makes him laugh. "Well, if and when the time comes, you have my blessing."

My face drops. Of all our parents and grandparents, he and abuela are the only two that will be there.

At my reaction, he tries to backpedal. "I didn't mean anything by that. I'm sorry."

I shrug it off. "Not you. Not the conversation we're having, either. You're avoiding the question. What makes you think I'm going to bail on you?" I repeat.

He lets out a long breath. "Carmen mentioned that you said you could easily get a better job."

"I did say that. Did she tell you the context of that comment?" I brace myself.

He shrugs his shoulder. "Partially. Very vaguely."

I breathe a sigh of relief and release the tension in my shoulders. "That conversation was complicated, and honestly had nothing to do with you." Not one hundred percent true, but close enough. "If you want to know, I'll tell you. But it's not pretty. It'll make you uncomfortable." Bringing my coffee to my lips, I take a sip. "It won't change the fact that I'm not actively looking for another job—and that if I have a problem with my job, I'll talk to you about it."

He studies me for a long minute, then bites his lip. "Tell me," he says softly.

"It's ugly, Richard. I don't want you to see me differently if I tell you." I bite my lip and shift my eyes away from his, staring at the space over his shoulder.

He swallows thickly. "If it were Carmen, I would want to know."

I raise my eyebrows. "If it were Carmen, you'd probably be in jail for assault."

He nods. "Please tell me."

I debate backing out of it, but I trust him. "At one of my first jobs, one of my seniors decided to take a special interest in me. He never went that far," I clarify, seeing the scowl forming on Richard's face. "He just liked to pull me into closets and get handsy with me. He threatened my job if I resisted him." I take a shaky breath. "I had bills to pay."

He growls softly. "You could have—"

"Stop, Richard." I interrupt him angrily. I take a deep breath. "I'd just found out I was pregnant, my parents had disowned me, and I had one friend in the world. She was married with two little kids. Don't tell me what I could've or should've done. I couldn't afford to lose my job. Don't judge me," I say, harsher than I mean to.

"Is she his?" he asks quietly.

"Lily?" I shake my head. "No. He never pushed it that far." I stop and take a sip of my cold coffee. "Anyway, my friend Beth and I have talked about it ad nauseam over the years. Lily has heard some of those conversations, and when she asks questions, I answer them."

He nods. "Sofi and I did the same with Carmen."

I breathe a little easier. I don't want him to dwell on that part. "The other night, the three of us were talking about workplace relationships and how complicated power dynamics are. We were talking about me and Carmen, Richard. The conversation honestly had nothing to do with you."

He opens his mouth to say something, but I put my hand up to stop him. "We've talked that out. You and me. We're fine." I pause until he gives me a short nod. "When we were talking about power dynamics, Lily said something about what happened before. In vague terms, because that's all she knows. But Carmen jumped on it and wanted to make sure that it wasn't you. And that it wasn't at your company."

He nods. "I'd never be able to live with myself if that happened to someone on my watch."

"I know," I say softly. "But Carmen asked me directly if I ever felt like my job was in jeopardy when you were pursuing me."

He closes his eyes and rubs his hand over his face.

"It wasn't particularly welcome, but I never felt like I would lose my job," I assure him. It occurs to me that I shouldn't be the one reassuring *him* of anything—but we've dealt with that. "For one, I like to think I know you better than that, after working for you for ten years." I swallow and take a nervous breath. "But also, because you'd be stupid to fire me over something like that. I could have a better paying job lined up in a week. You'd lose a lot more than I would."

He purses his lips together, speechless.

"Anyway," I continue, "for what it's worth—that's the context of whatever Carmen said to you." I give him a second to digest that, but then finish what I have to say. "I'm not interested in talking about what happened at my old company. I'm not upset with you for wanting to take me out, although I hope to God that idea is gone now, seeing as I'm sleeping with your daughter." *True, but misleading—at least so far.* "I never asked Carmen to say something so I could get a raise. I'm not actively looking for another job, and I'm going to trust that if there's ever reason for me to be, you'll talk to me about it. Me, not my girlfriend. And if she says something to you about me and work, please talk to me."

21

Carmen

As I pull into work, Sarah starts blowing up my phone. She's pissed off, and I have no idea why. I don't know what dad might have said to her. Other than maybe, *You're a rock star. Here's a huge raise so I'm actually paying you what you're worth,* or something unrealistic like that.

I text her to call me—twice—but she doesn't. I try calling her, but she sends me to voicemail. I think about calling dad, but I don't want to have that conversation at work. I'm not sure I want to have that conversation with him at all. I debate staying out here in the car for a few minutes to see if she answers my call, but I'm already running later than usual.

I pull up my text thread with Olivia and text her. *You're coming for turkey day next week, right?*

Free food, yes, of course, she replies. She must already be at work.

Do you have a few minutes for a call?

5m if it's important. you ok?

mostly, yeah

I send the text before hitting the call button.

"What's wrong?" She answers the call with no preamble.

"I need your advice, especially as a mama," I tell her. "And hi to you, too."

"Are you pregnant?" She sounds fake-shocked and confused.

I snicker. "No. I don't even know how that would happen."

"Do you need me to explain the birds and the bees to you?" She laughs.

"I have a problem with Sarah," I say, stopping her mid-laugh.

"Go on."

"Long story short," I say, "she's grossly underpaid. Not a big surprise, although I thought better of my dad." I pause. "Anyway, we were talking the other day about something else, and..." I trail off, not wanting to get into Sarah's personal shit. "She said she could easily get a better job within a week with a big pay raise, if she needed to."

Olivia makes a noise of agreement. "Most professionals could find a new job that fast if they wanted to. There aren't enough qualified people to fill open jobs," she points out. "Architects, lawyers, PR people."

"She's the best in the city, Liv. She's better than my dad. I hand-picked her for the cultural center before I met her."

"Okay. She's good at her job and she's underpaid. What's that got to do with you, though?"

"I kind of hinted to dad last night that he doesn't pay her enough, that she could go anywhere she wanted to, and that he's a misogynistic pig. Then left for the night."

"Very adult of you." I can hear her wry smile through the line.

"I honestly didn't think he'd bring it up to her. They're both professional at work, level-headed, and keep personal stuff out of the office."

"But he did, I take it. It's barely past eight. How does drama happen before normal people even get coffee in their veins?"

"I don't know." I roll my eyes. "She blew up my phone while I was driving, and when I tried to text her back, no answer. She's not answering her phone, either."

"Did it ever occur to you that she might be adulting? She *is* at work—maybe building you a grand castle where you can do good things in the world?"

I shake my head. "Her texts sounded like she was ready to blow a gasket, Liv."

"I know you don't always see eye to eye with your dad," she points out softly, "but he's a good guy. Maybe they're talking it out."

I snicker. "Do you think I was wrong to bring up her salary to him?"

"How much does she make?" Olivia asks curiously.

"I have no idea. I told him I don't want to know. I just wanted him to think about it."

"Hmph." She's quiet for a moment. "I don't know, Carmen. Normally I would say it's not your place, but if you don't point it out to him, I doubt anyone else will. Plus seeing as you're paying his firm to build for you, I think it's a fair question."

My phone beeps at me. "That's her on the other line. Talk later. Love you."

"Love you back."

I look at the phone for a moment before swiping to answer the call—before I give myself time to talk myself out of it. I answer. "Hey. Are you okay?"

"We'll talk about it later," she says, ignoring me. "I need to get back to the office in a minute. Richard said Montgomery is escalating?" She's calm enough to dismiss me like that. *What changed in the past half hour?*

I want to growl at her. "Get back to the office? Where are you?" Montgomery can wait.

She sighs loudly. "Richard took me out for a cup of coffee so we could talk. It's—" She pauses for a long moment. "Whatever. Things are okay. I think." She doesn't sound convinced. "I'm walking back now. Tell me about Montgomery."

I take a deep breath and slowly let it out. I was expecting her to blow up at me after her texts, and now she's ignoring the whole issue. She wants to know about Montgomery. "He's trying to get a protest event organized at the mall next Friday."

"Black Friday? The biggest shopping day of the year? That's insane."

"That's what Mike and I were thinking. This is a different tactic for him. Mike and Ali are working on a plan to counter it. Ali's our event coordinator," I tell her. "I have a few other ideas in mind to counter him, too."

"What do you need from us?" she asks. "It's private property, so we're very limited. We need to be careful."

I chew on my lip. "I thought of that, too. It could be either a blessing or a curse, depending on which side the mall's owners support. We have a plan in place, though. I don't think we need anything from you guys, but you should be aware. It's probably time to contract a guard on-premises to keep an eye on things."

"Okay. I'll talk to David and get him on that. You think Monday will be soon enough? How much noise is he making right now?"

"As long as the site is locked up, Monday should be fine. It's just chatter right now. I honestly don't know if this will gain traction or not. We're planning for the worst-case scenario but hoping for the best."

"Good plan." She laughs softly. "Let me know if there's anything else you need from my end. Keep me updated."

"Sarah." I stop her from ending the call. "We need to talk."

"Yes, we do," she says curtly. "Call me when you're out this afternoon. I need to get back to work now." She hangs up on me.

I knock on her apartment door. Lily answers; she's much quieter than normal. "Hey, kiddo. How was your day at school?"

She shrugs her shoulder. "Fine." She looks over her shoulder. "Mom, I'm going to Sophie's. I'll be back after dinner." Sarah grunts an acknowledgment, and Lily brushes past me without a second glance.

Okay, then. Judging by Lily's attitude, this is going to be fun. I put my purse on the counter before going into the kitchen. "You need help with anything?" I ask her, trying to act like nothing's wrong.

"Nope. Everything's done. Another ten or fifteen minutes." She washes her hands and dries them on a dish towel. "You can sit down if you want." She nods toward the kitchen table.

"You didn't have to send her away for dinner," I start. I really hope this won't turn into something unpleasant. We have nothing to hide from Lily. Sarah will tell her anything that happens, anyway.

She snorts softly. "I only made enough for two. Beth always makes extra. She has a big husband and three growing teenagers."

"Oh. I'm sorry, I didn't think about that. I could have come over later." For some reason, it hadn't occurred to me that she only made enough for the two of them. Abuela always makes tons of extra food.

She shrugs indifferently. "It is what it is. There's enough for her to eat over there. I don't like to waste food. I usually only make what we'll eat."

"I know food prices have gone up a lot the past couple of years." I swallow. "It's just that abuela always makes enough for leftovers. Sometimes we send them over to Olivia for the kids."

She stares at me for a long minute. "I can afford to feed my family, Carmen." Her voice is cold as steel.

I meet her eyes. "That's not what I meant. I just didn't think—"

"Obviously." Her voice is hard.

I sigh in exasperation. "I'm sorry, okay?" I bite my lip. I don't know what she wants to hear from me right now. When she doesn't say anything, I venture a question. "What did he say to you this morning?"

She shakes her head. "He and I talked. We're fine." She glances at me and sighs. "Do you want something to drink?"

"Sure." I nod absently. "So you blow up my phone like the world is ending, then basically ghost me about it all day."

She pours me a glass of water and drops a few ice cubes in it before putting it on the table in front of me. She nods for me to sit down. After I sink into the chair, she settles across the table from me. "Like I said, he and I talked. We cleared up a misunderstanding. Things are fine."

"Your job?" I ask curiously.

"Is fine," she answers briefly.

I raise an eyebrow. "Is he giving you a raise?"

She lifts an eyebrow, and the corner of her mouth twitches in amusement. "We didn't talk about that. Although it wouldn't surprise me if HR calls me into the office one of these days. Was that your goal?"

"To get you a raise?" I ask in confusion.

"To make it seem like I can't afford to pay my bills or buy my goddamn groceries on a salary I work my ass off for?" A buzzer goes off in the kitchen. "I already feel inadequate enough without you throwing fuel on the fire, Carmen." She gets up, turning away from me, to get the food out of the oven.

But not before I see her wet eyes. *Fuck.* I follow her toward the kitchen, stopping in the doorway. "No, Sarah," I say firmly. "This was about you being paid what you're worth. You're the best architect in the city. You're aware of that, right? You're the reason my dad's company is building my legacy. You know I don't settle for anything less than the best."

She shakes her head, her shoulders dropping. "I'm definitely not that." She sighs, pulling the pork chops out of the oven. "What do you want, Carmen? Why are you here?"

"I wanted to make sure you're okay."

She pokes the potatoes with a fork and nods to herself before plating the food. "I'm fine." She sets both plates on the table. Grabbing the salt and pepper, she puts them on the table before sitting down.

I groan as I sit down again. "Will you talk to me?" I sigh in frustration.

She takes a bite of her pork chop, savoring it slowly before taking a drink. "About what, exactly?" she asks quietly. "Your dad was under the impression this morning that I was looking for a new job and I was ready to bail on him. We talked, straightened things out. You know, that little thing called communication that adults do?"

Ouch. "I never told him that you were looking for another job. I just mentioned that you could any time you wanted to."

She nods patiently. "Which could be said of essentially any professional."

I grit my teeth. "All I did was ask him to think about how much he paid his two most important employees, and if he felt it was fair compensation for the work they did."

She takes another bite of her food, making me wait. I swear she's trying to get under my skin. "Which led to me looking for a new job, of course."

I slam my fork down on the table and stare at her. "You realize this has nothing to do with you, right? I'm pissed at him because he's supposed to be one of the good guys. Yet he still treats you like shit. And his entitled ass is too oblivious to even realize it."

That stops her. She cocks her head and looks at me in surprise. She bites her lower lip with a frown. "He doesn't treat me like shit, Carmen. He respects me and the work I do. He respects everyone on our team. Men and women." She stops, taking a sip of her water. When she puts it down, her voice is more controlled. "Sure, in a perfect world, I'd get paid more because I deserve it. But we don't live in a perfect world."

I look down at my plate and pick up my fork, pushing my food around a little. I take a bite of the potato, and buttery herbs explode in my mouth. She missed her calling. She should have been a chef. "You're right, but he could do a lot better. It sucks when you have your parents up on a pedestal, and you realize that they really don't belong there." I swallow uncomfortably.

"I wouldn't know about that," she says quietly. She shakes off the shadow that crosses her face. "So then you do what you can to educate him. Don't throw me under the bus to my boss of more than a decade—to someone whom I respect." She swallows thickly. "He's always had my back, Carmen. He's taught me everything he knows. He's given me opportunities to grow. He's not perfect, but he's not a bad boss."

"*Not bad* isn't the metric we should be aiming for," I mutter, looking down at my plate. We're silent for a few minutes while Sarah eats, and I push my food around on my plate.

"If you don't like pork, I can save that for Lily," she says pointedly.

I close my eyes and sigh. "I'm sorry. I just hate to see people not living up to their potential or being recognized for it." I cut up my meat and take a bite. *Damn, she's a good cook.*

"Carmen, don't take this the wrong way, because I know you had more than your fair share of heartache growing up, but not everyone has the opportunities and the support around them to take big risks like you did."

I look up at her in surprise. "You have no idea how much I've had to overcome to get where I'm at." I'm floored that she would even say such a thing to me, especially after witnessing my body breaking down on me the other night.

She shakes her head. "No, I don't." She sighs softly. "But with your dad and your grandma, and the community you had around you, you had the support you needed to. Not everyone has that."

I frown at her. "I thought you had Beth, and Bob and Teresa, and a bunch of people from ballet. What about your family? You never talk about them."

She bites her lip and studies for me for a long minute. "Carmen, are you serious about us trying to make things work?" she asks, sounding tired.

"Do you think I'd be here if I wasn't?" When she puts her fork and knife on her plate and picks them up, ready to get up and walk away from me, I stop her. "Yes, I want to make things work with you. I can't even explain why, since all we seem to do is argue." I swallow away the fear I feel in my gut. "I want to make you happy, and all I seem to do is make things worse." I fight back the tears. "Maybe I should just leave." I glance toward the door, my heart heavy. "Do you want me to go?"

Shaking her head, she leans back against her chair. She lets out a long breath. "No, I don't want you to go." Her shoulders slump. "When your dad hired me ten years ago, I was working for a reputable company. I was young and vulnerable, and all the men I worked with knew it. Most of them were okay. A few of them weren't. I'm not going to get into it. Suffice it to say that it wasn't the best place to work."

"That's the place Lily was talking about?" I ask quietly.

She shrugs a shoulder. "One of them. Your dad took me on when I had a toddler, and the only support I had was Beth. She had three kids under ten and had her hands full. She wasn't working at the time, and Justin wasn't making much. They had a two-bedroom apartment for the five of them. She had her own life to deal with." She takes a drink of water. "I couldn't count on her for a lot of help. I was young, I had very little experience, and he was flexible and understanding the first couple years I worked for him."

I take a bite of my pork chop and sit back, quiet.

"I pulled my weight. I learned at every opportunity I had. I grew. He literally taught me everything he knows." She laughs softly. "Then he gave me opportunities to learn more and hone my skills to be better. But at the beginning, I had no one. Your dad gave me a lifeline, Carmen. I don't know where I'd be without him." She looks up at me. "So, yes. I know that the situation at work isn't ideal. I know I'm worth a lot more than he pays me. But despite his shortcomings, I wouldn't be where I am without his support. I would never consider jumping ship just to get a raise. If I need more money, I'll ask for it. I'm sure I'd get what I need."

I chew on that for a minute. "You weren't young, Sarah. You were my age."

She laughs wistfully. "My life was in a very different place ten years ago, Carmen. Your dad, some of the people in that office—they've become family to me."

"Where does your family live?" I ask her curiously. "They couldn't help with Bug when she was little?" As soon as the words are out of my mouth, I wish I could take them back.

Her whole body stiffens. "I don't talk to them. They're not far away, but I don't see them. I haven't in a long time."

"Why?" I ask, confused. *Why in the world would her parents not want to be part of Lily's life? Why would she keep her from them?*

"Because I'm not welcome," she says stiffly, picking up her plate and heading into the kitchen.

My throat catches, and I look after her, stunned. After a minute, I pick up my plate and follow her. She has her hands in the sink, but they're still. Her shoulders are hunched over, and her breath catches in a sob. "Hey," I say softly, coming up behind her. She stiffens, but I wrap my arms around her. "That is so very much their loss," I whisper gently, my head resting on her shoulder.

I hear the door open and close. Lily. I tighten my arms around Sarah as Lily sticks her head in the kitchen.

"Didn't I tell you not to fuck with her heart?" Lily growls quietly.

Sarah turns to her. "Bug, can you give us some space, please? Carmen and I are okay. We're talking about grandma and grandpa."

Lily's eyes go wide. She comes into the now-crowded kitchen and squeezes in front of her mom. "Grandma and grandpa are bigoted piles of shit. They're not worth your tears." She wipes the tears from Sarah's face.

"Don't talk about your grandparents like that," Sarah says softly.

I fight a small smile. "Your parents are bigoted piles of shit," I repeat Lily's words. "They're not worth your tears."

Lily wraps her arms around both of us in a tight squeeze before giving me a grateful smile and disappearing.

22

SARAH

I pull the car up in front of the Tomsen house. It looks like Olivia's family beat us.

"I thought we weren't eating until four. We're two hours early," Lily mutters as she hops out of the car.

"I think Olivia and Miguel want the kids to get some energy out before we eat. Those kids have more energy..." I shake my head in wonder. "I'm glad you can dance to channel your energy into something useful," I tease her.

She stops, watching me as I close the car door and catch up with her. "Would you think about having more kids, if things work out with Carmen?"

My brow furrows. I hadn't really thought about it. "I suppose that would be a conversation for us to have. If we do, I'm sure you'll be part of it. You don't get enough of Nathan and the twins when we're here?" I try to laugh the conversation off. It probably is something Carmen and I should talk about, though.

Richard opens the door for us as we're heading up the porch. "Carmen and Olivia are out back with the twins," he says, giving me a gentle hug. "Happy Thanksgiving."

"Do Colombians have turkey for Thanksgiving?" Lily asks.

"This Colombian does," abuela laughs, pulling me in for a hug, then giving Lily one. "I'm the only Colombian here, you know. Carmen is only half. Olivia and Miguel's parents are from Mexico."

Richard laughs. *"Basta, mamá,"* he says, shooing her back toward the kitchen. "We always have a traditional American Thanksgiving," he tells Lily. "But the food won't be ready for a while. Do you want to dance or go play outside with the little ones?"

"I want to play with the twins!" Lily heads for the back door.

I glance at him as she bounds away. "Are things okay with you and Carmen?" I ask softly, not sure if I really want to know the answer.

He nods. "We've called a truce for the weekend. But yes, things are," he pauses, looking for the right word, "less volatile."

I raise an eyebrow, the corner of my mouth twitching up. "That's not the first time you've used that word for her, is it?" I'm going to have to remember that one. It's an apt description of her personality sometimes.

"You should go out there before she accuses me of hogging you." He laughs softly.

"Does abuela need any help?" I ask, hesitating.

"Miguel and I have it under control. Go enjoy yourself," he insists.

I head out the back, and Carmen gets up to greet me. "Hey you," I murmur, giving her a light kiss.

She moans softly, pulling my body closer to hers. "I missed you," she whispers quietly, pulling me in for a longer kiss. I close my eyes, melting into her.

"Get a room," Lily calls to us from the swing set.

Olivia laughs, getting up to give me a quick hug. It always feels a bit weird coming over here. I wonder if all Hispanics are huggers. Until I met Carmen, I think the only person besides Lily that ever hugged me was Beth. But it makes me feel like I'm part of the family here.

"You can save that for later." Olivia winks at me, sitting back down and doing a headcount of the kids.

Carmen rolls her eyes. "We need to sleep tonight. Tomorrow might be eventful."

I sit down next to Carmen, putting my hand on her thigh. "Hey," I murmur to get her attention. "I should warn you that Lily's been asking about kids. A few times. Don't be surprised if she brings it up."

Carmen glances at Olivia and nudges her leg gently. She nods toward the kids, motioning for her to give us some space. She turns back to me. "What did you tell her?"

I roll my eyes and swallow a laugh. "That you and I will need to talk about it." I glance over to the kids in the yard. "If we get to that point," I add quietly with a sigh. "I also told her that she'll be part of a discussion, if it comes to that."

Carmen glances at the twins, Lily and Olivia pushing them on the swings, and Nathan building castles in the sandbox. "She would be fourteen or fifteen at the earliest, Sarah." Her voice catches, surprising me. "Don't you sometimes look forward to when she'll move out? It would be starting over for you."

"You've really thought about this, haven't you?" *Not only about kids, but about kids with me, and Lily.*

"Yeah." She's quiet for a long minute. "Thanksgiving is always bittersweet. I have so many wonderful things in my life. So many people I love." She gives me a small smile. "But there's always the underlying feeling that something's missing." Her mom.

She studies me. "I miss her—but honestly, it's mostly just scattered memories. There's always the knowledge that she loved me with every fiber of her being. I don't think I could ever forget that. But it's not really a memory. It's just a warm fuzzy feeling." She laughs suddenly, and Lily and Olivia glance over at us. "Even though dad and I don't see eye to eye on everything, he molded me into who I am, Sarah. He and abuela gave all of themselves to me."

'That's sweet of you to say." Richard smiles, overhearing her as he comes out with two steaming mugs of hot apple cider. He hands one to each of us, then leans over and kisses Carmen on the top of her head. "I'm thankful for you, too," he teases. He smiles at me and squeezes my shoulder. "I'm grateful for you too, Sarah."

I chuckle at him, not sure how to take that. "Ditto, boss."

After he goes back inside, I turn back to Carmen. "By the way, a number of people in the office wanted me to pass along their thanks." At her look of confusion, I add, "HR is reviewing everyone's salaries and adjusting for competitive market rates for their respective jobs."

She frowns. "What does that have to do with me?"

I laugh at her, nudging her with my foot. "Richard and I have disappeared to breakfast a handful of times to talk, away from the office. Don't worry, we weren't talking about you." I grin at her. "Someone asked me if something was happening between him and me. We shut that down fast."

"He wouldn't be a bad catch." Olivia laughs, sitting back down next to Carmen.

Carmen groans loudly. "Can we *please* not talk about my dad like that? Besides, he's old enough to be your dad," she reminds Olivia.

"He's older than my dad," she retorts with a shrug. "But seriously, he's not bad-looking. He's rich and single. If I didn't already have the best man alive, I'd consider it."

Carmen makes a vomiting motion.

I shrug, teasing her. "He's not bad-looking, for a man. A woman could do a lot worse."

She leans over and brushes her lips across mine. "Don't joke about that. It hits a little too close to home," she murmurs into my ear. She raises her voice enough for Olivia to hear. "I'm going to see if they need help in the kitchen. You," she holds my gaze, "stay here. Two sets of eyes on those babies at all times."

Olivia moves over into the chair Carmen was in.

I turn to look at her. "How do you do it? Manage work, husband, three little kids. It seems like so much."

She snorts. "I don't do it by myself. Miguel is a great husband and a great dad. Richard and Carmen are always around if we need anything. Miguel's parents live around the corner, so between abuela and his mom, someone is almost always available to help when we need it."

"I can't even imagine. It was so hard with just one," I say quietly.

She shakes her head. "You didn't have much help when Lily was little, did you?"

I study her for a long moment, wondering how much Carmen has told her about me. I know they're close. "No, only my friend Beth. But she had a kid in elementary school, a toddler, and a baby. The same age as Lily." I smile, remembering nights when Justin would take JJ out of the house and leave the two of us with the littles. It wasn't so hard when there were two pairs of hands.

"Her bio dad isn't in the picture?" she asks.

I shake my head. "My parents, either," I say, warding off the question. Lily's sperm donor was my last-ditch attempt to be straight—or at least see if I could live that lie before I came out to my parents. My parents, who still think my *sinful ways* are a choice. My parents, who drilled into my head since I was too young to even understand what it meant, that *those abominations are going to hell.* It took me a long time to erase the damage that did. I'm not sure anything will ever undo the mental and emotional anguish they put me through as a teenager and young adult—how isolated they made me feel.

Olivia's wide smile brings me back to the present. "That's why you and Lily are so tight. Carmen always talks about how much she envies your relationship with her."

I snicker loudly. "She's almost a teenager. Trust me, it's not always sunshine and rainbows. God, the hell she gives Carmen sometimes, too." I burst out laughing. "The first time Carmen spent the night, she talked to Bug to check with her that it was okay for her to spend the night, and Bug turned it into a sex thing."

"Which it was." Olivia waggles her eyebrows at me.

"Which it would have been, if Carmen's leg hadn't acted up," I admit, "but Bug tried to make it about sex."

"Isn't she kind of young to be talking about that kind of thing?" she asks. "She's twelve, right?"

I laugh. "She knows about the mechanics of a man and a woman together." I shrug lightly. "When I was in school, I knew way too many kids who started experimenting with sex when they were thirteen or fourteen. I'd sure as hell rather her be comfortable talking to me about it than hiding it from me. She's not shy talking about things with me. She talks to Carmen and Beth a lot, too."

She nods, her gaze drifting across to the swings. "She's really good with the twins," she points out, glancing at me sideways.

"She's way too young." I dart a sharp glance at Olivia before I realize she's not talking about Lily anymore. When I look over at her, Fia is perched on her hip and she's pushing Talia on the swing. "She really is, isn't she?" I admit quietly.

I put my lukewarm apple cider on the table beside me and get up, walking out to Lily by the swing set. "Let me take her." I pull a sleepy Fia out of her arms and snuggle her into my chest.

23

SARAH

"Penny for your thoughts," Carmen murmurs to me as she closes the bedroom door behind us. She pulls me in for a soft kiss.

"If you keep that up, the only thought I'll have is putting my face between your legs," I tease her, pulling her body flush with mine.

"Promises, promises." She sighs softly, pulling away from me and flopping on the bed.

"I'm going to take a quick shower. You want to come with me?" I ask, raising an eyebrow in invitation.

She sits up, rubbing a hand across her face. "I'm worried about tomorrow, Sarah."

I take her hands in mine. "I know, sweetie. Let's take a shower—wash the turkey smell and baby food out of my hair and get some sleep." She strips down to her bare skin and follows me into the bathroom.

Turning the water on to warm it up, I turn to her. "Can I kiss you?" I ask her softly. She's been here with me physically almost every night the past week, but any time I try to touch her, she finds an excuse to wait. Having her naked in my bed for so many nights, but not being able to enjoy her body, is starting to frustrate me. I don't understand.

She smiles, taking my face between her palms. She brushes her lips across mine. But when my hands find the bare skin of her perfect hips, she smiles into the kiss with a chuckle. "You smell like turkey." She lets go of me, stepping into the shower.

Fifteen minutes later, we're crawling into bed naked together, and she's still keeping things between us chaste. She wraps her arm around my stomach and rests her head on my shoulder.

I kiss the top of her head. "Can I ask you a question?"

She tilts her head to meet my eyes. "What is it?"

The intensity in her eyes catches my breath. "Why are you here, Carmen?" She starts to pull away from me, but I tighten my arm around her. "No, stay. I don't want you to go anywhere. I just want you to talk to me."

She snuggles back into my shoulder. "About what, Sarah? We're full of turkey, and we have a big day ahead of us tomorrow."

I growl softly. "You've been in my bed six nights, naked no less, and you barely let me touch you." I close my eyes and fight the empty ache in my heart. "What's wrong with me? If you don't want me, why are you here?" A tear escapes from the corner of my eye, and I feel it burn its way down the side of my face. I've never been enough for anyone.

"You're perfect," she whispers, tracing a fingertip in circles along my bare stomach. Every nerve in my body comes alive at her touch, fire building low in my belly. "You're too perfect." She sighs.

I loosen my arm around her. "What does that mean?" I ask, pulling back from her enough to dislodge her from her comfortable spot snuggled into me.

She pulls away from me, laying back against her own pillow. "Do you think we're compatible? Long term, I mean?"

I cock my head and look at her for a long minute before answering. "We could be, if we decide that's what we want. But you need to talk to me about whatever's on your mind." I tuck a strand of hair behind her ear. "You don't think we can figure it out?"

"I don't know," she admits dejectedly. "I don't know if we want the same things in life."

"I would be happy having someone to come home to every night, someone I love." When she bites her lip with a frown, I take her chin and gently pull her gaze toward me. "Talk to me."

She chuckles wryly. "That's all it would take to make you happy?"

"Honestly? Sex would be nice," I tease her. "Eventually. When you're ready." Whatever's holding her back, I don't want to pressure her. "I'm just trying to figure out why you're here in my arms, but you feel so far away." I reach over and lace my fingers with hers. "What do you want in life?" I ask her gently.

"You," she says simply, her body deflating.

"And?" I urge her to continue. Obviously, that's not all.

"A family," she whispers, talking to the ceiling.

"Babies," I murmur. She nods, closing her eyes tightly. "Are those two things mutually exclusive?" I ask.

"I don't know. You tell me," she murmurs, not looking at me.

"Carmen, if you're thinking of having a family with me, can you look at me and talk to me?"

She rolls over and wraps her arm around my waist again, her head resting on my shoulder. She meets my eyes. "I want kids. I know you're older than me, and Lily's almost a teenager, and you probably don't want to start over. I've always wanted to be a mom, but I don't want to do it alone, and I'm afraid I'll never find someone who wants babies. At least not before I'm too old—"

I put my finger over her lips to stop her. "Carmen, slow down." I kiss away the tear on her cheek. "This woman that you want—have you asked her what she thinks about having more kids?"

She shakes her head. "I'm afraid of what you'll say. If you don't want more kids, can I accept that? Can Lily be enough for me?"

I hadn't thought of it that way, as her being Lily's other mom. Their relationship would be a different dynamic than my relationship with her, but I'm sure they would develop their own special bond. They already have, really. "Lily really likes you. I've never seen her give shit to anyone else besides me." I trace my thumb across her chin tenderly. "Is that what you've been thinking about the past week?"

She nods, exhaling slowly as she leans into my touch. "Would you think about having kids with me?" As she asks the question, I can feel some of the tension release from her body.

I brush my lips across hers. "I think we have a ways to go before I'm ready to make that kind of commitment," I tell her honestly. "You need to talk to me when something is bothering you," I whisper. "The past week, I've felt like there was something wrong with me. That's why you didn't want me."

She shakes her head. "No, it's not that at all. You know you're beautiful, right?"

I chuckle quietly, deflecting. "You want to play house, to see what it would be like living with us." I put my finger over her lips. "It's okay. I understand, sweetie. But if we do that, you need to act like we're in this together. Talk to me. Trust me." I trail a fingertip along her collarbone.

"Okay." She puts her hand over mine, stilling it. "I can't think straight when you're touching me like that," she murmurs, her breath uneven. "I'm afraid that once we have sex, I won't be able to think straight at all."

"Fair enough." I chuckle softly. "I'll take that as a compliment. Not sure if it's meant that way or not..." I raise my eyebrow in curiosity.

"I just have so many..." She searches for the right word. "Feelings. I've never felt this way before about anyone, and it scares me."

"Can I still kiss you?" I search her eyes for something. I'm not sure what I expect to find there. She's so hungry for me I can see the pain in her eyes.

"Yes, but will you answer my question first? If we can make this work, would you consider more kids?"

"Honestly? It hadn't occurred to me since Lily was little, not until she brought it up at your house today."

She nods, encouraging me to go on.

"I'm not sure I'd want to carry another one," I confess softly, "but if we can make this work, I'd be open to more kids if it's important to you." I rest my hand on her lower belly. It might be nice to enjoy parenting little ones again, if I had enough money and support that every day wasn't a struggle.

Her hand snakes over mine, lacing our fingers together. "You're serious?" she whispers, her breath catching.

I kiss her gently on the forehead. "I would say a lot of things to get into your pants." I chuckle, leaning my forehead against hers, "but I wouldn't mess around with your heart like that."

"You don't need to say anything to get into my pants, you know." Her voice chokes up.

"We have a big day tomorrow, sweetie. Can I hold you tonight?" I turn on my side and pull her back against my body. She falls asleep almost immediately, our hands interlaced over her belly.

24

CARMEN

I fit the earpiece in my right ear and cover it with my hair. I push the button on the device. "Testing. One, two, three, testing."

"Loud and clear." Jessica Rodriguez laughs, her striking blue eyes sparkling. "Way to be creative, boss."

"She's not your boss, I am." Mark Davis, a tall, broad-shouldered man covered in tattoos, nudges her.

I roll my eyes at these two. I've worked with this security team for events before, and their reputation is stellar. They goof around when things are calm, but as soon as something happens, they're on it. I like people who know how to have fun, as long as they're ready to buckle down when shit gets real.

I look around at the group we have here. Alex is the cute blond next door, in his mid-20s, and dressed to be nondescript. We really want to blend in and not draw attention to ourselves, and he's perfect to lead the team at the front entrance to the mall. Beside him, Mia is petite and full of energy. Jessica will be with them.

Mark will be with Jordan, who looks like he doesn't have a care in the world in his jeans and flannel shirt, and Amy, whose bright red hair and fancy dress seem like they would clash with Jordan's casualness, but the colors in his flannel match her dress. It works well, in a strange way.

"Okay, guys," I say, clearing my throat. Everyone's earpieces are working. "I have no idea what to expect today. We're hoping that whatever group gathers to protest will stay peaceful. We just want to pass out as many Pride stickers as we can near the doors. We want to have people quietly supporting us without actively getting involved. A couple of my team will be going around to different stores in the mall to see if they want to hang up Pride flags."

Mark nods. "Anyone who comes in to help needs to get an earpiece. I can meet them out here. We have a dozen extra. It's about safety for everyone, and it's about covering our asses if anyone wants to play he-said, she-said. The button on your earpiece turns it on so everyone can hear you. Use it to talk to me or anyone on the team. Be aware that everything you say, even with the mike off, will still be recorded on a separate stream. As long as things go smoothly, no one is ever going to listen to it, but we need to do that for safety—and any publicity issues we might deal with later."

I straighten my stance. "I know you guys have already been briefed on this, but the mall security hasn't been notified. If anything happens, we want them to react in a fair way. The head of security here is more progressive, but the mall owners—a group of businessmen who are generally hands off—are less so. If Montgomery hasn't tipped them off, we don't want to give them the chance to direct their security team against us. The local police force is aware of the planned gathering. They have a few plainclothes walking around, but they'll stay out of the way unless shit goes south. This is private property."

Mark shakes his head. "Nothing's going south today. All we're doing is handing out free stickers."

"Fucking fifteen thousand of them." Jessica snorts. I like this woman.

"If anyone needs anything and doesn't feel comfortable turning their mic on, everyone has me programmed into their phones," Mark reminds everyone.

"Me, too," Jessica reminds them. "If you feel like a situation would be better resolved with a less burly presence..." She smirks at Mark. "I won't be far."

"Spread out, people," he orders.

SARAH

I look at the line of young kids and their parents waiting for pictures with Santa, then glance across the way at the fifteen people hanging around in an unorganized group. One couple has a small sign that says, "Marriage is one man and one woman." Their showing is paltry so far. They don't have anything indicating that they're against the Cultural Center. The post online said 1:00 to 4:00 this afternoon, and it's already 2:30.

"Do you think it's going to fizzle out?" I ask Carmen, lacing my fingers with hers.

"Let's be patient. Wait and see," she says cautiously. We've been walking around the mall for the past few hours. Lily is people-watching, and she's brilliant at spotting people who might be willing to wear a sticker. Almost everyone she approaches takes one and sticks it on their chest or their sleeve.

"How do you always know?" Carmen asks her, after she passes another pair out to a straight couple that look like they're in their 50s.

She shrugs. "People notice the two of you holding hands. Some people look away, frown. Some don't even see you. Other people notice. They look for a second too long. It's all in the body language," she explains.

Lily looks around. She notices something, abruptly taking a step back into me. "Turn your earpiece on," she says under her breath. Carmen taps her earpiece.

A young man about Lily's age smiles and waves at her. She tries to hide the stickers between her hands. "Lily! How are you doing? Did you have a nice Thanksgiving?" he asks pleasantly.

"Chuck, how are you? Yeah, we had turkey and all the trimmings with the fam and some friends. How about you?"

He half-shrugs. "We went to a restaurant. My family is boring." He nods at Lily's cupped hands. "Are you passing out those flag stickers?"

She nods, and glances up at Carmen with a flicker of confusion in her eyes. She looks back at her friend. "Sure. You want one?" Her voice sounds forced, and Carmen puts a hand on her shoulder possessively.

He nods. "Sure." She takes one from the pile in her hands and passes it to him. He pulls the paper off the back of the flag and sticks it over his left shirt pocket. He glances at me and Carmen. "These your moms? I didn't know your mom was Mexican."

Lily takes a step toward him defensively. "She's not Mexican. She's Colombian,"

Carmen takes a step toward them and laughs lightly. "Half Colombian, anyway. Who's your friend, Lily?" she asks casually.

Why do I feel like I'm missing something huge here?

"Sorry, mamá." She answers Carmen with the Spanish word for mom. "This is Chuck Montgomery. He's in my class at school."

Carmen steps around Lily and holds her hand out to him. "Nice to meet you, Chuck. Are you here with friends for the Black Friday sales?"

Lily steps back toward me, and I squeeze her shoulder, resting my hand there.

"Sorry, Señora Reynolds. I'm bad at geography. He shakes her hand. "I'm not here with anyone, really. My grandad is around somewhere." He scrunches up his nose. "But I ditched him about an hour ago when he was trying on shoes. He has my number when he's ready to go." He pats the phone in his pocket with a shrug, then looks back at Lily. "Want to hang out for a while? If it's okay with your moms?"

Lily looks up and makes eye contact with Carmen. "Can I, mamá?" she asks softly. It's obvious from her body language that she doesn't want to go, but why is she putting on this show with Carmen?

Carmen shakes her head. "Maybe another time, *mija*. We still need to go to Kohl's, and we need to meet abuela in an hour." She turns her attention back to the young man. "It was nice to meet you, Chuck. Have a nice weekend with your family." She takes my hand and pulls me in the other direction.

We walk down the mall, and I follow her, confused. Carmen glances at Lily. "Are you okay?"

Lily nods dumbly. "Yes. That was the weirdest fucking thing ever."

Carmen holds up a finger, and her eyes glaze over for a minute. "No, Mark. Everything is fine. Chump Change is on premises, but he's keeping a low profile. He probably doesn't want to be noticed." She pauses for a minute while someone talks to her on the other end of the earpiece. "I'll explain a little later," she says quietly. "It's not relevant for the team. No, nothing has changed as far as security goes, other than we know he's here. We expected that. Nope, we don't need anything right now. I'll let you know if we do. Thanks, Mark." She clicks the earpiece off, then turns back to Lily. "Are you sure you're okay? You're shaking."

I realize that I'm shaking, too. "Can someone tell me what the hell that was about?" I ask unsteadily, looking between Carman and Lily.

Carmen looks at Lily. "Can we go sit down somewhere and tell your mom?"

Tell me what?

"Cinnabon." She nods, steeling herself.

"What is going on?" I demand, fear starting to grip me. *What's going on with my daughter that Carmen knows about and I don't?*

Carmen turns to me. "Everything is fine. Lily is fine. Breathe, Sarah." She raises an eyebrow, and I realize how tight my shoulders have gotten. She squeezes my hand. "Let's go sit down, and we'll explain it."

"It's okay, mom. He's just some rich kid from school. He's a homophobic asshat, though. Or he acts like it at school, anyway." Lily's forehead furrows in thought.

Carmen gets two cinnamon rolls and brings them to our small table. She passes plastic forks to Lily and me, then looks at Lily with a raised eyebrow.

Lily gives Carmen a slight nod, then digs into the gooey treat in front of her.

"A couple weeks ago, Lily was telling me about a boy in her class that was picking on two girls at lunch. They were holding hands, and this Chuck kid was apparently giving them a hard time."

I look at Lily. "Do you get picked on at school because of me?"

She shakes her head. "No, mom." She talks through a mouthful of dough. She swallows the food in her mouth. "Believe it or not, no one in middle school talks about their parents' sex lives. That's gross." Carmen swats at her, laughing. "Anyways, my friend Aiden clocked him one for being an asshat."

I chuckle. Of course, she would have friends like that. I'm proud of her. "Did your friend get in trouble?"

She shakes her head. "No. They both had to go talk to the principal, but apparently Chuck apologized and acted like Aiden's fist hitting his face was a"—she puts her fingers up in air quotes—"accident, since Aiden didn't leave a bruise. Ms.

Terpstra let it go. Aiden thinks Chuck got a good talking-to after he left, though."

I nod slowly. "So when you saw him coming toward us, you thought he was going to cause a scene."

"If the shoe fits..." She shrugs.

I look at Carmen. "You think he's Montgomery's kid."

"Grandkid, probably. It would make sense. But I didn't put two and two together until Bug used his full name just now." She snorts softly. "I bet his grandad isn't going to be happy seeing his precious grandson wearing a Pride flag."

Lily bursts out laughing, covering her full mouth with a hand. "His grandpa is behind the thing you guys are here for?"

Carmen nods. "He's a rich bigot who doesn't like queer people or minorities."

"Queer people are minorities," Lily points out candidly.

Carmen nods. "Anyone who's not straight, white, and at least middle class," she clarifies. "Basically all the people our Center is planning to serve, he has a problem with."

"So he's an asshat like Chuck."

All three of us laugh. I look at Lily. "You know you can talk to me about anything, right? You don't have to talk to Carmen or Beth about things. You can come to me."

She shrugs, nodding. "I know. But I don't need to talk to you about everything. Beth and Carmen have both told me that if they ever feel like my safety is an issue or you need to know about something I tell them—yadda yadda," she rolls her eyes, "you'll hear about it."

Carmen groans softly. "The team is wrapping up their surveillance. Are you two okay if I go debrief with them? I won't be long."

"Of course." I pull her cinnamon roll toward me. "Let me finish that for you." I grin at her with a wink. She glances at Lily.

"We're fine. Go." She makes a shooing motion with her hands, laughing.

"Do you want us to wait for you? Or do you just want to meet us at home?" I ask her as she picks up her purse.

A smile spreads across her face. "I like that. I'll meet you at home." She leans over and brushes her lips across mine.

Lily groans. "PDA is not cool, whether you're straight, gay, or alien."

After Carmen leaves, I turn to Bug as she's finishing her food. "You know you can talk to me," I repeat. I don't like that she's growing away from me.

She rolls her eyes at me with a snort. "I know, mom. But I can also talk to Carmen and Beth, even Richard and Justin. If it's something important, I know you're there for me."

"I know, honey. It's just hard that you're growing up, that's all. I worry about you."

She snorts, amused. "I'm probably the most boring kid in school, mom. There's nothing to worry about." She wipes her face with a napkin, then gathers up all our garbage from the table before standing up. "Do you actually want to stop at any stores before we leave?"

"Nope, let's go home."

25

SARAH

"That could have been a lot worse," Carmen murmurs, pulling the scrunchie out of my hair and running her fingers through it. "Come here," she whispers, pulling my face to hers. She brushes her lips against mine. There's an urgency in her kiss that I haven't felt since the night she ghosted me.

"Hey." I cup her face in my hand, pulling back enough to meet her eyes. "Are you okay?" I glance over across the living room at Lily's open bedroom door.

She swallows hard and nods, her eyes following mine. She lets out a long breath, shoulders sagging. "Yes. I just forgot how hard it can be to love someone, to worry about them when shit happens. Is she okay?" She motions toward Lily's room.

"She seems fine. Go talk to her," I encourage, slightly flummoxed at her sudden emotion—and the unsettling feeling that my daughter is more willing to confide in her than in me.

She puts her phone down on the counter and gives me a quick kiss. "Okay. Then you're mine tonight." She grins, her eyes roaming down my body.

I roll my eyes. "Did you touch base with your team yet? Let them know everything's okay? And your dad?"

She nods. "I sent out a quick text to everyone that it was mostly uneventful, details Monday. I haven't talked to dad yet. I'm surprised he hasn't texted me yet. Your team?"

I shrug listlessly. "My team isn't particularly invested. I'll brief them on Monday. Go talk to Lily," I tell her. "I'll text your dad that everything was okay today."

She nods before disappearing into Lily's room.

I pick up my phone and send Richard a message. *Mall was mostly uneventful. Only about a dozen people there. Quiet.*

Mostly?

Yep. Some kid approached Lily for a flag sticker, apparently a homophobe at school. That threw her off a little, but nothing happened. Everything else was quiet.

She's okay though?

Yep

Carmen's phone dings with a text, and I swipe down to check it. It's probably one of her team checking about the mall situation.

I stop. It's from a Valerie Mendez. *I'm in town for the weekend. You wanna hook up?*

I frown, glancing toward Lily's room. Carmen is still in there. Who is Valerie Mendez? Is Carmen hooking up with someone when she's not with me? Is that why she keeps hitting the brakes with me? I click her phone screen off with a sigh.

I knock on Lily's door before poking my head in. Their laughter stops immediately when I open the door. "I was thinking of ordering Trattoria's. Is that okay with you two giggly girls?"

"Sure. Whatever you want." Carmen glances up at me, nodding.

Lily looks up at me curiously, studying me for a long minute. "Pizza's fine, Mom." She frowns. "Are you okay?"

"Sure. Fine," I answer through a dry throat. I pull the door shut, suddenly feeling like a stranger in my own house. Did I somehow just get relegated to the boring, serious parent? I know it's healthy for Bug to have other adults to talk to, but I feel like I'm missing out on something important—like I'm being replaced.

I turn off the light and crawl into bed, quiet.

Carmen crawls in next to me, wrapping her arm around my waist and cuddling up to me. "Talk to me," she says quietly. I stiffen.

I try to relax my body. "About?" I ask her a little too harshly.

"Whatever is bothering you, Sarah. What is it?"

I sigh in empty frustration. "It's nothing. I just..." I look up at the ceiling in the dark. "I watch you laughing and playing house with Bug, and... I don't know. I have no idea why she was so freaked out by that kid today. She doesn't talk to me about anything, and now she's calling you mom?"

She chuckles against me, tightening her arm around my waist. "If I tell you something, can you keep a secret?" she whispers. "She'll probably kill me if she finds out I told you."

I turn to face her, the moonlight from the window making her eyes dance. "If she told you something in confidence, don't. You're sure it's nothing I need to worry about, though?" My voice is thick.

She snorts, her body shaking with laughter. "A thousand percent." She shifts and kisses my neck, her mouth right below my ear. "She likes a boy," she whispers softly. She kisses me gently on the cheek before laying her head back on my shoulder with a comfortable sigh. She keeps her voice low. "The one who slapped Chuck for being a homophobic asshat."

I let out a slow breath. "God, what am I going to do when she's ready to start dating?" I whisper. "What happens if she ends up having sex?"

Carmen puts a finger over my lips. "Stop, Sarah. No wonder she doesn't want to talk to you about boys." She laughs, burying her face in my shoulder. "He gives her butterflies. They hold hands between classes. You've got a few years before you need to start worrying about her having sex."

I nod slowly. "I'm glad she has you and Beth to talk to about stuff like that," I admit quietly. "She can talk to me, but I worry about her too much."

"Save that worry for a few years down the road. Now, erase this all from your mind. You know nothing," she tells me playfully. "Trust me, Sarah," she whispers, suddenly serious. "If there's anything I think you need to know when it comes to her, I won't hesitate to tell you. She knows that, too. Okay? Try to relax." She traces her fingertips along my stomach.

I close my eyes and try to catch my breath, as heat pools between my legs against my will. "Carmen," I choke out a whisper of protest through an involuntary moan, my body instinctively gravitating toward her touch.

I put my hand over hers to stop her. "Who's Valerie Mendez?" I ask her flatly.

"An old friend. She lives in California, and she comes back here a couple times a year. Her parents live here. We try to meet up when she's in town."

"You're going to hook up with her this weekend," I accuse her.

She gives me half a shrug. "I was going to meet with her for brunch Sunday. Does that bother you? I can cancel it if you want me to."

"So it's not a hookup?" I ask in disbelief.

She shakes her head. "No. I mean, we've hooked up before, when we've both been single—but seeing as I'm not single, we're just going to catch up over brunch."

"Oh." Somehow that hadn't even occurred to me.

"Do you want me to cancel? Or you and Lily could come with and meet her if you want to,"

I shake my head. "No, it's okay." I sigh quietly. I know she has friends that she's fucked before, and it doesn't bother me. Mostly, anyways. I guess I'm just jealous of what they've had and I haven't.

"Hey. The only person I want is you." I can feel her swallow, and I wonder how true it is.

"Okay," I murmur, turning on my side.

She rolls over and snuggles her back into me, then pulls my arm around her waist. She's quiet for a minute, and I can almost hear her thinking. She wiggles her ass into me and slides her leg back between mine, opening my legs enough that she can rub her backside against my core.

"What are you doing?" I whisper in her ear, lightly kissing the back of her neck.

She takes my hand, resting on her lower stomach, and guides it between her legs.

"God, you're wet," I murmur, my hot breath and soft kisses tracing along the back of her shoulder. I glide my finger over her clit, then hover at her entrance.

She whimpers, her breath suddenly ragged. She leans her head back and gazes at me in the moonlight. "Please, Sarah," she begs, voice raspy.

"Please, what?" I tease, my breath tickling the skin on the back of her neck.

She bucks against me, and I chuckle. Her hips undulate against my hand, one wet finger slowly circling her entrance. "Fuck me," she whimpers, "or I'm going to die."

"We can't have that," I tease. I run my tongue along the shell of her ear as I slowly ease a single finger into her.

She lets out a feral moan. "More," she whimpers loudly.

I slide a second finger into her and feel her body wrap itself around me. God, she's so tight when she clenches me like that. I pump into her harder and faster, until she's right on the edge. I feel her ready to come, and I pull my fingers out of her wet heat. I tap lightly on her clit.

She lets out a desperate moan. "Sarah, please," she begs, guiding my hand back to her entrance. As soon as I plunge my fingers back into her center, her body arches against me and I feel her walls quake around me. The animal noise in the back of her throat almost gets me off, too.

I hold her as her orgasm rocks her. Then we're both quiet, except for trying to catch our breath. I trace my wet finger over her nipple, and her body bucks against mine again. "Like that, is it?" I ask, chuckling against the back of her neck.

She moans softly. "God, I've waited for you to do that to me for months."

26

CARMEN

I cover her mouth with mine, hungry for more of her. "Sorry," I smile into the kiss, "did you want to sleep?"

She lets out a husky laugh, deep in her throat. "You don't get off that easily," she murmurs, her lips trailing down my collarbone. She palms a breast, and I arch into her touch.

"Try me again," I challenge her, every nerve in my body taut. God, I've never come undone so fast in my adult life. She takes her time exploring my skin with her hot wet mouth and her featherlight fingertips. Her every touch heightens my senses. I can smell my sex on her.

I pull her hand to my nose and breathe in the heady scent of my own arousal. She nips playfully against the flesh of my breast, and I pull her wet fingers into my mouth. She moans loudly and wraps her mouth around my hard nipple. She licks a circle around me and bites gently. I buck against her mouth, a bolt of lightning hitting my core.

She looks up at me with a dirty grin on her face. "You're close again, aren't you?" She raises an eyebrow at me knowingly. At the animal noise that escapes my throat, she pulls her mouth from me and shakes her head. "Mmm, we can't have that. Not yet," she teases. She shifts, straddling my thigh and pressing her wetness against me.

She's hot and wet, and I need to touch her. I want to feel her body tighten around me. As I reach for her heat, she grabs my hand, pinning it against the bed. She rocks against me, her breath fast, and kisses me lightly between my breasts. I tangle my free hand in her hair, trying to bring her mouth back to my nipple, moaning her name. She can't leave me on the edge like this.

She kisses my nipple softly, then blows warm air across my pebbled skin. A shiver of need passes through me. She looks up at me again, holding my eyes as she rolls her hips against my thigh. "Not yet," she murmurs softly. "Enjoy the journey, Carmen." She shifts her hips open further, and I can feel her hard against my skin. "I promise you'll get where you're going. Just slow down." She presses hard against me, then leans forward, our bodies pressed together. The feel of her hard nipples against my body makes me gasp.

"I need to touch you," I choke out, gasping for air.

She laughs softly, her body shaking against mine. "You will," she whispers gently, brushing her lips over mine. One hand is tangled in my hair at the nape of my neck, and she pulls me into a kiss. I take her bottom lip between my teeth before slipping my tongue into her mouth. *God, the way this woman makes me feel.* She rolls her hips against me again, and her nipples brush against my skin.

Her tongue is in my mouth, our lips locked, and I can feel her wet center tighten around my thigh. My hands slide around her ass, pulling her into me. She's so close I can feel it in her whole body, in her breathing. She moans softly. But then her body is relaxing against mine. *She was almost there. Why did she stop?* She kisses me gently once more before moving down my body with a slow, maddening trail of lips and teeth.

She spreads my legs, pushing my knees apart, and I open myself to her. She tortures me with languid nips and kisses up my thighs. I press my core closer to her mouth, and she blows warm air across my clit. "Please, Sarah," I moan loudly. My hands are in her hair, desperately leading her to my sex. "I need you," I whimper.

She stops, inhaling my heady arousal. "You're so beautiful," she murmurs under her breath. Her tongue circles my clit, and my body jolts at her touch. She spreads me apart, her tongue finally sliding up my swollen folds.

Then her tongue is inside me, and my body quakes in pleasure. I cry out loudly, closing my eyes as the waves overtake me, stronger than the first time. Just as I come down from the wave, Sarah's fingers are inside me, first one, then two, and her mouth is on my clit. She pulls me into another explosion of nerves, rolling for a long minute, until my body collapses against her. I gasp for breath, disoriented.

"Sarah," I plead through my post-orgasm haze, trying to catch my breath. "Wow. Hold up. At least let me catch my breath."

She laughs, her warm breath against my swollen core. "You have another one in you?"

My breathing evens out, and I nod weakly, every nerve in my body still on fire. She suddenly slides two fingers into me again, caressing my inner ridges, and circles my clit with her tongue. As soon as her mouth closes around me, my body rocks again, harder this time. I gasp, crying out as she draws out the longest rolling orgasm of my life.

After, as I lay there limp, fighting for air, she slowly kisses her way up my body. She takes a hard nipple in her mouth, and I buck against her again, groaning. "Sarah, enough," I surrender softly, still trying to catch my breath.

She chuckles against my skin. She lays next to me, cupping my face in her hand. "You said I could make love to you after I fuck you." She raises an eyebrow in amusement.

I lose myself in her eyes for a long minute. "Save that for tomorrow," I tease her. I reach over and trace a circle around her nipple with my fingertip. I nudge her playfully. "God, I think that was the longest orgasm ever."

She laughs. "You do look pretty boneless right now." She looks pretty satisfied with herself. Deservedly so, I admit to myself. She wraps her arm around my waist and lays her head between my breasts with a sigh of contentment. "I—" she starts. She stops herself.

I kiss the top of her head. "You what?" I ask softly, trailing a finger down her forearm.

"I—" She pauses, her breath fast. She shakes her head slightly. "I hope we didn't wake up Lily." She chuckles.

Oh shit. I didn't think about that. "She'll be alright. She has her earplugs." I laugh. "But I'll try to keep it down a notch next time." I tilt her head back to look at me and take her face in my hands. She stares deep into my eyes, her breath coming faster.

"Carmen," she whimpers my name. She inhales slowly, closing her eyes. "Touch me," she begs, pulling my hand over her beautiful breasts. A soft satisfied moan escapes her throat as I take her in my hand.

"Is that your happy noise?" I tease, my mouth on the hollow of her neck where this all started. I nip at the tender skin and kiss her gently. She moans louder. "I want to listen to you come for me," I growl fiercely, my hand reaching for her core.

I feel her whole body stiffen. For a split second, I think it's a reaction to my touch, but something feels wrong. I lift my hands and my mouth off her, pulling back.

"Sarah," I murmur, aching to touch her. "What is it?"

She wraps her fingers through my hair and pulls me back to her. "Nothing, don't stop," she says hollowly.

I lovingly kiss the skin of her collarbone, then shake my head. I shift my body to lay against hers, the comfortable interlaced position we've perfected over the past week or two. "Trust me, I want to," I admit, my voice husky. "What's going on in your head?" I ask softly.

She drops her hands and turns her head away from me. She swallows loudly.

I'm so lost. *What just happened?* "Sweetie, talk to me." She doesn't answer. "Do you want me to go?"

"No," she murmurs softly, grabbing my arm and holding onto our connection.

"Is it Lily?" This whole kid thing is weird, at least when it comes to sex. Especially since she's old enough to know what's going on—at least in theory.

She snorts quietly. "No."

"Okay," I puzzle out slowly. "We've been doing good at this communication thing tonight," I squeeze her gently. "Can you give me a clue?"

She turns toward me. "Do you always get off that easily?"

I snort loudly. "No, not really. I'm the queen of multiples, but never like that before. That was all you—and legit, I haven't had a real orgasm since before I met you. Like two months ago."

She frowns at that. "Why? You didn't even kiss me until a month ago, then I didn't even see you for a few weeks after that."

Thank goodness she doesn't outright bring up my stupid ghosting her. I half-shrug. "I didn't want anyone but you."

She leans into me and kisses me, her soft lips gentle and hungry against mine.

I pull away from her. "Did I do something wrong, Sarah?"

She shakes her head. "No. I just—" She stops, sighing quietly. "I've never been able to get off with anyone."

"What do you mean?" I ask her, confused.

She shrugs indifferently. "Just that. I've never had anyone give me an orgasm before."

I mull that over for a long moment. She's obviously turned on by women. "Never?" I repeat like a broken record. I can't even imagine. "Wait—but you can get yourself off, right?"

She nods, laughing quietly. "I'm actually quite an expert at it."

"You like it when I touch you?" I ask, suddenly questioning every movement of her body language.

"God, yes," she snort-laughs.

"Okay. So I make love to you, and when you're ready, you can finish it. Will you let me watch?" *God, that sounds so hot.* I can feel myself getting wet again.

She shrugs. "Sure? I've never done that before, either, but why not? Isn't that weird, though?"

I laugh softly, trailing my fingers up her bare stomach. "As long as you're happy, it doesn't matter how you get there." Her back arches up at my touch, and I grin. "You were really close when you were riding me." I nip at her collarbone. "Why'd you stop?" I ask her softly before inhaling her skin and licking my way down to her breasts. "God, you're beautiful."

She moans softly, bringing a hand up to palm herself. She's going to have to give me a chance, at least. Maybe not tonight, but tomorrow. The next day. "It was your turn," she answers, her breath already ragged.

I kiss along the bottom of her breast, licking, humming. "Next time you're that close," I bite her hardened nipple gently, "it's your turn, *mi amor.*" My tongue trails wet circles around the nub, then I take it in my mouth. I suck gently.

Her moan gets louder. One hand grabs my head, her fingers in my hair, holding my mouth on her. Her other moves between her legs, her fingers sinking deep into her wet sex—slow at first. She lets out a feral moan. *Fuck, if she keeps that up, I'm going to come again.* Her fingers speed up, and I can hear the slap of her palm against her wetness.

Even without being inside her, I can feel she's almost there. I take her other breast in my hand and brush my thumb over the nipple as I suck harder at the one in my mouth.

It breaks her.

Her body bucks up against me, her breathing hard. The wild breathy groan that escapes her throat brings me over the edge with her, and we both end up panting, limbless.

We lay there in satiated bliss for a long minute, catching our breath. Maybe five, I don't know.

"Fuck," she says softly.

Yep, I'd agree with that. "I thought..." I shake my head, chuckling. "I thought it would take more, when you said..."

She groans softly. "Someone's been working me up for the last two weeks—then spending the night in my bed so I couldn't do anything about it."

I laugh softly, my head against her chest. I shift and pull her lips to mine. "Any time I'm in your bed and you want to get off, I won't complain if you do that. Not if I can listen to you come like that." I pull her wet fingers to my mouth, slowly sucking her juices off them. I moan softly. "Can I eat you out?" I whisper, trying not to beg.

"I don't think I can come again after that." She sighs contentedly.

"Okay," I murmur, trying to hide my disappointment. Maybe she doesn't like when women go down on her. I thought that's what she was fantasizing about before, though. "Can I touch you at least?" I know I sound desperate.

She takes my face in her hands. "You can, but temper your expectations. That's all I'm saying. I'm not built like you. I've never had two orgasms in one night, much less five."

I hold her eyes as I slide my hand between her legs. I drag my finger through her wet, swollen folds, then circle her clit. Her breath catches. She whispers my name. I brush my lips over hers, my tongue begging entrance as I slide two fingers into her. Her body contracts around my fingers, and I thumb her clit. "No expectations," I whisper before moving between her legs.

I push her knees apart, and she falls open for me. Luscious, beautiful, swollen wet sex. I moan, trying to hold another orgasm back. I pull her knees over my shoulders, bringing her center to me. I breathe in her earthy arousal.

"Carmen, please," she whimpers softly.

I kiss her swollen lips, suck on them, and she starts to squirm. "Please what?" I respond playfully. "What do you want, *mi amor?*"

Her soaking flesh quivers for me, and I lick up her wet folds. I tongue her, but not long enough to get her off. She's close, if she lets herself. I take her clit in my mouth, and her body bucks against me, needing more. I slowly slide one finger into her, and that feral sound comes from her again. I slide a second finger into her, caressing deep along her ridges. I nip at her clit, my teeth gently scraping over it before my fingers start moving harder and faster. I swirl my tongue around her bundle of nerves, then suck hard as I reach deep inside her.

And she breaks again.

I come with her, her loud groan almost painful-sounding, and I hold her until her muscles stop quivering. Then I let her hold me, my sated body against hers, our limbs tangled in sweat and sex, until the sun comes up on a brand-new day.

27

CARMEN

I look up at the clock, surprised that it's almost lunchtime already. I click over to the last slide and look around at my team. "It's been three weeks of quiet. I anticipate he'll up the ante again after the New Year. That gives us two weeks. Carlos, Natalie," I smile to my philanthropic specialists, "keep reaching out to big donors. Long-term pledges are best, but any donations are appreciated. Make sure small businesses know that."

"Keep doing what we're doing," Michael nods happily, "and keep praying this guy keeps a low profile through the holidays."

I nod to him. "Emily, Lucas, keep posting in friendly places about the outreach programs we'll feature once we open." My phone buzzes on the table, and I see Lily's number flash up on my screen. I frown, wondering what in the world she would be calling about in the middle of the school day. "I need to take this. Good job, everyone." I nod to them and duck out of the conference room.

I swipe to answer the call, willing myself not to panic. "Bug? What's wrong? Are you okay?"

"I'm fine, mamá," she answers. "I need you or mom to come pick me up from school, though."

"Why? What happened?" I demand, concerned.

"Nothing. I was just involved in a thing with some other kids, and they're sending all of us home for the afternoon. No one's in trouble. I didn't do anything wrong. You can talk to Ms. Terpstra when you get here if you want to."

"Why did you call me instead of your mom?" I ask her. I know what she's doing. She wants me to come get her as her mom instead of Sarah.

Lily groans. "You know she's busy on that project at work. I thought I'd try you first."

I sigh softly. "I'll come get you. I'll be there in about twenty minutes."

"Oh, my God. Thank you," she breathes softly. "I should warn you," she adds hurriedly, "Chuck's grandpa is coming to pick him up."

I walk into the middle school office and glance around. Lily is sitting in the principal's office with Chuck and two other boys, the door wide open. The secretary motions me toward the office. "They're in there, Ms. Reynolds." I open my mouth to correct her, but then close it. I don't even know if they'd let me pick her up if I did.

Lily looks up at me from inside the office. I can tell she's itching to get up and come to me, but she holds herself still. "Ms. Terpstra, my mom is here. Can I go?"

I stride to the principal's desk, reaching my hand across. "Carmen," I introduce myself. "What's this about?"

She nods toward an empty seat along the wall. "Sit down please, Ms. Reynolds." An older gentleman walks in on my heels. "Mr. Montgomery. Pleasure to see you again." I detect a hint of sarcasm in her voice as she indicates for him to sit down, too. I avoid looking directly at him. It wouldn't be good for him to recognize me.

"Lily, Chuck, and Aiden are not in trouble. I want to be clear about that," Ms. Terpstra begins. "Colten," she motions toward the boy sitting alone on the other side of Lily, "tried to start something with Chuck. Chuck tried to walk away, and when Colten didn't want to let it go, Aiden and Lily peacefully stepped in between them. The three of you did exactly what you're supposed to do."

"Why are they being punished, then?" Mr. Montgomery barks impatiently.

"They're not being punished. We're just sending everyone home as a precaution, that's all," she replies firmly. "There was trouble brewing. Things died down as soon as the problem was removed." She glances at Colten. "But we don't want it to flare up again. There are only two class periods left of the day. I'll make sure all your teachers are aware of the situation. You can get your assignments online."

I breathe a sigh of relief, mentally soothing my internal disquiet for not calling Sarah right away. Lily's not in trouble.

"Thank you, Ms. Terpstra," Lily says politely. "Can we be excused now?"

The principal laughs softly. "Yes, you two can go. Aiden, too, as soon as his mom gets here. Sign out at the desk, please."

I follow Lily out the door, surprised at how quickly she wants to get out of here. She scribbles her name on the sign-out sheet and *mom* behind it before we head out. Behind us, Chuck and Mr. Montgomery sign out, too.

"Dirty Mexicans," Mr. Montgomery mutters under his breath. Lily puts her hand on my arm and shakes her head.

"She's Colombian, not Mexican," Chuck corrects him. "And don't talk like that about my friend's mom," he says quietly.

Lily pulls me out the door, the corner of her mouth twitching up.

We get into the car, and I turn toward her. "Why did you need to step between Colten and Chuck?" I ask her.

"Colten was being an asshat to Chuck's friend, and when Chuck stood up for him, Colten tried to go after him. Aiden and I just got in the way to stop it." She shrugs.

"This is the same Chuck that Aiden clocked a few months ago for being an asshat?" I ask her, already knowing the answer.

She nods, biting her lip with a frown. "Chuck's best friend came out to him right before Thanksgiving. Gay, bisexual, something. I don't know." She shrugs again. "Not really my business. I just wish people would leave them alone."

I nod, starting up the car. "Do you need to text your mom or Beth not to pick you up from school?"

She shakes her head. "No. I already texted Beth and told her I had a ride."

As we pull into the parking lot, I turn to her. "You need to tell your mom what happened. Tonight when she gets home," I tell her firmly.

She groans. "Do I have to? I didn't do anything wrong."

I chuckle. "No, you didn't. I'm proud of you for standing up for him today. But you still need to tell your mom, Lily. Trust me. She'll be less mad if she hears it from you than if she hears it from me."

She nods reluctantly. "I know. I will," she promises. "Are you coming back for dinner?"

"I was planning on it—but I'm not leaving you here alone, so unless Beth wants you early, you're stuck with me for the afternoon. I'm going to try to get some work done, though. You can work on homework until the time you normally get out of school."

"I'll text mom that I'm home and you're with me." She sighs quietly. She takes her backpack into her bedroom and shuts the door on me.

Sarah comes home a little after five, slipping her shoes off right inside the door. She glances at me with the laptop and papers spread all over the desk. "To what do we owe this pleasure?" she asks, leaning over to give me a quick kiss.

"It's Friday, it's a beautiful afternoon, and I wanted to see your beautiful face," I tease her.

She laughs brightly. "Good answers. What's the one you're leaving out?" she asks, her eyes narrowing.

I shake my head. "Lily wanted me to pick her up from school. She's in her room." I nod to her still-closed bedroom door. "A thing happened at school. Nothing big. She wasn't in trouble or anything," I explain vaguely.

"What do you mean, a thing?" Sarah asks in concern, her voice rising a register. She raises her voice the slightest bit. "Lily Anne Reynolds!"

She sticks her head out her bedroom door. "Oh, hi, Mom. Can we get pizza tonight?"

Sarah shakes her head. "Not tonight, not with ballet in the morning. Maybe tomorrow, though. What happened at school today?"

Lily shrugs her shoulder. "Nothing exciting, really."

"Lily." Sarah draws out her name. "Carmen said something happened. Talk to me." She fills up a glass with water and some ice. She passes it to Lily, nodding for her to sit down at the table. Sarah sits down halfway between me and Lily. "Please?"

"Mom, it seriously wasn't a big deal."

"It was enough that you needed to get picked up," I say. "You're not going to get in trouble. Talk to her," I tell her firmly.

Sarah glances at me, then back at Lily.

"Seriously, it wasn't a big deal. A kid was bullying my friend Chuck. Chuck tried to walk away, and Colten didn't like it. So Aiden and I just stepped in his way. There's been a lot of tension at lunch the past couple months, mostly queer kids getting picked on," she says defensively. "The school is doing what they can. I didn't do anything wrong. I didn't get in trouble. Ms. Terpstra said she just wanted to let us all go home, because if we went back to class, it might get people riled up again. I only missed two classes. The teachers already sent me the homework, and I'm already done with it. I'm done with all my homework for the weekend. She," Lily motions to me defiantly, "wouldn't let me play on my phone until all my homework was finished." She gives me a dirty look.

"Why didn't you call me?" Sarah asks, confused.

Lily shrugs. "You get weird about gay stuff. You'd probably get all up in the principal's face to know what they're doing about the problem. You'd freak out on me. You'd definitely freak out with Chuck's grandpa there. Pick a reason."

"Chuck, the kid from the mall?" Sarah asks.

Lily nods slowly. "Yeah. I guess his BFF is gay or bi or something. He found out right before Thanksgiving. He's actually super supportive of his friend. It's kind of sweet." She smiles softly. "Colten was trying to pick on him, and Aiden and I decided to conveniently get in the way." She shrugs her shoulder. "I didn't do anything wrong, Mom. I just stood up for one of my friends. Literally. I just stood between two people to protect my friend." She sounds defensive, almost angry.

Sarah nods slowly. "You let Beth know you had a ride home. She knows you're with Carmen."

It's not a question, but Lily nods. "Of course. I didn't want her to worry." She glances between me and her mom before straightening her shoulders. "You might not always like my decisions, but I'm responsible and I would never make you or Beth worry."

Sarah takes a deep breath, then lets out a long sigh, her shoulders deflating. "I know, Bug." She glances between the two of us thoughtfully, then looks at Lily again. "I'm proud of you for standing up for your friend."

The corner of Lily's mouth quirks up and her shoulders relax. "I should have called you."

Sarah nods absently. "Baby, could you go to your room for a few so I can talk to Carmen?"

Lily nods and quickly disappears into her room without another sound. Sarah turns and looks at me.

She studies me for a long minute and sighs. "You've been here with her for—what—the past four hours?"

I half shrug, nodding. "More or less. She did all of her homework before I let her do anything else."

She shakes her head at me in disbelief. "Did it not occur to you to call me and tell me where my daughter was? Four hours, Carmen." There's fear and anger—and exasperation—in her voice.

"She was at school and she was at home. She was always in a safe place," I say quietly. "She didn't do anything wrong. I figured she could fill you in when you got home."

"The school just let you take her?" More disbelief.

I nod, confused. "Why wouldn't they? I talked to the principal to see what happened. I signed her out in the office."

She frowns, a look of alarm flitting across her face. "Only Beth and Justin are authorized to pick her up. They should never have released her to you." She shakes that thought away. "Why would you go pick her up from school without talking to me first?"

I study her for a long moment. "She said she wasn't in trouble. Everything was fine. It was nothing to worry about. I didn't really think it was that important."

She stares at me incredulously. "The school calls and says my daughter was involved in an incident and a parent needs to pick her up, and you don't think it's important." She shakes her head in disbelief. She takes a deep breath and lets it out slowly. "I need you out of here."

She turns away from me and goes into her room, shutting the door.

I stick my laptop and papers back in my bag, then look over at Sarah's bedroom door confused. I knock softly. "Sarah." When she doesn't answer, I add, "Talk to me, Sarah."

"Just get out of my house, Carmen," she says angrily through the door.

I let out a frustrated sigh. "Can we talk about this?" I ask her through the door.

She opens the door, her face red and puffy with anger. "I said to get the fuck out of my house, Carmen. And fucking stay away from my daughter."

28

CARMEN

I get into my car in shock. *What the fuck just happened?* She didn't even seem mad at Lily. What the hell was that even about? I connect my phone to the speaker system in my car and dial Olivia before pulling out of the parking lot.

"Carmen? What's going on?" she asks, sounding surprised at my call. Which is fair, since I rarely call without texting, and never just before dinner time.

"Are you guys home? I need ... to talk. To figure some shit out. It's Sarah," I tell her.

I can hear the frown in her voice. "Are she and Lily okay?"

"They're fine," I tell her, "but Sarah's upset with me, and I don't understand why."

"Come over. Dinner's almost ready. It's just rice and beans, but there's enough for you. What happened?"

"Honestly, I have no idea. Lily called me from school today because she was involved in a thing and needed to get picked up."

"A thing?" she asks curiously.

"She stopped a fight by getting between a bully and the kid he was trying to pick on. She wasn't in trouble, but the principal let all the kids involved go home for the afternoon. She didn't want to rile things up again by sending them back to class. There were only two class periods left of the day, anyway."

"Good for her." Olivia's grin comes through the line. "Why didn't she call her mom?"

"Sarah's overly sensitive when it comes to gay kids getting bullied," I start. "Lily just didn't want to deal with that."

Olivia doesn't say anything for a long minute. "That's insensitive." She lets out a loud sigh. "Didn't you tell me her parents basically disowned her for being gay? Aren't those the kinds of kids you want to serve with the Center??"

I sigh softly. "Yes, and yes. It was the wrong choice of words, Liv. But that's why Lily called me instead of calling her mom."

"And the school let you take her? Are you on her safe list?"

"Of course the school let me take her. Lily said I was her other mom. The office didn't ask any questions, and I didn't correct them. She's safe with me." I don't really understand why that's relevant. I pull the car into their parking lot. "I'm here. I'm on my way up."

She pulls me into a hug when I get up to their unit, and Fia runs over to me.

"How's my favorite Fia?" I ask her, picking her up and snuggling her under my chin.

"Tía Ca-ca!" She giggles, wrapping her arms around me. I prop her up on my hip and reach down to tousle Talia's head as she wraps her arms around my knees.

Olivia shoos Talia to go play with her brother. "Come in. Dinner's almost ready." I follow her toward the kitchen but stay in the door frame, out of her way. "So why is Sarah upset with you?"

"I don't know. That's what I don't understand. I stayed with Lily until she got home. I made her get all her homework done. We told her almost as soon as she walked in the door."

Miguel looks up at me from the living room. "You didn't talk to Sarah before you picked Lily up?" He glances at his wife.

I shake my head. "No. Lily wasn't in trouble. She didn't do anything wrong, so I just figured we'd tell her when she got home from work."

"How long between when you picked her up and when Sarah got home?" Olivia asks quietly.

"It was only three or four hours," I say in my own defense. "We were at home the whole time."

Olivia opens her mouth to say something, then closes it. She gives Miguel a pleading look.

He leads me over to the couch, gently pushing me to sit down, Fia in my lap. "Close your eyes for a minute, Carmen. Feel your baby in your arms."

I close my eyes and squeeze her. She giggles before laying her head against my chest.

"Imagine for a minute that Olivia and I are gone, and it's all on you to take care of our kids. You're their only parent. This little girl is one hundred percent your responsibility."

"I would. You know that." I swallow thickly.

"I know." He puts a hand on my arm and squeezes gently. "Now imagine you have a new partner, someone you've been seeing for a few months. They don't have your permission to take your kids. You've never talked about it. The school legally can't release them to anyone but you, your dad, and abuela. How would you feel if that partner took your kids and you had no idea where they were? Even if it was someone you knew and trusted—if they didn't tell you?"

"Worried," I answer softly, my chest tightening. "Even if they're with someone I trust, I would freak out if I didn't know where they were."

"If you needed to pick Nathan up from school for some reason, would you call one of us first?" Olivia asks softly from the kitchen.

I look up at her. "Of course. You're his parents." I sigh softly against the warm child in my arms. Groaning, I hold Fia a little bit tighter. "I would be a horrible mom."

Miguel looks hard at me, then shakes his head. "No, you'll make a fantastic mom, Carmen. You just have to be careful. You're starting to think of Lily as yours, but she's not. At least, not yet."

29

SARAH

Lily knocks softly on my door, sticking her head in without waiting for an answer.

I wipe the angry tears from my eyes and look up at her. "I'm not mad at you," I say quietly.

"I know. You said that already. You shouldn't be mad at her, either. I'm the one who called her. Even if the school doesn't have her on record to pick me up, I'm the one who acted like she was my parent. One of my parents," she clarifies.

I shake my head with a sigh. "I'm not mad at the school. They should be more careful, but I get it. I just..." My voice trails off. "I just never expected that of her." I glance at the clock on the wall and try to shake this off. Lily needs to eat.

"I'm going over to Beth and Justin's to eat, to give you a little bit of space—unless you want me to stay here. I can make something for dinner."

"Are you trying to run away from me? Do you hate being around me that much?" I ask her softly, trying to tamp down the hurt in my chest.

She snorts a laugh. "Are you serious? I don't hate you. I don't always like you, and I disagree with you a lot, but I don't think I could ever hate you." She frowns at me for a second. "I get why you're mad at her. She wants to be a mom so bad she thinks she can just come in and be one. Or act like it, anyway. She doesn't really get it."

"She's not your mom," I remind her tartly.

"I know that," she bites back. Her shoulders fall and she glances at me, a pained look on her face. "You just broke up with someone you were talking about creating a family with, Mom. I just thought you might want a little space. I'm sure Beth has enough food to feed me. Would you rather I stay and make something for dinner?"

I shake my head and try to settle the overwhelming emotions brewing inside me. "Can you go to Beth's?"

Lily walks into the room and wraps her arms around me tightly. "Are you going to be okay?" she murmurs into my chest. "I didn't mean for you to get into a fight."

"I'll live, I promise." I smile weakly, dropping a kiss on the top of her head. "Go mooch dinner off the neighbors." She starts to head out the door, and I call after her. "I love you."

She rolls her eyes. "Yeah, yeah."

After she leaves, I pour myself a glass of wine and sit down on the couch, pulling my legs up and wrapping my arms around them. I'm so lost. I understand why Lily called her, even though I don't like it. But how many times did Carmen promise she'd tell me if there was something with Lily that I needed to know?

I bury my face in my knees. I'm not even mad anymore—just vacant.

I hear the door open. I glance up, expecting Lily, but it's Beth. She brings a container of food into the kitchen before coming to sit next to me on the couch. "There's food in the fridge when you get hungry later."

"Thanks," I murmur, dropping my chin back onto my knees.

"I thought you already knew, since Carmen picked her up and Lily texted me. If I had any inkling that you didn't know, I would have called you. Then wrung her a new one."

I let out a small huff. "I don't blame you, Beth."

"Sophie told me what happened at lunch. Lily and her boyfriend are developing quite the reputation as peaceful crusaders for equality. Avery says even some of the high school kids are talking about them."

I lift my head and glance at her. "Lily's boyfriend?" I close my eyes and take a slow, deep breath. I shake my head. "Don't tell me. It's another secret she wants to keep from me."

Beth rolls her eyes with a chuckle. "Aiden. They hold hands between classes, Sarah." She reaches out and puts her hand on my arm. "I know you didn't have a relationship with your parents where you talked about this kind of stuff with them. Lily knows, too. But it's completely normal for kids her age *not* to talk to their parents about things like that."

I breathe a small sigh of relief. "I know."

"I hear more when she's talking to Sophie, or when Avery is teasing her, but she talks to me, too. A little. She gets the same safe-sex advice my kids all get, peppered in when Justin or I feel it's appropriate. You don't have anything to worry about in that department, not for a while at least."

I give her a small smile. "What would I do without you?" I can't imagine my life without her friendship and support.

Beth snickers. "You'd have to show her how to put a condom on a banana."

I roll my eyes. "I'd have to learn first."

Beth breaks out in a grin. "She knows how. Avery and Sophie, too. We made a game of it one evening when the boys were out. They all know where there's a box of condoms in the house. And if the box is almost empty, to put it in my underwear drawer if they're not ready to talk about it."

"Stop." I choke out a muffled laugh. "I'm not ready to think about that with her."

Beth shrugs good-naturedly. "My oldest is having sex, Sarah. I have to think about it. I'm not ready to be a granny."

"God, don't even talk about that." I rest my chin back on my knees with a sigh.

"What are you going to do about Carmen?" she asks quietly.

I look at her and shake my head. "I have no idea. I don't think I can trust her anymore."

She bites her lip and nods. She opens her mouth, then closes it. She's arguing with herself about bringing something up.

"Say it," I tell her. "Whatever it is, just say it."

She inhales slowly. "You won't like it." She meets my eyes.

"When has that ever stopped you from saying what's on your mind?" I say acerbically.

"Okay. But don't get me wrong. She one hundred percent fucked up by not telling you that she had Lily."

"Noted. But...?" I push her.

"I want you to think for a minute. Pretend like you two have been together for a few years. You share parenting duties equally. You trust her with Bug completely. Just two moms, just a happy family."

It makes me sad to think that. That's exactly what we were considering when we talked about having more kids together.

"If Bug called you today to come get her, and Carmen was busy at work, do you think the situation would warrant calling her and interrupting her day?"

I squint my eyes at her for a long moment. "She wasn't in trouble. She didn't do anything wrong. I would probably just wait 'til she got home to tell her." I shake my head. "But Carmen's not her other mom. We've never even talked about a situation like that. She should have called me," I say stubbornly.

She nods. "Yes. She should have."

"She acts like Olivia's kids are hers, too," I say softly. "But she respects Olivia and Miguel as their parents. She doesn't try to take over that role."

"But you two have been talking about becoming a family, which would include sharing parenting roles," she points out.

"Where did you hear that?" I ask sharply.

She shrugs her shoulder. "A little Bug who lives on the other side of your bedroom wall hears things sometimes." She sighs.

"I'm not excusing what she did, Sarah. But I think it's worth asking why."

She did it because she feels like she's Lily's other mom. I don't need to ask why.

"You should drink that wine." She nods her head toward my still-full glass of wine on the coffee table. "There's food in the fridge when you're ready to eat. Do you want me to keep Bug overnight?"

I shake my head. "Of course not. She can come home when she's ready."

"Are you going to be okay?"

I nod reluctantly. "I always am," I answer softly.

"Do you need anything from me?" She nudges me softly as she stands up.

"Make my daughter talk to me more?"

She chuckles. "Give that about ten years, my friend." She leans over and gives me a hug. "You know where to find me if you need me."

It's about ten o'clock when my phone rings. It's Richard. *What is my boss calling me about this late on a Friday night?*

"Hello?" I answer, confusion coloring my voice.

"Sarah. It's Richard. Tomsen. From work. Carmen's dad."

"Richard. You're programmed into my phone. I know who you are. What's wrong? Is Carmen okay?" I ask curtly.

He chuckles softly. "Sorry. Carmen is... Yes. She's home and safe. She told me what she did."

"Okay." I bite back a sarcastic comment. I'm surprised she even mentioned it to him. They haven't exactly been getting along like best friends lately.

"Are you okay? Is Lily okay?" He sounds concerned.

I bite back a snarky comment. I'm not in the mood to put up with her shit from him, too. "We're ... both home and safe," I tell him, throwing his own words back at him. "Why are you calling, sir? It's ten o'clock on a Friday night."

"Because Carmen fucked up bigtime today, and I wanted to call and check on you. I'd be livid if I were you." He manages to sound gentle and spiteful in the same breath. His voice softens. "Are you okay?"

I choke back a sob and try to pull myself together until I can get him off the phone. "Lily's safe in bed. I'm—" I hear her bedroom door open, and she gives me a questioning look. I sigh in frustration. "Okay, not in bed. Hold on a sec," I tell him.

"Who is that?" Lily asks, coming into the living room.

I roll my eyes at her. "It's Richard. My boss. Why aren't you in bed?" I ask her shortly.

"I heard someone call, and you didn't seem happy about it, so I came to rescue you. Tell him I take forty-nine percent responsibility, but she's the adult, so she gets fifty-one percent of the blame. He's not allowed to take her side."

I stifle a snort and hand the phone to her. "Tell him yourself." I shrug my shoulder, exhausted. I just want to go to bed.

"I heard," I hear him chuckle through the phone. Lily puts him on speaker as he continues. "Bug, I wasn't taking Carmen's side.

She messed up today, and I just wanted to call and make sure you and your mom are okay."

Lily grumbles something under her breath. "I'm fine. Mom's not. She just fucking broke up with someone she loves and was planning to have a family with because I made a stupid call this afternoon."

"Lily," I warn her. "You don't talk to adults that way. It wasn't your fault—don't blame yourself."

Richard lets out a long loud exhale. "Sarah, let me know if there's anything I can do for you. As a friend, as your boss, as a single parent who's dealt with more than my fair share."

I close my eyes and shake my head. "I'll be fine." I steel my voice. "I always am. But I appreciate the concern," I add, my voice softening. "Now, if you two don't mind, I'd like to go to bed already."

30

SARAH

I pull the car into the parking lot Wednesday night after Lily's dance class and stopping at the store for the last few things we need before Christmas. We'll spend the day with Beth and her extended family. I only needed enough groceries for the two dishes we're bringing. I've got gifts wrapped for everyone. Everything is ready for the holidays.

"I don't remember the stores being so busy before; we're still a few days from Christmas. It seems like everyone in the whole city was at the store today." Lily chuckles, securing her dance bag on her shoulder before grabbing two bags of groceries.

I grab the other two bags of groceries and the Chinese food we picked up at the last stop. I shut the car door with my hip and hit the key fob to lock it up. "Tomorrow is Christmas Eve. Today and tomorrow are probably the busiest days of the year to be at the store. Everybody and their mother are out getting last-minute gifts and shopping for food."

"It doesn't feel like Christmas," Lily grumbles softly as we walk into our building.

"We'll turn the tree lights on and put some Christmas music on." I give her my best smile. "You do that while I put the groceries away." I juggle the groceries around while I dig out my keys. "Do you want to watch a Christmas movie tonight?" I could use some help getting into the holiday spirit, too.

She shrugs. "Why not?" She drops the bags of groceries in the kitchen for me before taking the Chinese to the table. She turns the Christmas lights on before we sit down to eat.

Half an hour later, cleaning up from dinner, she stops in front of me. She wraps her arms around me. "You know I love you, right?"

I squeeze her tight. "Sometimes I wonder," I tell her honestly. "To what do I owe the wonderful pleasure of you admitting this out loud?"

She stiffens, letting go of me. She takes a step backward. "You're going to kill me."

"Doubtful. What did you do?" I'm emotionally spent after the past week, ignoring Carmen and trying to get ready for the holidays when I don't feel the spirit of the season.

She looks up at me sheepishly. "Carmen is coming over to talk to you. You don't need to talk, but at least listen to her, Mom. Please." The pain in her eyes surprises me.

I half-shrug a shoulder. I really don't feel anything anymore. "Okay. I don't know why it matters so much to you, but okay."

"Because I hate to see you hurting. I love you, and it sucks seeing you like this—especially since it's partly my fault."

I sigh in resignation. "It's not your fault, Bug. You're a kid. Kids make mistakes."

She looks at me dubiously and snorts. "Adults do, too, Mom. You make mistakes all the time. I get over it and move on because we love each other." The doorbell buzzes, making me jump. "Don't forget that when Carmen is here."

I frown at her as she goes to the wall to buzz Carmen in. I sink into one of the chairs at the table. I make mistakes all the time? What is she talking about?

"I'm going to go let her in, then I'm going over to Beth's so you guys can talk." She gives me a light kiss on the cheek. "Be civil to her, at least," she orders gently as she disappears out the door.

Carmen walks in a minute later, tentatively calling out that she's here. She sees me sitting at the table; she takes a visibly deep breath and closes the door behind her. She drops a Christmas card and gift on the counter and turns to look at me. "Sarah." She chokes out my name. Her eyes scan me. She must be disappointed by what she sees because her face falls.

"Carmen." I feel obliged to acknowledge her. I can see the pain in her eyes, hear it in her voice, see it in her body language. I wish I could feel something—anything—about any of it. "It's not going to make a difference, but say what you've got to say. I told Lily I'd listen."

Studying me for a long minute, she sits down across from me with a sigh. "Look. I fucked up and I'm sorry."

I shrug my shoulders. "Apology accepted." It still doesn't change that I can't trust her.

She stares at me, speechless. She shakes her head to clear her shock. "It's not that easy," she mumbles incredulously. "So you don't hate me?"

I hold back an exasperated sigh. "I never hated you. I don't hate you. But you betrayed my trust. That can't be fixed."

She studies me with sad eyes and nods. "I understand. But I want you to know something."

She watches me expectantly, so I raise an eyebrow.

"It may have been misguided, but it was done out of love."

My eyebrow inches up doubtfully.

"Okay, it *was* misguided," she concedes. "But still—it was done from a place of love. I feel like that kid is mine, Sarah. I love her like she is."

"But she's not," I point out drily. I understand why she did it, but it's not an excuse.

She nods sadly. "I know."

We're both quiet for a few minutes. I wonder if she's finished.

"Dammit, Sarah. At least say something," she pleads softly.

"I don't know what you want me to say."

She groans. "Tell me how you feel. Yell at me. Cry. Throw something. I don't care. Just talk to me."

I shrug my shoulder. "I don't feel. Anything. Angry. Sad. Hurt. Nothing. I don't feel anything. It just doesn't matter."

She nods. "Dad said you seemed empty."

I look up at her, almost curious. "That's a pretty accurate description."

"You shut down when you're hurt," she says softly.

"It's a survival mechanism," I respond defensively.

She reaches across the table and takes my hand. "Maybe in the past, that's what you needed to do to survive, Sarah. But surviving isn't living. You deserve so much more than that."

"Maybe," I shrug half-heartedly. "You deserve better than me."
I exhale softly. "You deserve someone who can love you. Someone you can love back."

"I can love you, Sarah. Even if you never love me back, it won't
change how I feel. About you or Lily." She closes her glistening
eyes and takes a long minute before she opens them again. "Do
you think it would be okay if I still talk to Lily sometimes? I swear
to God that I'll talk to you if there's anything you should worry
about. I learned my lesson. She's yours. She's not mine."

"She blames herself for all of this, you know," I tell her, suddenly fighting back tears. "She's a kid, Carmen. It wasn't her job
to be the adult." My voice cracks, and a rush of feelings over-
whelms me. "Now I can't trust you, and she doesn't even want
to talk to me. So I fucking lose both of you. There's nothing left,
nothing that matters." I lay my head down in my arms, burying
my face, and try to regain control of myself.

She gets up and comes around the table, kneeling at my side.
She puts a gentle hand on my arm. "Lily still loves you, even if
she doesn't always act like it. Why do you think she's so worried
about you? If she didn't love you, she wouldn't care so much."

I take a deep breath, trying to calm myself down. I look down
to her, on her knees by my side. I wipe the tears from my face.
"You can talk to her, even see her sometimes if you want to," I
concede.

She grabs my hands tightly with a gut-wrenching sob. "You
trust me enough to let me see her?"

I close my eyes and sigh, realizing that I do. I do trust her with
Lily. "Yes. You love her, and I don't think you'd ever let anything

happen to her." I groan softly. "Will you get up already? I feel like you're begging, and that's unbecoming." I pull her up to her feet, then she pulls me to mine. "Besides, she loves you, too. Just don't let her talk you into anything stupid. Or if she does, at least run it by me first."

"Oh, God. Thank you, Sarah." She rasps, leaning over and giving me a quick kiss. As soon as she realizes what she's doing, she steps back and stutters. "Oh, my God, Sarah. I'm sorry. I didn't mean to—" She closes her eyes with a groan. "Fuck," she mutters under her breath, running her hand across her face. "Fuck, fuck, fuck."

I watch her reaction, a twinge of amusement tickling my gut. "God, relax already." I sit back down at the table, not sure if she has more to say. For the first time since that night, my emotions are swirling, confusing and overwhelming. "I'm not mad," I tell her quietly.

She drops her hand and studies me for a beat. "Like 'you'd let me do it again' not mad, or 'you're not going to call the cops on me' not mad?"

"Don't push your luck," I warn her. "I'm not ready for that. I don't know if I ever will be."

She closes her eyes and purses her lips together with a sigh. She nods. "I'll go and let you be," she says softly. "Thank you for letting me have Lily back. I promise I'll take care of her."

"I know you will." I give her a small smile.

"There's a gift for Bug. It's ballet stuff. You can open it and make sure it's okay before you give it to her, if you want." She bites her lip, standing up. "There's a card for you, too, if you'll read it." She closes her eyes again for a long minute, then meets my eye. "Please, Sarah. Please read it." Her voice cracks, and she turns away from me. She takes a deep breath, squaring her shoulders, and turns toward the door.

She stops in the doorway and turns to stare at me, her eyes full of something I haven't seen before. Hope, longing, aching pain, and something I can't put my finger on. She turns away from me.

31

CARMEN

I pull the car in front of the house so Miguel and Olivia can park in the driveway. Alexi and Ella are supposed to be coming by, too, but I don't think they'll be here until dinner time. This way, I can get in and out easier when Lily is ready to go, or when Sarah wants her home.

"You're okay being here without your mom?" I ask her as we get out of the car. From the little Sarah said the other night, it sounds like Lily feels at least somewhat responsible for our breakup.

She shrugs. "I've been here plenty without her. I'm fine. I'm more worried about you."

I bite back a comment about my heart missing her because Lily doesn't need to hear it. "I wish she were here with us, but I'm glad you're here, at least. Did you open your present yesterday after I left?"

She shakes her head. "I was going to wait until I got home tonight—hopefully convince mom to read your card, too." She gives me a hopeful smile.

I hope she can convince her to read my card, at least. "It'll probably be an hour or two before Miguel and Olivia are here with the kids, so you can hang out with me or abuela. I bought you a new pair of ballet shoes. They're downstairs, so if you want to dance while you're here, you don't need to bring yours." I open the front door for her.

"Wow. You guys go all out with the decorating, don't you?" She laughs, looking around at the brightly lit Christmas tree next to the fireplace and the ten stockings hanging from the mantel. "You have a lot of stockings." She walks along the mantel. They're grouped by family. Miguel, Nate, Fia, Talia, and Olivia. There's a small space before Sarah, Lily and me. "You have them for me and mom, too," she marvels.

"You can take your mom's home for her, if you want to. Most of the stuff in it is from my dad and abuela. They normally fill the stockings." Maybe she'll accept gifts from them, even if she won't take anything from me. "You're family, Bug, whether or not things are okay between me and your mom."

"Hey. You said I could do whatever I want until the kids come, right?" she asks suddenly, looking up at me.

"Yes," I answer cautiously, dragging the word out a little. "Why? What do you want to do?"

She laughs, looking around the living room. "You always mention your suite, instead of your bedroom." I suppose I do, at that. I never thought about it. "Can I see your suite?"

"Sure, if you want to. It's not very exciting." I chuckle good-naturedly. "Come on." I look around for my dad to tell him where we're going, but I don't see him. Maybe he's in the kitchen with abuela.

I lead her upstairs and direct her to the right at the landing, through the large French salon doors. Without thinking, I hit the handicap button to open the door for us.

"Holy shit. Who has doors that open like that in their house?" she asks, awestruck, walking into the sitting room.

I shrug. I'm so used to it that I never even think about it. "Remember I told you I was in an accident when I was about your age?"

She nods, lowering her eyes. "When your mom died."

"Yes, when my mom died. I was in a wheelchair for a while after the accident. My dad installed that so it was easier to take care of me. When I started walking again, it made things easier, too, especially while I was on crutches. It's hard to open doors when you're on crutches."

"Oh. I didn't think about that. I thought it was just some rich-people thing." She glances around the sitting room, then peeks into my bedroom. "This is bigger than our whole apartment," she murmurs in awe.

I never thought of it that way. "Your apartment is cozier." I grin at her.

She shrugs. "The walls are too thin."

I fight back a chuckle. I'll give her that one. "There's a bathroom over there. Otherwise, it's just a bed and empty space. I don't really have a lot of stuff."

"Do you miss her a lot?" Lily says quietly, turning around to look at me. Her eyes are damp.

"Like my heart is ripped out," I admit quietly. "But I have to respect her wishes, so I'll give her space. At least she lets me see you."

She shakes her head. "No. I mean your mom."

I let out a long sigh and sit down on the sofa. "Sometimes. It's been long enough that I don't have a lot of memories of her. Most of the memories I have are more like fuzzy feelings. I feel her love, more than anything. Sometimes I don't get along with my dad. A lot of times, I don't like the way he acts. We fought a lot when I was a teenager."

"Like me and mom?" she asks, swallowing a lump in her throat.

I huff out a laugh. "A lot worse. You're not even a teenager yet, Bug. Things will get harder before they get easier." She sits down next to me, and I pull her into a hug. "You're a strong-willed kid. Your mom is doing an amazing job with you, but you're going to give her a lot of headaches over the next few years."

"I don't think it can get worse than it is." She half-shrugs a shoulder.

"Honestly, kiddo, a lot of that is up to you. It's hard. Your mom doesn't understand what it's like to be a kid."

"Exactly," she agrees emphatically.

"It was worse with me and my dad. He didn't understand what it was like to be gay or Latina or a twelve-year old girl who just lost her mom." I swallow the lump in my throat. "I didn't realize at the time that he knew a lot more than I did, though. About life in general."

"You're lucky you had your abuela," she points out, leaning against me.

"Very lucky." Nodding in agreement, I look at Lily. "Try to go easy on your mom. She loves you with everything she's got. If you need her, she'll be there for you."

"I can't imagine losing her." She sighs softly. "I can't imagine losing either of you." She wraps her arms around me, squeezing me tight.

"Your mom's not going anywhere," I assure her. "Neither am I." I close my eyes for a minute, enjoying the closeness of her in my arms. "But Lily—I'm not your mom. I'm like Beth. I'm a trusted adult, and you can always come to me. You can talk to me about anything. I love you. But I'm not your mom. You have to understand that."

She nods, holding me tighter.

I hold her tight for a minute longer, then give her a little shake. "It's Christmas Eve. Let's go downstairs and find something fun to do."

"Is it okay if I dance for a while until the other kids get here?" she asks, subdued.

"Of course. You can do whatever you want. *Mi casa es tu casa.*"

Half an hour later, I finish wiping up the kitchen again.

"Gracias, mija," abuela says gratefully. "Now, go sit down and wait for your other babies to get here. Everything is as done as it's going to be right now."

I dry my hands and hang the towel over the oven door handle. "Do you know where dad is? I haven't seen him since I got back with Lily."

"He was in his office working on something, last I knew." She nods in that direction. "Do you need something?"

I shake my head. "Nope. I just wanted to check on him." I give her a quick kiss on the cheek. "You're sure you don't need any other help right now?"

She shakes her head and shoos me out of her kitchen.

I knock on the office door, but when dad doesn't answer, I poke my head in. I thought I heard him talking. Maybe he's on the phone. I frown, pushing the door open the rest of the way. "Dad?" He's not here.

I'm about to turn around and close the door when I hear his voice. I step into the office and glance around. Surprised, I find him on the TV screen, downstairs in the dance studio with Lily. He's sitting on the floor; she's sitting in his lap crying.

I fight the urge to run downstairs. I quietly close the office door and turn the volume up. "What's wrong, Lily?" She's sobbing uncontrollably, burying her head in his chest.

"You're not hurt." He can tell by her body language it's not something physical. She shakes her head. "Is your mom okay?" She shakes her head again. He takes her face in his hands. "Is she physically hurt, Bug?"

I hold my breath, waiting for her answer. *No,* she shakes her head. I let out a breath and sit down in my dad's chair, swirling it around and bringing it next to the TV. "I'm afraid she's going to die of a broken heart," Lily manages to say through sobbing hiccups.

My dad laughs wistfully, shaking his head. He pulls her head to his chest, rocking her. "Trust me. You can't die of a broken heart, even if it feels like you're going to." His voice cracks, and a single tear trails down his cheek, landing in Bug's hair. "She might feel like it right now, but I promise she won't."

"I couldn't live without her. Sometimes I hate her, but I don't know what I'd do without her."

He rocks her gently, letting her get all her feelings out. I remember so many nights after mom died when he held me like that, absorbed all my pain. It never occurred to me back then that he had his own, too.

A few minutes later, Lily looks up at him, calmer. Mostly, anyways. "I don't know how to fix it."

"Your mom is not going anywhere, Lily. You don't need to worry about that. If anything ever happened to her—God forbid—between Beth and Justin, and me and Carmen, you have a lot of people who love you and would take care of you." He wipes the tears from her face. "But that's not going to happen."

"She hurts so much right now. You have no idea how hard it is to watch someone you love in so much pain."

I choke back a cry at the pain in his eyes. He looks at her with a sad smile. "It's hard to watch someone you love when they're hurting. But you know, what's happening between Carmen and your mom isn't your fault. If they're meant to be together, they'll figure it out. One or the other of them will decide to fight for it." They're both quiet for a moment, letting that settle. "As long as they're both here on this earth, they can fix things," dad says softly.

"Do you think you could take me home? I want to be with my mom."

32

SARAH

I take the last piece of fudge off the plate of treats we took home from Christmas with Beth's family. Breaking it in half, I give a piece to Lily. "You have one more gift from me and the one from Carmen. Which one do you want to open first?"

I was surprised when she didn't take the one from Carmen with her yesterday, but she didn't stay there very long. When she got home, she seemed unusually clingy. She didn't say anything about what happened, but I could tell she was dealing with something. When I asked her, she just shrugged and told me she wanted to be with me.

"I'm not opening the one from Carmen until you're ready to read her card," she says quietly.

"I'll make you a deal," I say, sitting down next to her on the couch. "You open her present now, and I'll open her card tonight. I'd rather be alone for that. Is that fair?"

"You promise?" She looks at me hopefully.

"I promise." I may regret that later, but I want Bug to have a good Christmas. I grab the gift from the counter where Carmen left it two days ago and pass it to her.

"Did you peek already?" she asks, watching me.

I chuckle. "No. Carmen told me I could, but I trust her."

She studies me for a long minute, biting her lip. Then she nods, turning her attention to the gift. Ripping the wrapping paper off, she opens the box and pulls out a brand-new pair of expensive-looking pointe shoes. "Wow." She looks up at me with huge eyes. "Do you have any idea how much these cost? They're top of the line. It's what real professionals wear."

I laugh softly. "You're as good as the professionals, Lilybug. You deserve to have the best."

She turns them around in her hands, admiring them, then sets them on the coffee table. She pulls out the next thing from the box. It's a DVD with instructions for all the solos in *Swan Lake* and *The Nutcracker*. She looks at it for a moment before putting it on the table next to the pointe shoes. She looks in the box again. "This thing is huge," she exclaims, pulling a book out. She tosses the box on the floor out of the way.

Setting the heavy hardcover on her lap, she admires the cover before opening it. "Wow," she whispers in amazement. "It's the history of ballet in pictures." She flips through, stopping to skim over a few random pages before turning to another section. The grin across her face grows wider. "This is so cool!"

"You should text her or call her later to thank her." I laugh. I reach over and give my daughter a hug. I'm glad she has so many people in her life who love her.

"I will, I promise. She'll know that you're opening her card once I tell her I opened my present," she warns me. Missy looks up at both of us, tapping the box flap of Lily's empty box.

"It's fine. Don't worry about us, baby." I sigh softly. Grabbing the last gift from me, I hand it to her.

She bites her lip and nods. Taking the small gift in her hands, she gives it a little shake. She tilts her head and looks at it curiously for a minute before ripping off the wrapping paper. Crumpling it into a ball, she tosses it into the box at her feet.

Missy jumps in and pounces on it. Lily grins, rolling her eyes at the fluffball's energy. She pushes the box with her foot, just enough for Missy to lose her balance as she grabs the ball of wrapping paper and falls over, frolicking around with it. We look at each other and burst out laughing her antics.

"Open it," I tell her impatiently, nodding at the gift.

"You old people and your lack of patience. I'm savoring the moment." She raises an eyebrow at me, her eyes glistening with humor. Opening the box, her face lights up. It's a gold necklace with a gold and ruby pointe shoe charm. "It's beautiful, mom," she murmurs. "Will you put it on me?" She takes it out of the box, carefully unhooking the clasp, and turns her back to me. She hands me the necklace and pulls her hair out of the way. "It's my birthstone."

I clasp the necklace, and she turns around to look at me. "I love it," she says, her eyes watery. She wraps her arms around me, holding me tight.

"Hey." I wait until she loosens her grip on me, and I pull back to meet her eyes. "Are you okay?"

She nods, laughing softly. "I just like the necklace." She reaches for the pendant and rubs her fingers over it. "Thank you."

"You're welcome, of course." I kiss her forehead softly. "You've just been acting a little *off* since you got home from Carmen's yesterday. Are you two okay?"

She gives me a sheepish grin. "We're fine, Mom. Richard just said something yesterday. About not taking the people we love for granted. We never know how much time we have with them." She leans back against me, and I wrap an arm around her shoulders. "Did you know that Carmen was my age when her mom died?"

I swallow the lump in my throat. I had known it on some level, but I had never thought about it in terms of Lily's age. Carmen barely remembers her mom now. "I'm not going anywhere, Bug. For better or worse, you're stuck with me."

"He said I'm going to make you crazy sometimes, that it's part of growing up. But I should remember that you're important, and that I would miss you if you weren't here."

I huff out a chuckle. "He's a wise man," I grant her. "But you're not going to get rid of me that easily." I tuck a strand of hair behind her ear, a surge of pride gripping my heart. "I know you have Carmen and Beth and Justin to talk to, and I'm glad. But you know you can talk to me about anything, right? I will always love you. No matter what."

She glances up at me curiously. "Even if I kill someone?" she deadpans.

"Depends on who, maybe," I reply seriously. Lily snorts, her body shaking with laughter. I roll my eyes at her. "I'm serious, Bug. I know what it's like when your parents don't love you. Me and you, we don't always like each other very much. We don't always agree on stuff. That's all okay; it's normal. But I will *always* love you."

"Yeah, yeah." She rolls her eyes at me. "I'm going to go talk to Aiden for a while if he's done with his family Christmas stuff. You're going to read Carmen's card, right?"

I nod. "I will. I told you I would." I elbow her gently. "Aiden, huh?"

She blushes, the tips of her ears turning pink. She nods. "I like him."

I grin at her, then pull my arm off her shoulder. "Just make sure if you're video chatting with him that you're covered up."

She groans at me as she gets up. "See why I don't tell you things?"

I laugh. "It's my job to keep you safe. Sometimes when you start liking someone, you end up making stupid decisions. I'm just trying to keep you safe."

She studies me for a minute before turning away from me. "Stupid decisions, eh? Read her card, mom." She disappears into her room.

Touché.

I look after her for a long minute before walking to the counter. I pick up the card, turning it over and over in my hands. I inhale slowly, then head for my room.

> *Mi amor* Sarah,
>
> As much as I want to fix things between us, it's more important to me to respect you and your wishes. I made a colossal mistake treating your daughter like she was ours.

I do love her that much, but it was disrespectful of me to assume I could take on that role in her life. You will always be her one and only. You have done such an amazing job raising her to be a beautiful, caring person. She is well on her way to becoming a strong, independent woman—just like her mom.

When that independent streak of hers frustrates you both, I want you to know that I will always be there for her. I will always have her back, and yours. I vow to do better by both of you in the future. You have my heart and my soul always. Carmen

I turn the card over in my hands again, looking at the front. *All I want for Christmas is you.* Then underneath the word *you,* she writes *to be happy.* All she wants is for me to be happy. I open it back up and read the letter again. She sure as hell knows how to tug at my heartstrings.

My phone dings, and I consider ignoring it. It's probably Carmen. I'm sure Lily told her I was reading her card.

I grab my phone and swipe open my messages. Not from Carmen, then.

Richard: *Merry Christmas! Ignore me if you're still busy with Christmas stuff.*

Richard: *I just wanted to check on Lily after yesterday. You too, of course.*

Sarah: *Merry Christmas to you guys, too! We're winding down for the night.*

Richard: *How's Lily?*

Sarah: *Clingy and more emotional than usual. What happened yesterday?*

Richard: *Can I call? Easier than texting.*

Sarah: *Sure*

The phone rings a minute later, and I answer it on the first ring. "Hey. Merry Christmas," I tell him.

He chuckles. "To you, too. You both have full stockings over here. You need to come by and pick them up before the end of the year." He's quiet for a second. "They're from me and Isabela, if that makes a difference."

I close my eyes and shake my head, knowing he can't see me. I don't want to talk about Carmen. "What happened with Lily yesterday?"

"Before Olivia and Miguel came with the kids, Lily wanted to see Carmen's suite upstairs."

A pang of jealousy shoots through me. I haven't even been up to her room.

He sighs quietly. "I don't know if you've been up there or not, but Carmen has handicap buttons to open the door. I installed them after the accident. It made taking care of her a lot easier. Then when she was in a wheelchair and on crutches for the few years after, it helped her gain a little bit of independence from us." His painful memories make me realize that even with Bug's attitude, she and I have it easy by comparison.

"Anyway," he continues, "she was teasing Carmen about it being a rich-people thing, and it..." His voice trails off. "Not that it rubbed her the wrong way, but... She's hurting too, Sarah. She started talking about when she lost her mom. I think she intended for Lily to think about how lucky she is to have you, but I think it scared her. The idea of losing you."

"She's not going to lose me," I tell him fiercely.

"I know, Sarah." His voice is suddenly tired. "There are no guarantees in life, but nothing's going to happen to you. Besides, I don't think that's what was bothering her so much. Did Carmen tell you she went downstairs to dance until the other kids got here? I was in the office, and Lily was sitting in the corner down there in the studio by herself, just sobbing."

"No." I swallow thickly. "Carmen isn't talking to me right now."

He makes a strange, choked noise in his throat. "She's trying to respect your space, *mija*. She loves you and she doesn't want to push." I can hear the disapproval in his voice. "Anyway, I don't think she even saw Bug down there. I went down to talk to Lily and then took her home. She didn't even say goodbye to Carmen or abuela. She just wanted to be with you."

"Did she talk to you? I don't know what to do for her, other than just be there for her." Missy jumps into my lap and turns in a circle before plopping down on me. I absently scratch between her ears. He doesn't answer me for a long moment. "Richard?"

He sighs. "She seemed more upset with you and Carmen being apart than worried about *losing* losing you. She's worried about you. You're not yourself, Sarah."

"I'll be okay," I assure him.

"Can I offer you some advice? Not as Carmen's dad—what she did was horrible." He pauses, and when I don't answer, he continues. "I know I'm your boss at the office, Sarah, but you and Lily have become family to me. I've watched you go from a struggling young mom to a confident amazing woman over the past ten years. I'm proud of who you've become, that's all. I hesitate to say like a daughter, but you get my drift."

I murmur a quiet assent.

"I just..." He trails off, and he's quiet for a minute. "I know what it's like to lose the love of my life, Sarah. I'd do anything to have another day with her." His voice cracks. He clears it before continuing. "Whether it's Carmen or anyone else—if you really love someone, don't waste time being upset or angry over things if you can find a way to fix it. Life is short. Don't waste it being mad at each other."

I curl up with Missy on my lap, reading and rereading Carmen's words long into the night.

33

CARMEN

I look around my sitting room and pull my knees up to my chest. My eyes roam my space, stopping on the French doors that open to the main landing. My gaze drifts to the handicap button on the wall. A rich-people thing, Lily said.

Obviously, it wasn't that. It was installed after the accident. It made taking care of me easier for dad and abuela. It never occurred to me that most people would never even think about putting such a convenience into their house. We had the money and it made things easier, so dad made it happen.

As much as I lost in that accident, and the heartbreak and challenges that came after, I never thought about money. Even starting my own business, I never thought about money. Well, that's not completely true, but I never *worried* about money. I never wondered if there would be enough.

I always had my family's love. I never doubted for a minute that mom and dad loved me. Even before mom died, I'd talked to her about cute girls in my class. She loved me unconditionally. I don't know when dad realized I was gay, but he never made me feel less for it. It never even occurred to me to hide that from him.

I think I understand why Sarah is struggling so much with what I did. She keeps saying it's about trust, but it's not—not really. She trusts me with Lily, and Lily is the most important thing in the world to her. It's not that. If there's one thing that defines her, it's being Lily's mom. I came in and tried to take that away from her. To take away the most important aspect of her identity.

I'm worse than her pile-of-shit parents.

My phone dings. I ignore it. I'm not in the mood to deal with anyone. A few old friends are in town for the weekend, looking to catch up, but I'm not in the mood to see anyone but Sarah.

My phone dings again. Reluctantly, I reach for it, only smiling when I see it's from Lily. She must have opened my gift.

Lily: *thank you so so much for the cool ballet stuff. it's super awesome*

Carmen: *Glad you like it. How was your Christmas?*

Lily: *it was fun*

Carmen: *You left early yesterday. You okay?*

Lily: *yep, just decided I wanted to be with mom, that's all*

Lily: *don't be mad, I still love you*

Carmen: *I will never ever be mad when you choose your mom over me. You have enough love for both of us, but she's #1.*

Lily: *I think she's reading your card now*

Lily: *no, your dad is on the phone with her*

Lily: *anyway, I'm gonna go video chat with Aiden. later*

Carmen: *Stay covered please. Love you.*

Lily: *I was planning to get naked for him. night*

I ponder for a minute before sending Sarah a text: *Can you call me for a minute? It's about Lily.* I know that'll get her attention.

A minute later, my phone lights up with a call from Sarah. "Hey," I answer. "Don't hate me. She's probably joking and I'm probably overreacting."

"Carmen..." Her voice trails off. "What are you talking about?"

"I think she was joking. She said she was going to video call with Aiden, and I told her to stay covered. She told me she was planning to get naked for him."

Sarah bursts into quiet laughter. "I'll check on her in a little while, but I'm pretty sure she was joking, too. I told her the same thing, like twenty minutes ago."

"She told you about him?" I ask, surprised.

"She mentioned she was going to talk to him. She's been really clingy the last few days."

"That's my fault," I tell her quietly. "We were talking a little about my mom."

"Are you okay?"

I chuckle lightly. "About my mom? Yes, Sarah. It was a long time ago."

"I didn't mean about your mom, Carmen," she chides me. "Are you okay?" she asks me again, more insistent this time.

I swallow thickly, shaking my head. I don't want to do this tonight. "If I lie and say I'm fine, will you drop it?" I whisper hoarsely. *God, I miss her.*

"Do you really want me to?" she asks, her voice breaking.

"You know me, Sarah. I shut down when I'm hurting. Do you really want me to get all blubbery on you?" I try to make light of the situation, but my voice is hollow.

She chuckles. She's quiet for a long moment. She takes an audible breath. "Will you come and be blubbery with me?" she asks, her voice watery. "It doesn't mean things are okay yet, but if we want to work things out..."

"It's almost ten," I point out to her. Is she inviting me to stay?

"I know." I can hear the grin in her voice. "You can stay, but..." her voice trails off hesitantly.

"But don't expect to be making hot passionate love to you tonight?" I tease her. "I'm not," I assure her quickly. "I'm not expecting anything you aren't willing to give," I promise her.

She clears her throat. "Well, that, too, but..."

"Sarah," I drag her name out slowly, a light threat to my tone. "Just talk to me. But what?"

She sighs softly. "I'm going to brunch with Ella tomorrow. They're only in town for a few days, and she wanted to catch up."

Oh. Ella, who smudged her lipstick in a bathroom make-out session. "Maybe I should stay home then." I frown, trying to swallow my disappointment. We had a fight barely a week ago, and she's already looking to hook up with someone else?

"My God, Carmen. We're just going out for brunch. She's one of my idols. Professionally speaking," she clarifies. "We're eating *food* for brunch." She sighs in exasperation.

"Okay," I grumble softly. "It's just that—"

"Oh, don't even fucking start with that. How many women have you had lunch or coffee with the past few months that you've fucked before, Carmen?" Her tone is biting, and I mentally think about the string of empty hookups I've had over the past few years. "Don't answer that," she says sharply. "I don't want to know."

Ouch. "If it matters to you, I haven't thought about anyone other than you since the day I met you," I tell her quietly. "It doesn't bother me if you see Ella tomorrow."

"Good," she murmurs firmly under her breath. "Are you coming over?" Her voice is suddenly soft. She needs to see me as much as I need her.

"Hi," she says hesitantly, opening the door for me to come in.

I close the door and follow her into the living room. "Sarah," I breathe her name quietly. I need her to turn around and look at me. I need to see her, to look into her eyes, to gauge what I'm up against.

She turns around and holds my gaze for a long minute but doesn't shorten the distance between us. "Go say good night to Lily first. She knows you're coming."

Lily bounds out of her room and grabs me in a tight hug. "Thank goodness you're back."

"Lily. What did I tell you?" Sarah warns.

"Things aren't fixed. You need to talk. Yadda, yadda." Lily turns toward her mom, then looks at me. "Fight it out and get it out of your systems already. Then go have noisy wild sex all night and make up already. I have my earplugs."

"Lily Anne Reynolds, that's enough," Sarah barks at her, emotions fraying.

"Bug, apologize to your mom. That's not appropriate."

"Sorry, Mom," she acquiesces quietly. "I love you. I just want you to be happy, that's all."

Sarah nods at Lily. "I know, sweetie. But right now, that's between me and Carmen. You need to let us figure things out."

Lily nods silently.

That may be enough for Sarah, but not for me. I turn to Lily. "Do you remember the first night I stayed the night, when I came in to talk to you?" I ask her. She nods. "Sex between your mom and me, if there is or not, is between me and her. I don't ever want to hear you, even joking, telling someone else to have sex. It's not a joke, and it's never your place to make that decision for someone else."

"Yes, ma'am," she murmurs, looking down at the floor.

"Hey." I wait until she lifts her eyes to mine before continuing. "I'm not mad, *mija*. But you have to respect other people. Even if you and your friends talk about sex, hopefully not for a few more years, but still—even when you and your friends talk about it, that never ever gives you a right to push them to do something. It doesn't give them a right to push you, either."

Lily nods, silent for a minute. "My body, my choice. Your body, your choice." She sighs in frustration. "I just want you guys to be okay again. You're both miserable, and it's stupid."

I pull Lily to sit down on the couch next to me. Sarah leans against the wall, watching us. "Yes, we're both miserable," I tell Lily quietly, "but it's not stupid. I made a big mistake, and I hurt your mom. We're going to try to figure out how I can fix that, but you can't do that for us."

Lily nods. "But she said she didn't trust you before, and now she does. She trusts you with me, and I'm the most important thing to her."

I fight a smile. "Yes, you are. But my mistake was bigger than that. I have a question for you." Lily looks at me expectantly. "If someone asked your mom who she is, what do you think she would answer?" I feel Sarah's eyes on me, too.

Lily frowns for a moment but decides to play along. "She's an architect—a damn good one. A lesbian—a not so good one. At relationships in general, anyways. My mom. Beth's best friend. A good cook."

"Which one of those is most important to her?" I ask Lily.

She shrugs. "Being my mom, obviously. The rest is just gravy."

I turn back to Lily. "The most important thing in your mom's life is you. Her whole life is about being your mom. What I did, when I picked you up from school and didn't talk to her first—some of it was about trust. But I screwed up, Bug, because I wanted to be part of your family so bad that I thought I could share that job with her. Even if your mom and I find a way to make things work, even if I become like another mom to you, I will never ever be able to replace her. I would never want to."

Lily nods, her face lighting up with understanding. "But that's what you did at school. You took away her most important job and acted like you could take her place." She shakes her head. She looks over at her mom, then back at me. "No matter what, you could never replace her."

"Exactly," I tell her. "I was never trying to replace her, of course. I just wanted to be like her."

Lily laughs. "Everybody would be lucky to have a mom like her. But she's mine," she says possessively.

I huff out a small laugh. "Yes, she is. Now, go to bed so I can talk to your mom and see if she can find a way to forgive me."

Sarah tosses me a T-shirt and waits for me to crawl into bed. She's wearing a pair of shorts and a T-shirt when she crawls into bed next to me. "It's easier to talk in the dark, when I can touch you," she whispers softly. "But I don't trust myself, so..."

"Clothes," I finish for her.

"So, clothes," she repeats softly. "Can I hold you?" she chokes out, reaching across the distance between us.

I swallow, loud in the quiet of the bedroom. "If you do, I'm going to lose it and you're going to have a blubbering mess on your hands," I warn her softly.

She reaches out to me, her hand trailing down my arm. She links our fingers together and brings them to her lips. "Talk to me," she whispers.

I shake my head. "I'm sorry. I could repeat that for days, but," a quiet sob escapes my throat, "but that's the only thing that matters. I'm sorry." She pulls my head into her chest and holds me tightly. I let myself feel all the pain and fear and hurt I've been suppressing for the past week.

34

SARAH

Ella studies me across the table, biting her lower lip before she takes a sip of her lukewarm coffee. It's been a pleasant morning getting to know each other better, but mostly it's been an amazing discussion about the future of architecture in a world that's rapidly changing. Some of the ideas that she and Alexi are looking at are truly groundbreaking. A lot of the environmental aspects they're focusing on have the potential to be revolutionary in the industry.

"I want to show you something," she decides out loud. She waves to the waiter for the check and sticks her card in the leather folder. "My treat," she laughs, waving away my feeble attempt to fight her for the bill.

"I can afford to feed myself," I smile tightly. I don't like feeling like I owe anyone anything.

She places a hand over mine, a slow smile blooming across her face. "I know. You got a pretty hefty raise recently. But it's still my treat. Will you come back to the hotel with me? I want to show you a project we're thinking about."

Go back to the hotel with her? I raise my eyebrow at her curiously. "Is this an architectural project?"

She licks her lower lip, then pulls it between her teeth with a blush. "Yes, Sarah. Purely professional. You're a brilliant young mind. I just want to pick your brain a little." She says all this with her eyes studying my lips.

"Professional," I repeat dubiously, nodding. "Sure, why not?"

We walk, since her hotel is just down the block. She slips her arm around my elbow, shivering. "I'm not used to this cold," she murmurs as she pulls me closer.

I internally roll my eyes. Maybe I should have been more clear with her that I'm not looking for a hookup. I certainly didn't encourage her, but I guess I didn't obviously dismiss the idea, either. I turn to her, swallowing. "What do you mean that you heard that I got a hefty raise?" I ask, frowning.

She bursts into laughter. "You know my husband and your boss are best friends, right?"

I nod, raising an eyebrow. "You guys normally talk about employee salaries?"

She giggles, leaning into me. "No, of course not. Richard felt really shitty once he realized that he wasn't paying you what you're worth. Not just you, his whole team."

"I never intended to be the catalyst for that, but Carmen called him on it."

"Well, good on her." She smiles at me, opening the door to the Grand. She leads me through the lobby and toward the elevators. "We're on the fifth floor." She lets go of my arm to punch the button for her floor.

"What's this special project you want to show me?" I ask her as we get off the elevator, wondering if there really is a project, or this is just her way to get me back to her room.

She pushes the door open to her room, and pulls her coat off, tossing it on the bed. "Make yourself comfortable." She nods toward the bed. Pulling off my coat, I drop it on the bed next to hers. She goes over to her laptop bag and pulls it out, connecting it to the big TV on the wall.

I breathe a sigh of relief that this is indeed a professional call. Even though Carmen and I haven't figured everything out yet, I'm not giving up on us. It was nice to have her back in my arms last night, even though we did more crying than kissing. The fact that we're both hurting so much gives me an odd sense of hope. We both want it to work out between us so badly, I'm hopeful we can find a way.

Ella looks up at me curiously, the corner of her mouth twitching with amusement as she brings up some general concept plans up on the screen. "I'm sorry. Were you expecting something more hot and naked? I got the impression you had someone else on your mind."

I shake my head. Am I that transparent? "No. I do have someone else on my mind. We're having issues, but we both want to try and make things work. Did Richard tell you about that, too?"

She raises an eyebrow at me in surprise. "No. He doesn't usually share his relationship issues with us. Unless things are good, of course." She's thoughtful for a moment. "Then you might consider my proposition. Alexi said you wouldn't, but if you're having relationship issues with him..." I wonder what the hell proposition she's talking about.

I consider correcting her about me and Richard, but let it pass when she shrugs and turns toward the TV screen. "Our next big project. A floating city. Completely sustainable, including its own energy and food production. We want to create three or four different versions for different climates. The energy sources and plant life would vary, but otherwise, the basic framework would be the same."

I look at the plans on the screen as she flips to the next image and continues explaining. "Energy source is the most important, after the actual build—for a variety of reasons, but especially because we don't have an energy-efficient process for desalination. Yet. We're investing in a few small teams around the world who are onto something, though."

"Are you planning for them to be docked, these floating cities?" I ask, my eyes scanning the details on the screen.

"Initially, but the end goal is that they wouldn't need to be." She flips to the next set of pictures. "The bigger the area, the more plants we can have, and the more natural we can make it look and feel. Even something as small as a square mile could feel like you're in a grassland or a forest."

"This is science fiction," I tell her quietly, awed. "You hear about this kind of thing as something in the future. We don't have the technology to do this yet." I turn and look at her. "Do we?"

She shrugs. "With material sciences, we have a few options that would stand the test of time."

"Would it stand the test of salt water long term?" I ask her doubtfully.

She turns to look at me, her eyes wide with excitement. "Honestly, the biggest obstacle is finding a more energy-efficient desalination process. Virtually all the other technology and materials we need already exist."

I frown, shaking my head. "Then why don't we have countries actually building them? The desalination is a long-term problem. As long as it's docked and near land, that's a literal non-issue."

She bites her lip, tilting her head. She studies me. "Because it's a big investment. Which is not as much of a problem as you'd think it might be. The bigger problem is finding architects and scientists who are experienced in multiple aspects of the project and are willing to learn and collaborate on it. We have a few mega investors who will fund the initial stages of the project if we get the right set of talent on board."

It occurs to me that I'm being wooed. Not into this woman's bed, but to work for her. On a truly groundbreaking project. "It's an ambitious project," I say cautiously.

"It is," she affirms, her tone conservatively optimistic. She closes the laptop and sits down on the end of the bed, looking up at me. "Would you consider it?"

I look at the now-dark TV screen and turn to study her. "What, exactly, would I be considering?" I ask her slowly.

She looks up at me and pats the bed beside her. Sitting down, I pull my leg up under me and turn to face her. "Double what you're making now. Stock options, if the company ever goes public. That would be long-term, though. We anticipate five to eight years for the planning stage, to make sure we have all our bases covered. By that time, your kiddo would be old enough that you could travel or relocate. Once we start building, we'd want you there, at least part of the time, but that's years down the road. Until then, your location isn't an issue."

"Why me?" I ask her, shocked. Floored is more like it. I don't have the qualifications to be on a team like this.

"You have the experience. We've seen how much you've grown over the past ten or twelve years. You're constantly learning what you need for new projects. If you continue that, you'll be one of the most valuable people on the team. You have the ability to see the big picture and how the big systems work together without losing sight of the smallest details. You're smart, Sarah."

"Have you talked to Richard about this?"

She looks down at her hands, fiddling in her lap.

"You and Alexi have been his friends for three decades, Ella," I accuse her quietly. It's really low for them to approach me like this. To take his best architect out from under him.

"We had no idea if you'd even be interested. You're in the middle of a project, so even if you decide to come work with us, it won't be for months yet. Ultimately, I told Alexi it should be your decision if and when you want to talk to him about it—if you're even interested."

35

CARMEN

"You've been really quiet tonight," Sarah says softly as we crawl into bed.

I swallow as I wrap my arm around her waist. "I like you better naked, but you in a tank top with no bra on is kind of delicious." I nip lightly at her bare collarbone.

She closes her eyes, moaning softly. I feel her nipples harden against me. "Carmen," she breathes my name.

But it's a warning, not an invitation. Not surprising, since she spent half the afternoon with Ella. I sigh softly, rolling away from her. I lay on my back, staring at the ceiling. "Why am I here, Sarah?" I ask with soft exasperation.

She props herself up on her elbow and looks at me. "What do you mean? I want you here. I thought we were going to try to figure things out between us."

"Right. I did, too," I throw back at her, meeting her gaze in the semi-darkness.

She frowns, gently tucking a stray hair behind my ear. "Is this about Ella? I told you nothing would happen between me and her. I thought you were okay with me seeing her today."

I scoff. "When I thought it was just for brunch." I heard Alexi and dad talking this afternoon. Alexi seemed convinced that Ella was bringing Sarah back to the hotel for a rendezvous after they ate. "You know, as long as her husband is okay with it, I guess whatever floats your boat."

She sits up and studies me. "Carmen, nothing happened between us. The only time anything did was that kiss at the gala. I would never cheat on you."

"We're not exactly together, are we?" I scoff, sitting up and raising an eyebrow at her.

She lets out a long slow breath. "I have no desire to be with anyone but you. As long as there's a chance we can make this work, I would never consider being with someone else." She takes one of my hands in hers. "Besides, you're in my bed. So yes, we are together—in my mind, at least."

"So you didn't spend hours in her hotel room this afternoon," I say dubiously.

She bites her lip and looks down at our hands linked together. She sighs.

I pull my hand away from hers. "You did," I accuse her, barely a whisper.

She closes her eyes and shakes her head, her shoulders deflating. "Do you think I'm a liar, Carmen?"

I shake my head. "Of course not. But.."

She takes my face in her hands. "Why do you think something happened between me and Ella today then?" she asks gently.

I swallow thickly. "I heard Alexi say something to dad about Ella taking you back to the hotel room."

Sarah snickers. "What did Richard have to say about that?" She seems almost amused.

I chuckle. "I don't think he really understood what Alexi was implying." I take a deep breath, not sure I want to know the answer to my next question. "Did you go back to her hotel with her?"

She runs her hand over her face and sighs. "Listen and let me finish, please."

So she did spend the afternoon alone with Ella at the hotel. "Sure." I shrug.

"Nothing happened between us, Carmen. She wanted to—" She closes her eyes, searching for something. "Can I tell you something without you talking to your dad about it before I have a chance to?" She reaches for the lamp next to the bed and turns it on.

What? I wasn't expecting that. "I guess? I don't normally talk to him about personal stuff anyways..." I trail off.

She shakes her head. "It's not personal stuff. It's work." She meets my eyes, her forehead furrowed. "She offered me a position—to come work for them on a revolutionary project. She was showing me the project, trying to sell me on it."

"Oh," I murmur dumbly. Then again. "Oh." My first thought is that it's pretty shitty of them to try to take Sarah away from dad. But then it hits me. "A revolutionary project. Something that could make your career," I say quietly.

Her laugh wavers. "I like to think I've done a pretty good job of that myself already." She glances at me. "With your dad's help, though. I wouldn't be half as good as I am without him, Carmen."

I grumble softly. "You're one of the best in the Midwest. You know that." I lean over and kiss her playfully. "Architects, I mean. Kissers, too, I'd wager."

She chuckles softly. "Did you do your research on that front, too?" she teases.

I roll my eyes. "Seriously, what are you going to do?"

She huffs in exasperation. "I have no idea. Talk to your dad, first of all. No—scratch that. I'm going to talk to Richard, as my boss, and as someone who has been a mentor and teacher and cheerleader for me for the past decade—then find out more about the project that Alexi and Ella want me for."

I nod slowly. "Sounds like a good start."

She yawns loudly, stretching. "Honestly, it sounds like a dream project. But I need time to sit with it, think about how it would affect things. Besides, even if it's something I decide to consider, it's something I would need to talk to Lily about—and you," she says pointedly.

"Me?" I ask in surprise. "Why me? You'd finish the Cultural Center, right?"

Sarah bursts into laughter. "Of course I'm finishing your build." She sighs, cupping my cheek and rubbing a thumb against my jawline. "Things might be rough at the moment, sweetie, but I see a lot of you in my future. Maybe even some little Tomsen-Reynolds running around."

"More than one? You mean, besides Lily?" I ask her, shocked.

She shrugs. "If that's what you want. I think it would be nice to have more babies if I had a partner in the process."

She gets the biggest professional opportunity in her life, and she's thinking about me and babies. "You would let me get in the way of a career move like that?" I ask her in amazement.

She bites her lip, shaking her head. "If you can learn to trust me enough to fucking talk to me when something is bothering you," she pokes me in the ribs, "yes. Have you not figured out that I lo—" She stops herself, sighing, then whispers, "that I love you."

36

SARAH

I glance across the table at Richard. "Thank you for meeting me for breakfast." I give him my best smile. Of all the conversations I've had with him over the years, I've never been this nervous before.

He glances at me in my work clothes, noticing my professional demeanor. It's the Monday between Christmas and New Year, and no one is working in the office this week. He was obviously surprised when I called him yesterday to request a breakfast meeting today.

He waits until we've both ordered before folding his hands on the table and giving me a firm look. "What's going on, Sarah? You're acting out of character." When I don't answer right away, he raises an eyebrow, hiding a small smile. "Is this about Carmen?"

I chuckle softly. "No. Not yet. Besides, you've already given us your blessing. Remember?" I tease him.

He laughs, a smile spreading across his face. "Fair point. Work, then?" he asks more seriously.

I take a deep breath and nod, exhaling slowly. "Ella made me a proposition this weekend."

He nods, not surprised. "Professional or personal?" he asks curiously.

I raise an eyebrow at his question. Is he asking what I think he's asking?

He rolls his eyes. "She's a woman who likes to have her cake and eat it, too." He laughs. "I've known them for thirty years, Sarah."

I shake my head vigorously. "No. I'm with Carmen. I would never cheat on her."

He puts his hands up in acquiescence. "Carmen doesn't talk to me about your relationship, and I know things haven't been all roses between you two." He sighs softly. "All that's none of my business, anyways. Alexi just said something the other day that made me think..."

I snort back laughter. "She was feeling me out. I think she actually got the idea that you and I are having relationship problems and trying to work things out. So Alexi was hinting to you that his wife was going to try to hook up with your girlfriend."

He raises an eyebrow in amusement. "Ella," he says. "She's been asking a lot of questions about you the past few months."

I bite my lip and nod. "She offered me a job, Richard."

That shuts him up.

Conveniently, the waiter shows up with our food right then. Richard slowly takes a bite of his breakfast, stalling. "What kind of job?" he asks finally.

I take a sip of my coffee before answering. "Have they talked to you about their floating cities? It sounds like a project they've been planning for a while."

He nods slowly, studying me for a long minute. "It's an ambitious project. I don't understand a lot of the newer technology, but that's their wheelhouse. It seems like science fiction to me, but Alexi seems to think that all the technology and materials they need already exist."

"Yes, except an energy-efficient desalination process. They're investing in a few teams that are working on that, though," I add, relaxing the tension in my shoulders.

"Are you thinking about it? Taking the job?" he asks.

I take a bite of my pancakes, thinking. "I just found out about this two days ago, Richard. I haven't made any decisions."

He laughs quietly. "You would be a good fit for their team, Sarah. It would be an amazing opportunity for you to be part of a project like that."

I frown at him, confused. "You won't be upset with me if I decide to take it?" I ask him, surprised.

"I'd expect you to finish Carmen's build, of course. But you're one of the best architects in the country, one of the most versatile."

I shake my head. "Not one of the best in the country. You're exaggerating. But thank you." I grin at him. "Honestly, it feels like I'm betraying you to even think about it. When you hired me, I was inexperienced and struggling. You taught me everything I know."

He laughs. "No. I taught you everything I know, and then you kept going. You surpassed me a long time ago. You're not going to hurt my feelings if you decide to take this job, Sarah. Regardless of what you decide, I'm proud of you, of the professional you've become. You have a lot of potential, and I never want to stand in the way of that. You're thinking about it, at least," he presses me with only a hint of question.

I nod reluctantly. "Thinking about thinking about it." I shrug half-heartedly. "If I decide it's something I want to explore, it's something I need to talk to Lily and Carmen about, too."

He raises an eyebrow, a sparkle in his eye. "I take it that means things are going well with Carmen?"

"Mom." Lily looks at me across the dinner table. She glances at Carmen, then back to me.

I glance between the two of them, my brow furrowing at the serious tone of her voice. "What is it, sweetie?"

She takes a deep breath. "I have a favor to ask."

I raise an eyebrow. "Ask away," I tell her, wondering what's going on in her head.

"I have a friend... A guy friend," she specifies. "He's confused. Bi-curious or something, I don't know. I don't really understand why people need to put labels on each other." She shrugs a little. "Anyway. He's afraid to talk to his parents because he doesn't think they'll be very supportive."

"That's a scary place to be," I tell her.

"I thought maybe he could talk to you or Carmen. I think he needs an adult he can trust. You always talk about that being important," she says sheepishly.

I glance up at Carmen, then back at Lily. "It is important. Is this a close friend or just someone you know at school?" I ask curiously. It doesn't really matter, but finding a way to talk to someone else's kid without them knowing could be tricky.

She hesitates for a minute and glances at Carmen again. She sighs. "You remember Chuck, from the mall?" When I nod, she continues. "It's him. I'm not super close to him, but he and his friends have been hanging out with our queer-friendly group lately. I suggested that he talk to one of the counselors at school, but he doesn't really want to."

I look at Carmen. "He's Montgomery's grandson, right?" She nods. I bite my lip thoughtfully. "So it would probably not be good for you to talk to him. Have you talked to Olivia about this? Legal issues about talking to minors without parent permission, I mean?" It's obvious that Lily talked to Carmen about this before she mentioned it to me—which, surprisingly, doesn't bother me.

"I didn't give her details, but she said if he and Lily meet somewhere public, like the mall or something, and you're with her, there shouldn't be any issues. I didn't ask about my connection to his grandfather. It's not relevant."

"You're the one who has experience dealing with what he's feeling, Mom," Lily points out. "I know that it's not your favorite conversation topic," she scrunches her face, "but you know how he feels."

I nod in agreement. It's not a subject I really want to talk about, but I can at least listen to him. "Maybe we can meet him at the mall some time this week—stop at the food court for lunch or something," I suggest to Lily.

A few hours later, Carmen and I are curled up on the couch watching a movie when Lily comes out of her room. She wiggles between us on the couch. "Can you take me to the mall on Wednesday afternoon for a few hours so I can hang out with my friend Chuck?" She turns to me and asks nicely.

I laugh. "Yes, I can. You didn't need to wiggle between us for that," I tease her.

She shrugs. "Sometimes it's just fun to annoy you."

I shake my head and chuckle. "It's not annoying. It's fine." I stifle a yawn and glance at the clock. "Speaking of annoying you, I want your opinion on something."

Lily grins. "I'm all for little brothers or sisters running around, but don't expect me to change diapers."

I close my eyes with a small huff.

"Good to know," Carmen jumps in, "but don't hold your breath on that just yet, kiddo."

Lily turns back to me. "Okay. What is it, then?"

"I got a really cool job offer," I start. "It would be with a different company."

She frowns at me. "You mean you wouldn't be working for Carmen's dad anymore?"

"If I take this job, then I'd be working for some of his friends. They do really cool projects. They want to build a floating city."

She frowns, looking at Carmen, then back at me. "That sounds like something from a movie. What does it have to do with me?" she asks, confused.

"I would probably work remotely for the next few years. So I'd probably be at home more. Otherwise it wouldn't change much, not for the next few years. It might mean traveling a lot or moving after the first few years."

She shrugs dismissively. "Seems like something you need to talk to Carmen about more than me. I'll probably be looking at college by then. You two will probably be changing diapers by then. Screaming babies might make it hard to work from home."

Carmen tries unsuccessfully to hide her laughter. "I might be able to find a room at the office where you can set up—screaming babies or not."

I groan silently. "Lily, I'm serious. Think about it, okay?"

She shrugs, climbing off the couch. "Do whatever makes you happy, Mom. Seriously." She leans over and gives me a hug. "I'm going to bed. Love you both," she says, leaning over to give Carmen a hug.

After she disappears back into her bedroom, Carmen closes the space between us. "So dad wasn't mad about the job thing?"

I shake my head. "He said he's proud of me. He thinks it would be a good opportunity for me if I want it. He told me to let him know once I make a decision."

"I don't know enough about your field to be able to say if it would be an amazing opportunity or something super risky, but it sounds promising," she says.

Neither of us mention what Lily brought up. If she and I make things work, this job opportunity could very well be a deal breaker. If I take the job, the reality is that I'll need to relocate in a few years. Carmen has an established business here. If it were just the two of us, I could travel back and forth when the time comes, but that's not fair to her if we bring more kids into the mix.

37

SARAH

Lily waves to Chuck, and the memory of her stepping back in fear of him last time I saw him unsettles me.

"You're sure you're okay talking to him?" I ask her quietly, putting a hand on her shoulder.

"Of course, Mom. Seriously." She glances up at me, seeming to realize what I'm thinking about. She frowns. "You know he's the one that Aiden and I were standing up for when we got sent home that day, right?" She sighs softly, her shoulders dropping. "When I made the stupid mistake of calling Carmen."

Oh. I think I knew that at some point, but I never really thought about it. "Fair enough," I say, putting a smile on my face as Chuck joins us.

Lily gives him a one-arm hug and a smile. "We were just going to go get some lunch. You want to come with? My mom's treat." She laughs, completely at ease with this kid.

Wow, the difference a month makes.

"Sure, if it's not a problem. My dad's picking me up in a couple hours. He had to go into work for a bit."

"What does your dad do?" I ask him, trying to make polite conversation.

He shrugs. "Some finance or money stuff. He works for my grandpa."

"Can we find a sit-down place, mom?" Lily asks. "Someplace quiet, maybe?"

"Sure. Your choice," I tell them.

They decide on a burger place, and we sit at a booth in the back of the restaurant, far enough away from other customers that I hope Chuck feels comfortable talking.

Once we have drinks and we're waiting for our food, Lily jumps right into it. She looks at Chuck. "I talked to my mom. You can trust her." He looks nervously at Lily before he turns to me.

"You're in a safe space, Chuck," I tell him gently.

Lily groans. "He kissed a boy and he liked it. It's kind of not fair. I haven't even kissed Aiden yet."

Chuck laughs at Lily. "Jealous much?" he teases her. He turns back to me. "I think I like both. Boys and girls." He shrugs a shoulder, embarrassed. "I haven't kissed a girl before, but I definitely like them."

I chuckle softly. I'm so glad this kid has Lily and other friends at school that help him feel comfortable with who he is. "You don't have to kiss a girl to know that you like them. Sometimes you just know." I see the waiter coming with our food and wait until he's gone before I continue. "For some people, they aren't attracted to someone based on their gender. They're just attracted to the person, and the person's gender isn't really a factor."

"That sounds like me. I don't know what that makes me, though. Sometimes it seems like everyone wants to know what I am," he says with a slight frown.

Lily shakes her head. "They can go fuck off. It doesn't matter what they think."

Chuck glances at me, no doubt wondering if I'll reprimand Lily for her language. I don't.

"You don't need a label, Chuck. You might find one that you feel fits as you get older. Whether you do or not, it's not really anyone else's business anyway."

He's silent for a moment as he pops a fry in his mouth. "It matters what my family thinks, though," he says quietly.

"You think they'll have a problem with you being queer?" I ask him.

He grabs another fry, chewing it slowly. He takes a drink and sighs. "My sister is a freshman, and she heard something. She's been teasing me. She obviously doesn't care—other than to get on my nerves—but I don't know about my parents."

I smile about his sister. "Be grateful that you have a sister who likes to tease you that doesn't care." I chuckle. "If your sister doesn't care, why do you think your parents will?" I ask him curiously. It's usually the whole family.

He laughs. "I will never be grateful for my sister. She likes to make my life miserable."

"Only because she loves you." Lily gives him a pointed look.

He acts like he's thinking about that, then shrugs. "Mom will probably be okay. Her sister sometimes dated women when they were younger. But then she married my uncle."

"What about your dad?" I ask him.

He scowls. "He comes from a shitty family. He's not as bad as they are, but they don't like anybody who's different. My grandpa was even rude to your wife when she picked Lily up from school the other day."

I don't plan to correct him, but Lily sighs. "Carmen is my mom's girlfriend. They're not married. Yet." She glances at me. "I fucked up when I called her to pick me up from school the other day. It caused a lot of problems." She sighs. "She's not my mom, and it was wrong of me to act like she was."

I glance at Lily. "Watch your language." I do reprimand her this time. "What did he say to her?"

"He called her a dirty Mexican. Behind her back, literally. We walked away, Mom." She puts a hand on my arm. "Let it go. He's not worth it."

I inhale slowly. Lily's friend needs me to be a rational adult here, not fly off the handle on how much of an ass his grandfather is. "You think your mom and your sister will be supportive?" I ask him gently. Let's start out with potential positives.

He bobs his head. "My sister for sure. She would tease me, regardless. That's what big sisters do."

"Little brothers, too," Lily elbows him in the ribs with a grin. "You do the same thing to her." He rolls his eyes guiltily.

"Do you want to talk to your parents about it? Or at least your mom? When I was your age, the hardest part about not talking to my parents was that I felt like I had to hide who I was," I tell him. "Like—the people who were supposed to know me the best and love me, they didn't really know who I was."

He frowns at me, then takes a bite of his burger. He shakes his head. "I'm proud of who I am, and they can take me as I am," he says firmly. "I think I'm going to ask my sister to talk to my mom with me. I can deal with dad later. He's less likely to act like grandpa if I've already got mom and Nancy on my side."

"That sounds like a good plan," I tell him honestly. "Do you guys want to get some ice cream for dessert?"

38

SARAH

I knock softly on Richard's office door. Carmen is in the living room with Fia wrapped up in her lap, sound asleep. Olivia is sitting next to her with Talia. I think Miguel is outside with Nathan and Lily in the snow, but I'm not sure. "Hey, you got a minute?" I ask, poking my head in.

"Sure. What's up?" he asks, a smile breaking across his face. He has all his favorite people here today, including the four grandkids that aren't technically his—they're still his pride and joy. He spins his desk chair around and nods to the other chair in the room.

"I'm going to call Ella tomorrow," I tell him without preamble. I've made my decision, and there's no point in dragging things out.

He nods. "Finish things out with the Cultural Center. I'll start moving the bridge project to Bob. He can work on the early stages until I find someone to replace you."

I shake my head. "I'm going to tell her no, I can't do it. I figure if I don't talk to you first, you'll hear it from her. I'd rather you hear it from me." I smile sheepishly.

"What? Why?" He stares at me in confusion. "It's the perfect opportunity for you."

I shake my head. "It would be a fantastic opportunity. It would be perfect if I could stay here. For the next few years I could—while we're in the planning stages, but I would need to move in a few years."

"By then Lily would be looking at colleges," he points out. "If you need to move before she's done with high school, she could stay here, and you could visit often."

I chuckle. "That would be an option, if it came to it. But I can't. Carmen's life and business are here. I won't make her choose between her work and mine. I can stay where I am. If you were serious about me taking over when you retire, it's better for you, too."

He steeples his fingers, studying me. "Have you talked to Carmen about it?"

I shake my head. "I don't want her to feel like she needs to choose."

"Is that because you're afraid she won't choose you?" he asks frankly.

I frown, studying him. "No. The opposite, in fact. I'm afraid she'll want me to take it. Then when we need to move, she'd resent me."

"Can I give you some fatherly advice?" he asks quietly.

I nod, knowing what he's going to say.

"This is a big decision for you. But if you're planning to spend the rest of your life with someone, it's not just your decision."

I sigh softly. "I get it. I'll think about it. I don't think she's going to change my mind, though. I still have a job, don't I?" I ask him with a twitch of a smile.

He rolls his eyes. "Of course. That's not even a question."

"Hey, beautiful. How was your day today?" Ella asks me with a wink as I answer her video call.

I laugh at her flirting and look around at the closed conference room. I didn't want to do this at home, but I also don't want to do it in front of the whole office—or in front of Richard. "It was good. It's been a bit of a slow day. It always is, coming back from a long holiday."

"How's the Cultural Center coming along?" she asks curiously.

I shrug my shoulders. "It's on schedule. We have a bit of a PR nightmare with a local homophobic and racist group that's causing some trouble, but Carmen and her team are on it. We're on schedule for the grand opening in June."

"After that you're mine, right? Please tell me you're going to come rock this project with us." She gives me a huge grin. Obviously Richard didn't talk to her yesterday. I half expected him to.

"Actually," I start carefully. The smile drops from her face, replaced by a frown of confusion. "I'm truly honored that you sought me out, but I'm going to pass. I appreciate the vote of confidence, though."

Her mouth drops open, and she just stares at me for a long moment. "What?" she asks after a long minute.

"I appreciate the opportunity, but it's not the right fit for me right now," I tell her carefully. "I can't commit to a position knowing that I'll need to leave Delmont in a few years."

"If it's about Lily, we'll make sure you can stay until she's finished with high school. We might need you to make a few trips out to the build site, but we can work with that." She's thought through all my potential objections.

"It's not about Lily," I tell her. "Although I appreciate your willingness to be flexible with that—it's not just Lily."

Her eyes widen and her mouth falls open again. "You're going to make a go of it with Richard? He'll be retiring soon."

I snort out a laugh. "He's got a solid ten or fifteen years left to work before then. But no, it's not him." I snicker, amused.

"Well, whoever it is, they can always move with you," she points out rationally.

I shake my head. "It's Carmen, Richard's daughter. She has her own business here."

Her eyes bug out of her head and she's speechless for a moment. "You didn't—" She clamps her hand over her mouth. Her forehead furrows. She shakes her head and lets out a huge guffaw. "Never mind. I don't want to know." She shakes her head again, clearing her thoughts. "Sorry. For some reason, I didn't see that coming."

"Neither did Richard, at first," I tell her drily, holding back a laugh. I have a feeling I know where her dirty mind was going for a minute.

"Did you talk to Carmen about it?" she asks curiously.

"A little," I tell her. Very little, if I'm honest. But it won't change anything.

"I'll accept your answer," she says slowly, "but if you're serious about being with her, you need to realize that means more than sharing your bed. It means communicating and sharing everything. The good stuff and the bad stuff, the responsibilities and decisions. If you're going to be part of a successful team, you need to talk to her and get her input, too."

It feels strange to get personal advice from someone I respect so much on a professional level. "I know."

"Okay." She nods slowly. "I'll let you go. But Sarah?"

"Ella?" I raise an eyebrow at her in amusement.

"The job offer is still open, if you talk to her and she changes your mind. We want you on this team, and we'll work with you as much as possible. All you have to do is say the word."

39

CARMEN

It's been more than three months since Montgomery's attempted rally at the mall, and Mike and I are completely befuddled as to the radio silence. There's been nothing on social media, not even Truth Social. In fact, we've been getting more donations rolling in, primarily from big financial corporations in the Midwest. It doesn't make any sense.

"What's the frowny face for?" Lily asks me across the dinner table.

I shake myself out of my thoughts. "Just work, nothing important," I tell her. "How was school today?" She's been involved in an afterschool project to make minority kids feel more included. About a dozen students and a handful of teachers are involved.

"It was okay. We have this place set up where kids can anonymously write about why they feel different or alone. They can put their name or ID number if they want to, and they can mark a box if they'd be interested in meeting other kids they can relate to," she explains. "It started pretty slow, but in the last few weeks, we've had signs up around the school. It's really sad how many kids feel alone about stuff people don't like to talk about."

"Like what kind of stuff?" Sarah asks.

She shrugs. "Everything, really. Politics—Ms. Terpstra said we won't touch that." I chuckle. *Wise woman.* "I think every student who's not white has written that down at least once. Religion. Queer kids. Curious kids. Poor kids. Rich kids. Kids who have sick parents, who've lost parents, who have alcoholic parents." She pauses for a minute, before adding, "Abusive parents."

"That has to be hard. Do you read them, or do the teachers read them?" I ask her gently.

She shakes her head. "After the first one of those, Ms. Terpstra looks at stuff first."

"That's good," Sarah says softly. "Do you know if they're doing anything to help the kids?"

Lily's face lights up. "If a student wants to connect with a peer, Ms. Terpstra or one of the teachers finds a way to let them know. I think they're working on setting things up for the kids with more serious situations, but that's for the adults to worry about."

"I wonder if I could volunteer to talk to any of the kids who've lost parents," I say quietly.

"We're getting an app that kids can use outside of school. They're talking about adding something like that, where parents or other local adults can volunteer, but it's not ready yet."

Sarah frowns. "Is there already an app like that?"

Lily shakes her head. "No. Someone that Chuck's dad knows is building it for us."

"Wow. That's an expensive thing to volunteer," Sarah says, surprised. "Does that mean he talked to his parents and things are okay?"

Lily laughs. "Yes. He talked to his mom first. They talked to his dad together. His dad was more supportive than he expected." She bites her lip before continuing. "His dad actually quit his job, because when he found out what his grandpa did, he didn't want to work for him."

I look over at Sarah, my brow furrowed. "We haven't seen or heard anything from Montgomery since Thanksgiving weekend at the mall. Nothing. All of his socials are quiet."

Lily giggles. "Chuck's dad told his grandpa that if he didn't quit that shit, he couldn't see Chuck anymore. And when he was looking for a new job, he made sure everyone knew why he quit working for his father."

"Your daughter is an amazing person," I whisper to Sarah as we climb into bed that night. "You know that's all on you, right?" I lean over and give her a gentle kiss.

"It's not all on me," she chuckles softly. "She's got a lot of wonderful people around her. You influence her more than you know," she tells me, sighing quietly.

"Maybe some, but she wouldn't be who she is without you." I'm quiet for a long moment. "We've been getting a lot of big donations for the Cultural Center from big financial corporations the past few weeks—companies all over the Midwest."

"Chuck's dad, you think?" she asks.

"It would make sense. We haven't heard a peep from Montgomery. Michael and I have been trying to figure out why."

She's quiet for a minute before she starts tracing her fingers along my bare stomach. She sighs softly and rests her palm on my lower abdomen. "You make a great mom, Carmen."

I lace my fingers with hers. She hasn't mentioned babies since Ella offered her the new job. "I'm not her mom, Sarah. I won't take that from you."

"It's not the same, but you are, in a way. You will be even more, if we give her a brother or sister," she whispers.

"We need to talk about your new job first—what happens when you need to move for work, or at least travel a lot," I point out. I've let her sit with the idea for two months, and honestly, it's time we talk about it.

"I turned it down, Carmen. I'm not going anywhere." She squeezes our hands together, her thumb rubbing in slow circles on my stomach.

"I thought it was a really good opportunity," I say, surprised. I expected her to talk to me before making a decision.

She half-shrugs. "It would be, but not if it takes me away from you. Even if we stayed here, I'd have to travel a lot. I won't do that to you if we have little ones."

My heart drops. "You turned it down without talking to me." My mouth is suddenly dry. "It would have been the perfect fit for you. You would have loved the challenge of it."

She gently squeezes my hand. "Maybe. But if I have to choose, I'd rather stay here with you. We both have solid jobs here. Your family is here. Our friends are here."

I shake my head in amazement. "So you made this decision based on us being together, but you didn't include me in making the decision." I close my eyes and bite my lip. "If we weren't together, you would have taken it." It's not a question.

She half-shrugs. "Sure, especially since Ella said they'd work with me as much as necessary so Lily can finish high school here. But that's not the point, Carmen. I don't want to go anywhere if you're not there."

"No," I say, my argument sounding hollow in my ears. "The point is that you unilaterally made a decision that affects our family without even talking to me. You even asked Lily." *Right in front of me.* "I thought you wanted time to think about it, so I gave you time."

She shakes her head. "I told your dad and Ella both, right after the New Year."

"Without even talking to me about it." I pull my hand from hers, rolling away from her. Yes, it's ultimately her decision whether she wants to take the job or not, but if she wants to build a family with me, then she should respect me enough to discuss it with me.

"It seemed obvious, Carmen. If I took the job, I'd have to eventually leave Delmont. You have your business here. I would never ask you to walk away from what you've built, sweetie. We can talk about it, but that's what it comes down to." She rolls toward me and props herself up on her elbow. "Tell me I'm wrong."

"You're wrong," I say quietly through clenched teeth. "Maybe that's what we would have decided together. Maybe not. It's too late to ask for my opinion now." I roll onto my side, away from her. I don't want to be in a relationship where my opinion doesn't matter.

40

SARAH

When I wake up in the morning, she's already gone for the day. It's not the first time, but it's rare for her to be up earlier than me. She didn't leave me a note, so I uneasily assume she's at work. Still, last night she went to sleep upset, so I need to talk to her.

She doesn't respond to my good morning text, but I don't think much of it until lunch, when Richard stops by my desk. "Have you talked to Carmen today?" he asks softly, keeping his voice low.

I glance up at him and frown. "No. Why? Does she need something?"

He shakes his head. "She didn't really say. She just asked if I'd meet her for lunch."

"That's weird," I say quietly. "I told her last night that I turned down the job from Ella. She wasn't thrilled about it."

He studies me for a long moment. "That was more than two months ago, Sarah. I thought you—" He stops himself, shaking his head. "I'm not getting involved." He taps his index finger twice on the desk, a nervous tick I've only seen a few times from him over the last decade. "I'll be back after lunch. You need anything while I'm out?"

I shake my head. "No. I'm good. Thanks."

Half an hour after he gets back from lunch, I call her. She doesn't answer. I call her work number, and I get voicemail. I send her another text, this time to call me.

Finally, I get a text back. *busy afternoon. see you tonight*

I breathe a sigh of relief. *Okay, love you,* I send back.

When we finally get home from ballet class and dinner, it's after seven. Lily drops everything off and heads for her room and a shower. I saw Carmen's car in the parking lot, so I know she's here, but I don't see her. Then I notice my bedroom door is closed.

"Hey. Are you in here?" I knock softly before opening the door. She's sitting on the end of the bed, looking lost and alone. I step toward her. "Hey. Are you okay?" *Something is wrong.*

She inhales slowly, then straightens up as she exhales. "Will you kiss me?" she asks softly, her voice breaking.

"Every day for the rest of your life," I promise her, my heart in my throat.

She takes my face in her hands, her eyes searching mine, before she kisses me. Softly at first, but then more desperately, a whimper escaping her chest. She pulls back from me. "God, I love you, *mi amor,*" she breathes softly. She closes her eyes tightly, stepping back from me with steel in her posture.

"Carmen? Talk to me." I try to take her face in my hands, but she shakes her head.

"I'm sorry, Sarah. I can't do this," she chokes out. "I can't be in a relationship, especially a marriage, where I don't have a fifty-fifty say in things—when you don't care enough to get my input on things that affect both of us."

I step toward her, and she steps back. "I'm sorry. I just don't see a way it would work without you giving up everything you've built here. I'm not willing to take that away from you."

She shakes her head angrily. "But it's okay for me to take away the most important opportunity of your career."

"Oh, sweetie." I sigh softly. "You didn't take anything away from me."

'No," she snarls softly, "you didn't give me a chance. If we talked about it, maybe we could've found a way. Maybe we wouldn't. But at least fucking respect me enough to talk to me about it."

"I do respect you; you know I do," I argue, trying to keep my voice calm.

"Is this how it would be if we stayed together? You make decisions and try to pacify me so I accept them? I know you're used to being on your own, making your decisions without me. But don't make your decisions based on me if that's how you're going to do things."

She picks up her overnight bag, which was sitting next to the bed. I hadn't noticed it there. "Carmen, stop," I beg her. "Let's talk about this."

"I can't do this, Sarah. If you can't be fifty-fifty with me, I just can't." She storms past me, angry tears streaming down her face.

41

CARMEN

I pull into the garage and hit the remote to close the door behind me. I try wiping the tears from my face, but it's pointless, since my sorry ass can't stop crying. I don't know how long I sit there, bawling my fucking eyes out.

It's not even about the job. Sure, I want her to take the job because it would make her happy. It would give her lots of opportunities. After talking to Ella and realizing how much they offered her, I could even afford to stay home with the kids, if we had them—or work part-time and run my business remotely. We could make it work.

If she would just respect me enough to ask for my opinion. I can't be in a relationship where my partner doesn't want my opinion, chooses not to get my input about things that are important. I can't live like that. I won't.

I don't know if I can live without her, though. Her and Lily. I always thought that Olivia and Miguel's kids felt like my own, but it's different with Lily. She talks to me, trusts me, loves me—and hates me—in ways that I can't imagine from anyone other than my own child. I won't let Sarah take that away from Lily.

There's a soft knock on my car window, and I look up in the darkness. Dad. He opens the car door. "Come on, *mija*. Come inside." He puts his hand on my shoulder, and the pain in his eyes rips me apart again. He gently pulls me out of the car and into his arms. I don't know how long I sob into his chest, his arms wrapped tightly around me.

"I don't think I can live without her," I mumble into his chest. "But I can't be with someone who doesn't include me in the important stuff, either."

He kisses the top of my head. "I know, *mija*. I know." He loosens his arms around me. "Let's go in. Abuela is worried about you."

Abuela wraps me in a warm hug when I walk in. She hands me a hot cup of *aguapanela,* hot cinnamon and sugarcane water, that I haven't had in years. "You haven't made this for me since mom died," I sniffle, looking at her.

"Sit down and talk to me," she says softly.

I sit down on the big couch, dad on one side of me, abuela on the other. Dad wraps his arm around my shoulders, and I lean into his solidness. Abuela takes my hand, and I turn to talk to her. "We were talking about starting a family. Having kids together. Then she got an amazing job offer. She turned it down without even talking to me because she didn't want me to have to choose between staying here or moving with her."

Abuela nods. "She was willing to give up an opportunity to be with you. You're more important than the job is."

I shake my head. "She didn't even talk to me about it. How can we be equal partners if she doesn't talk to me about important decisions?"

"Hasn't she been on her own her whole life?" she asks me gently.

"That's not an excuse," I argue, trying to tamp down my anger. "I can't live that way."

Abuela laughs. "I don't think you can live without this girl either. You need to talk. Yes, maybe she needs to learn to share the responsibility, but she won't do that without you to help guide her. Relationships are hard work. You can't run away every time something is hard. Not if she's worth fighting for."

Dad's phone dings, and he pulls it out of his pocket. He sends a quick reply text, then puts his phone down. "Call Lily later," he says quietly, squeezing my shoulder.

I nod absently. I look at abuela. "I am going to fight for it, just not the way she wants me to." I look at dad. "I have a question. If you don't want to answer, I understand, but you know her best. Professionally, I mean." He raises an eyebrow, and the corner of his mouth curls up. "This job with Ella—how much do you know about it?"

He sighs thoughtfully. "The basics, I guess. It's ambitious, like all of Alexi and Ella's projects."

"Sarah's ambitious. She always has been, from what my research showed me. She passed your skillset at least four or five years ago."

He winces. "Fair assessment. But try to be nice to your old man," he chuckles.

"So this really is the perfect opportunity for her, professionally speaking."

He's thoughtful for a moment before nodding. "Professionally speaking, it would change her career trajectory. She's already one of the most versatile architects in the country. Working with Alexi and Ella would elevate her even more." He looks at me long and hard for a minute. "But you have to understand that, for some people, there are more important things in life. A lot of really talented people pass up good opportunities every day, Carmen—for valid reasons."

"Do you know how much they offered her?" I ask him dubiously. When he shakes his head, I tell him. "Twice what you're paying her." He whistles in surprise. "Money notwithstanding," I push him, "this really is the perfect opportunity for her."

He half-shrugs. "I was surprised when she turned it down, to be honest, especially as fast as she did. But I can understand why. She can continue to learn and grow where she's at, and there will always be projects that put her talents to use here."

"Don't take her side," I grumble.

"I'm not taking sides, *mija,* just telling you what I see from where I'm at."

"Which is what you were asking for," abuela reminds me gently.

I nod, sighing quietly. There has to be a way we can work things out where she can take the job if she wants it.

"For what it's worth, Ella said the offer is open, even though Sarah officially turned it down. That's not going to change.

They want her on that team. They respect her choice, but if she changes her mind, the job is hers," dad says.

"Are you going to be mad at me if I change her mind?" I ask him, half-joking.

He shakes his head. "As long as it's what she wants."

I give both of them hugs before I head upstairs to the privacy of my empty rooms. It's been more than two months since I've slept in my own bed. I turn my phone on and pull up my text messages. A few from Sarah, asking me to call. One from Lily.

I send a quick text to Olivia. *I know it's getting late, but can you talk in 10-15?*

Then I call Lily.

"Are you okay?" She asks as soon as she answers.

I huff a broken laugh. I love this child. "No, not really. But I will be. Your mom will be, too," I promise her. I'll do everything in my power to make sure of that.

"What happened?" she asks quietly. I have a feeling she's in her room, but her mom can probably hear us if she wants to.

"Is your mom okay with you talking to me?" I ask. I don't want to do anything to upset Sarah.

"She doesn't care." I can hear her roll her eyes at me. "She mostly told me, anyway. But I want to hear it from you, too."

"You remember that job your mom was talking about a few months ago, that Ella offered her?"

"Your dad's friends, right? The one where she'd have to move in a few years?" she asks.

"Yes, that one," I sigh. "She turned it down."

"Because she didn't want to make you move with your business. And with rugrats," she says quietly. "She doesn't want to take babies away from Richard and abuela, either."

That stops me in my tracks. "Maybe that was the right choice, but she never even talked to me about it." I try to keep the bitter accusation out of my tone. This isn't about Lily choosing sides.

"She didn't? Why not?" she asks, confused. "Why wouldn't she talk to you about it?"

I sigh softly. "I don't know, Bug. Your mom's used to making decisions by herself. That's how it's always been for her. I love her, but I don't know if I can deal with that."

"You shouldn't. She's always talked to me before she makes any big decisions. She still decides herself, but she at least listens to me."

I nod silently. "I'm sure your mom will let you come see me. Maybe we can do something Saturday or Sunday, okay?"

"Yep. Love you," she says.

"Love you back, Bug."

After I hang up with Lily, I pull up my texts with Sarah. *Look, I love you, but I need some space right now. Can you give me that please?*

After checking that Olivia can talk, I call her next.

"What's up, beautiful? I haven't heard much from you the past few months."

I scoff at that. "I saw you two weeks ago with the kids at my dad's."

"Your dad's. Right." She laughs. "So you've officially moved in with her then? When are you getting married?"

When I don't answer, she sighs softly. "What happened?"

"I just walked out on her," I admit quietly.

"You guys have to learn to talk to each other. You can't do that once you start popping out kids." She laughs softly. "What did she do this time?"

When I'm done explaining about Ella's job offer, Olivia whistles. "She asked Lily about it, but never asked you about it?"

"No, and she didn't tell me she turned it down until two months after the fact."

"Maybe it just wasn't that important to her," Olivia suggests. "There's more to life than work, Carmen."

"I don't understand why everyone is taking her side about this. That's not even the point. She should have talked to me about it."

"Hey," she says gently. "I'm not taking anyone's side, sweetie. But you know I'm not going to sugarcoat anything either. Yes, her ass should have talked to you about it. But if you guys are as serious about each other as it seems, and you're thinking of bringing babies into this, I can understand why she wouldn't even consider it."

"So if you got a job offer making twice what you make now, you wouldn't even consider it?"

She snorts out a laugh. "If it was for twice what I make, we'd move just about anywhere. Miguel would stay home with the kids. But he doesn't have his own business here, Carmen."

"Liv, she's so driven. She's come so far in the past ten years—she passed my dad years ago. She thrives on a good challenge. This is honestly a dream job for her. I don't want her to give that up for me."

"Honey, she's happy where she's at. She can create a family with you, and she's probably just thinking of the wonderful life you guys can build together here."

42

SARAH

It's been a month since Carmen left. She's texted me a few times. She's taken Lily almost every weekend for an afternoon. We've emailed about work plenty. She even called me about work once. Lily hasn't said anything about us. Richard just shrugs and says he's not getting involved.

So when she calls me out of the blue Thursday night, it takes me by surprise. "Hello?"

"It's me."

"I know," I say quietly. Lily's home with me, so that's not why she's calling. "Is everyone okay? Richard? Abuela?" I know Carmen is okay, as okay as either of us has been the past month. I can hear it in her voice, even in two paltry words.

"Everyone's fine, Sarah." She sighs softly. "I want to talk to you."

"Okay. About what?" I shake my head in confusion.

"Us," she says firmly. "Do you think I could come over for a few minutes? I won't stay long."

I let out a long breath. "You keep saying you need space. Is there still a chance for 'us' anymore?"

"If you want there to be, yes," she answers firmly. "I want there to be," she adds softly.

"Okay. Then come over so we can talk." I don't know how she wants to fix this, because I'm still not taking a job that will take her away from everything she's built here. But I'll listen.

Twenty minutes later, she's sitting at the table. She gives Lily a quick hug and sends her off to her room so we can talk. "What's up?" I ask curiously—curious, but cautious. This is the first time she's reached out to me since she walked out over a month ago.

"Listen before you react, okay? I love you. I want to spend the rest of my life with you. So don't get upset about this. Hear me out."

I frown. "I'm listening." I bite my lip, trying to figure her out.

She takes a nervous breath, letting it out slowly. "I talked to Ella. I wanted to understand what this job was, to understand why she's so determined to have you on her team, to see if there was a way that we could make this work." I open my mouth to protest, but she puts her hand up to stop me. "It's still one hundred percent your decision, and I will stand by whatever you decide, as long as you'll sit down and talk to me about it."

"If we're going to make things work, then it's not one hundred percent my decision. We'll make it together. I understand what you were talking about, Carmen. But you're going to have a hell of a lot of convincing to do if you want to talk me into it."

She nods amenably. "Fair enough."

"You have to understand that I'm happy with my job here."

She reaches across the table and nods, taking my hand in hers. "Tomorrow, I want you to come to lunch with me and Ella.

We're going to try to convince you that this job is the right choice. All I ask is that you listen. Ask questions if you want, but keep an open mind."

"That's all?" I ask, swallowing thickly. "Just listen?"

"Yes, and we'll talk about it before you make a decision."

I bite my lip and study her for a long moment. "Why are you doing this?" I ask her. "I've been making decisions on my own for so long, it's hard for me to change that."

She shrugs. "You've been taking Lily's input into consideration for years. Maybe not fifty-fifty, but you always talk to her and ask her opinion on things. I don't think it's that big of a stretch to include me, if you make it a conscious choice."

I guess she has a point. "You honestly think you and Ella can convince me to reconsider the job?"

She holds back a grin, but the corner of her mouth twitches. "If you listen to us, yes. I think most of your reasons for not taking it can be worked around, and I think you would really enjoy the job."

"Sure. I'll listen with an open mind, and we can talk about it. Is your dad coming tomorrow, too?" If we could find a way to make it work, the job would really be an amazing chance for me to grow a lot. I'm not sure there's a way around all the obstacles in our way, but I'll entertain the idea.

She shakes her head. "No. Not unless you want him there, anyway. He knows I called Ella a few weeks ago, but he doesn't even know she's here right now. I don't think Alexi is flying out with her. I was planning to tell him tonight that the three of us are going to talk about it, though, so he's not hit out of left field if you change your mind."

"Good idea." If I decide to go, it'll be hard on Richard until he finds someone to replace me. I noticed he hasn't given me a new project yet. The Cultural Center is almost finished, and I've been working closely with Bob on the bridge build. It wouldn't be hard for him to officially take lead on it.

It's weird leaving work to go talk to Ella and Carmen. Richard doesn't say much about it, other than to squeeze my shoulder and tell me he supports me, whatever I choose.

When the hostess at Bistro19 leads me to the table where Ella and Carmen are already sitting, Ella pulls me into a giant hug. Carmen awkwardly gives me a one-arm hug.

Ella looks between us, confused at the awkwardness between us, then shakes her head. "I don't want to know. You're okay to talk, right?" She looks at me first, and I nod.

"Of course we are," I assure her before glancing at Carmen. How much has she told Ella?

"We're fine," Carmen reassures her. She turns to me. "We ordered drinks and appetizers. We figure we'll show you what we have, then eat. It'll give you a little time to think, ask us any questions you want."

I laugh nervously. "You make it sound like I'm at a job interview."

Ella shakes her head with a chuckle. "If anything, it's the other way around. I assume Carmen told you we're going to do our damnedest to change your mind."

I meet Ella's gaze. "You have an uphill battle, but I'm listening."

She nods, deciding to get down to business. "Okay, first thing. If we need you there before Lily is finished with high school, we'll fly you out only when necessary."

"Any time you have to fly out," Carmen continues, "whether you and I are together or not, Lily can stay with me or with dad. I talked to him last night, and he agreed that he would do that for her, and for you. If you'd both be happier with her staying with Beth and Sophie, that's an option, too. I talked to Beth. Obviously, we're talking a few years from now, so she couldn't promise anything. But if they're still here, she and Justin said they'll do everything they can to accommodate having her during the week."

"You would be home on weekends," Ella finishes. "We'll pay for your airfare commute until she's finished with high school."

I let out a low breath. "You talked to Beth about this?" I ask Carmen.

She nods cautiously. "Beth and Justin. They said their oldest would almost certainly have moved out by then. If Ava, is that her name? If she's still living at home, they might need to move some rooms around, but they'll make it happen—if that's what you and Bug decide is best."

"Avery," I correct her on Beth's oldest daughter. "You talked to Beth and Justin?" I shake my head incredulously.

Carmen nods, the corner of her mouth twitching up. "You're not allowed to be mad at her."

"Also," Ella continues, "depending on where exactly we decide to build, and what she decides to study—assuming she plans to continue her education," she clarifies, "we might have connections at some of the better universities. We're almost certainly looking at the West Coast, but we haven't settled on an exact location yet. Assuming her grades are up to snuff." Her mouth turns up in an amused smile. I'm sure she knows that Lily's grades are up to snuff.

I look at Carmen. "What about your dad? He would need time to replace me if I leave."

Ella takes this one. "I've talked to him several times over the past few months, and again last night. He's been planning to hire another architect either way, because if you stay with him, he's going to start training you to take over the business—not officially for several years, but still. If you come work for us, he still has years to find the right addition to the team and promote the right person for the job."

I furrow my brow at the two of them. "Why do I feel like you two have been ganging up on me for weeks?"

Carmen reaches over and puts her hand over mine. "Because I honestly believe this is an amazing opportunity for you. If we can make everything align right and you can make a rational informed decision, you'd really love this job. I just want you to feel like it's a possibility, a real choice."

"That's a lot of hypotheticals," I tell her quietly, half-hoping that they'll be able to assuage all my possible objections.

Carmen nods tentatively. "I know, *mi amor,* I know." She sighs softly. "I'm going to be presumptuous for a minute, now. Bear with me, please?" She gently squeezes my hand.

"Go on," I encourage her, feeling a little lighter.

"If we can make things work with us—"

Ella interrupts her. "What do you mean if? You two are so—"

Carmen's glare stops her. "If we can make things work, and I *want* to make things work," she continues, pulling her hand from mine and straightening her shoulders, "I can hire someone to run the Delmont branch of Tomsen Media. I've already talked to Michael and Natalie, and if Michael isn't in a good place to step into the position, I can find someone else. They would work directly under me, and I could work remotely."

"We can even provide an office space for her," Ella adds, "as long as it's just one or two people. If you decide to grow your company in that location, you'll need to find your own space," she tells Carmen.

I shake my head in disbelief. "You weren't kidding, were you? When you said you were going to find a way to make it happen."

Carmen laughs softly. "We'll find a way to make it work *if* you decide you want to take the job. That's your decision completely. We just want to take away any potential obstacles."

I inhale slowly, biting my lower lip.

Carmen studies me for a long moment, opening her mouth to say something, then closing it again with a deep exhale.

"Whatever it is, just say it," I tell her firmly.

She purses her lips together, then nods decisively. "If we decide to bring more kids into our family, whether it's here or somewhere else, I'll bring in a VP anyways. It really wouldn't change that much as far as my company is concerned. If we're on the West Coast, I can always fly back a few times a year, whenever it's necessary. But almost everything I do can be done remotely."

I swallow, my eyes locked on Carmen. "You would do that for me?" I ask weakly.

She gives me the most heartwarming smile. "I would give up my business for you if I had to," she says quietly, the rawness reflecting in her deep brown eyes.

I shake my head. "I would never let you." The hoarse whisper scratches my throat.

Ella clears her throat. "If you guys want to go play tonsil hockey in the bathroom to get it out of your system so we can continue..." She smirks at us playfully.

Carmen's face shifts, slowly but distinctly, to a worried frown as she turns toward Ella. "Do I need to worry about you with her?"

Ella rolls her eyes with a huff of amusement. "No, not even a little bit. If she's even remotely interested in the job, she's off-limits to me. I don't do employees. Period." She shakes her head. "Whatever is between the two of you, now or later, I don't get involved with my employees like that. Ever." She gives Carmen a hard glare, then turns her gaze to me. "Under any circumstances. I can't say I haven't been with partnered women. As long as it's consensual from *all* parties," she clarifies, "but if someone works for me, that's one hundred percent off the table. No exceptions. I don't mess with power dynamics in the workplace."

I let out a slow breath I didn't realize I was holding, and some of the tension in my shoulders relaxes. Carmen notices, and I see a flicker of concern in her eyes before she lets it go.

"Besides," Ella says softly, glancing at Carmen. "You're like a daughter to me. Things being what they are," she puts her hand over ours, "I couldn't look at Sarah like that anymore if I tried. I imagine Richard feels the same way." She chuckles in amusement.

Our drinks and appetizers arrive, and we talk more about the project. Before I know it, we're getting ready to head out.

"You need a ride?" Ella asks Carmen.

Carmen tilts her head at me. "She picked me up," she explains.

I chew on the inside of my cheek. "Richard is expecting me back in the office," I tell her. "My car is there, anyway. I walked."

She nods, the corner of her mouth slowly tilting up in a half-grin. "It's a nice day. I could walk with you, then we could go in and tell your boss that something came up." She raises an eyebrow at me playfully.

"What exactly are you going to tell him came up that I need to skip out of work early on a Friday afternoon for?" I laugh.

"Me." She laughs, biting her lower lip. "I'm pretty sure he won't put up much of a fight. You know you're not going to be thinking about work the rest of the afternoon anyways."

She's got me there. She and Ella have covered all of my biggest issues about taking the job. Carmen and I still need to talk about it. It's more complicated than they make it out to be, but she's right. I won't be thinking about work this afternoon. I sigh dramatically and look at Ella. "I'll take care of her."

Ella's eyes twinkle. "That's way more information than I need, ladies." Winking at me, she gives me a hug. "If you come up with any other questions or issues, call me. Once you've had a chance to think about things, let me know. You know we want you on our team, but no pressure either way."

"Thank you," I say, my heart full of something I can't put my finger on. Partly pride, because I really do understand why they want me on this team, but also because I'm immensely grateful that she's willing to give me space to make the decision.

Carmen and I walk back to my office, our hands linked together. She's quiet, in a comfortable way.

Eventually, I squeeze her hand. "You feel so strongly about this that you went through all this trouble and even had her fly out for lunch." It's not a question, really. "You even talked to Beth and Justin." My mouth goes dry. I don't really understand why she's going to all this work for something where she stands to lose so much.

"It's not the job I feel so strongly about, Sarah. Don't get me wrong. I think the job would be an amazing fit for you, but that's ultimately your decision. I want you to explore the possibility. That, and if we're going to make 'us' work, that you make that decision with me—at least with my input."

"Fair enough," I say quietly, squeezing her hand again. "What are you planning to tell your dad?" I ask as we enter the office building.

She shrugs lightly. "Just that I'm stealing you for the afternoon. He can have you back on Monday. He'll be fine."

We step into the elevator and the doors close on us, leaving us completely alone for the first time in too long. She pulls my hand to her, turning over my wrist and placing a gentle kiss on the heel of my palm. A gentle kiss with soft lips, hot breath, and a gentle nip of her teeth.

My breath catches. "Let's talk first," I whisper, meeting her eyes.

Nodding, she lets go of my hand. She takes a deep breath and squares her shoulders. "Right."

When we walk into the office together, Bob and Ethan look up at us. Bob fights back a smile as he turns back to his work, but Ethan breaks into a huge grin. He winks at me. "You two are so cute together."

I laugh, nodding at him to get back to work. I sit down at my desk to close everything up for the day while Carmen sticks her head into Richard's office. When I join them a few minutes later, they're laughing about something. Richard glances up at me. "You'll be back Monday, right?" he teases.

"Of course." I purse my lips together in amusement.

"Go, you two. I'll see you sometime this weekend, right? I think Olivia and Miguel are coming over with the kids on Sunday. There are two little girls who've missed you the past few weeks," he says, looking at me.

We find a quiet place to sit at the park and talk. Sitting next to me, she takes my hands. "Talk to me, *mi amor*. Penny for your thoughts," she prods me.

I swallow, my heart in my throat. "Why is it so important for you to do this?" I shake my head to clear it. "Don't get me wrong. I appreciate it. I just don't understand why you're trying so hard to convince me, when this job would cause so much upheaval in your life."

She purses her lips together in amused patience. "It's important to me that you actually consider it. I want to take away as many obstacles as I can, so you can take advantage of it. I don't want little things to hold you back if you want this job." She squeezes my hands.

I shake my head. "But you and Lily aren't little things. You're the most important things," I argue.

A smile tugs at her lips. "Yes, and now we've created a path forward where you can have your cake and eat it, too."

I bite my lip thoughtfully. "Okay. I can see it potentially working. Does that mean you think I should take it, then?" That would be the rational assumption, after all the work she's done the past month to make it feasible.

Her laughter floats on the spring breeze. "Tell me about the job. The stuff you'd be excited about. The stuff that scares you. All of it."

"It's a tremendous opportunity," I tell her. "The team that Ella showed me, the experts in so many different fields—it's the most incredible group of talent I can imagine. Some of these people have three or four degrees in different fields. The breadth of knowledge is literally mind-boggling."

"Mm-hmm." Carmen murmurs amusement in the back of her throat. "You're on that list. You would fit in."

"I would need to learn a lot of new things to understand some of these new technologies," I say quietly, "but it's pretty damn exciting, if I'm honest."

She nods encouragingly. "But?" She raises an eyebrow for me to continue.

"You still want a family, right? Beyond me and Lily, I mean?" She drops her eyes for a moment, biting her cheek. I take her chin and gently bring her gaze to mine.

"We'll need to talk more about it, but yes. I would like babies," she says hesitantly.

"You realize there might be a year or two when I'm traveling a lot, and you're home alone with screaming kids and diapers?"

A stupid grin crosses her face, and she shrugs. "Ella will try to keep you here as much as possible, and when Bug is finished with school, we'll move. Abuela and dad are here, Olivia and Miguel too, even Lily and Sophie could help some. It'll only be for a little while in the grand scheme of things, Sarah."

I shake my head, all of a sudden realizing a flaw in the plan. "We can't take the kids away from Richard and abuela." My shoulders sink, the reality settling in after getting so close.

Carmen laughs. "If we move out there to stay, abuela will come with us. I bet dad would, too, after he retires. We'll talk to them. I'm sure he won't want you to turn this down because of that."

"You think I should take it," I say thoughtfully, meeting her eyes.

She studies me for a long minute, then bites her lower lip. Her brow furrows slightly.

"What?" I nudge her. "What is it?"

"Ella. Would you be comfortable working with her?" Her eyes bore into mine.

I tense slightly. "What do you mean? Why wouldn't I be comfortable working with her?" Does Carmen not trust me around Ella anymore?

She closes her eyes and exhales slowly, shaking her head. "Have you *ever* had a job where a superior didn't try to get in your pants?" When I open my mouth to deny it, she shakes her head again. "Even at my dad's company. He was trying to get into your pants. Have you *ever* had a job where you felt safe from all that?"

I purse my lips together, not sure I want to have that conversation. Again. Especially in a public place. "Besides working for your dad, no," I answer quietly.

She meets my eyes again. "We need to talk to her. I honestly don't think she would ever put you in a compromising position, but I think it would be good to have a conversation with her and put the topic on the table. We can make it all about me if you want, but I want to talk to her about it. All three of us."

"It's not exactly a topic of discussion at most job interviews," I say sourly.

"I know, sweetie. But seeing as she's one of my dad's best friends, and seeing as you had a little rendezvous—" She wiggles her eyebrows at me playfully.

I roll my eyes. "It was barely a kiss, and she's married."

"She likes to have fun," Carmen says lightly. She scoots closer to me on the park bench and cups my cheek in her hand. "I also saw the tension go out of your body earlier when she said nothing would ever happen with you two. Even if you weren't consciously thinking about it, it was in your head. Will you do it for me?" She gently traces the pad of her thumb across my jawline.

She's right, even though I hadn't realized it until Carmen brought it up to Ella today. If I were single, I wouldn't be opposed to having no-strings-attached fun with her sometimes. But that's a moot point. I nod slowly. "Yes, of course."

She pulls my face toward hers, her eyes lidded. "Sarah." My name is just a breath on her lips. "Can I come home to you now?" Her voice cracks.

43

CARMEN

I look around at the crowd in amazement. When I started thinking about this Cultural Center for Delmont, I mostly thought of kids like me. Queer kids. Kids with darker skin. Young women and girls. But our opening ceremony has a more diverse crowd than I ever imagined.

The weather is beautiful for an outdoor event. The sun is shining. The kids have just finished another school year. Families are roaming around, and kids are laughing and playing. A large group of teenagers congregates over by the Pride tables. Everyone is high on endorphins, even the parents.

"Can I have your attention, everyone?" I speak into the booming microphone. "We're getting ready for the official ribbon cutting." I give the crowd a minute or two to quiet, and people start gravitating toward the stage area. Sarah squeezes my hand before moving away to give me the spotlight.

"Members of my hometown community," I begin, looking around at the crowd in front of me, "thank you for coming today to show your support for nurturing and empowering our community for a better tomorrow!" I pause as the crowd claps politely. "When I was young, I had the support of a wonderful family—parents who loved and accepted me for who I am, and the lucky bonus of being in a family who wanted—and could afford—the best for me."

I swallow a knot in my throat. "Most of the world isn't that lucky. It's my mission here to create a safe space for kids, young people, even adults," the crowd chuckles, "to be accepted, nurtured, and empowered to be the best they can be in their communities, in their jobs, and in their personal lives. We have a lot of programs starting over the next few weeks, so look around today. Keep an eye on the website and social media. We would love to see you all back here over the next few months. Parents, encourage your kids to get involved. We have groups for almost everyone." I glance over at Sarah and Lily. "I want you to meet Lily, who'll be going into high school this fall."

Lily nods, walking to the middle of the stage to join me. I hand her the microphone. She looks across the sea of people. Her eyes widen in wonder. "Wow, there are a lot of people here." She glances at me hesitantly.

She straightens her shoulders and turns back to the crowd. "This past year, I got involved with a program at the middle school to help kids who felt alone," she tells them. "It started with some of my queer friends, but once we started talking to more students, I realized that almost every kid at school has something they feel isolated about. Whether it's who they're attracted to, or the color of their skin; for some kids, it's their religion. I had a few girls tell me they felt like their future was limited because they're girls." She shakes her head, her voice gaining power. "People, there are four billion women in the world. Can you imagine the potential we have to make the world a better place!?"

At first, there's a smattering of laughter in the crowd, then a few younger people start to whoop and clap. The enthusiasm spreads through the crowd. Lily gives them a minute, but then steps forward, putting a hand in the air to quiet them. "We're moving in the right direction, everyone, but we're not there yet. Just think. If we can educate and empower every single person in our community, can you imagine how much good we could do in the world?" She's not shouting now. Her voice is quiet. "Kids that feel invisible because their parents are divorced. Kids that don't live in a safe home environment. People don't realize that queer kids, minorities, girls—are all at higher rates of discrimination and violence. They don't have the same opportunities as a lot of us do."

The crowd is silent, waiting for her next words. "At school, we're setting up a program that pairs kids with other kids who have the same experiences, with adults who have been-there, done-that. Some stuff is more serious, and the program tries to provide the right resources for their circumstances. Thanks to the Tomsen family and donors to the Cultural Center, that program will be expanded to the whole community. Programs and safe spaces will be created when there's a need for them. So parents, encourage your kids to get involved."

She turns to hand me back the microphone. "Did I do okay?" she whispers. The mic catches her question, and the crowd chuckles.

"Perfect, *mija*." I drop a light kiss on the top of her head. I take the mic and turn back to the crowd. "Kids, encourage your parents to get involved, too. More adults volunteering helps us offer more and better programs. It also helps kids connect with safe adults and mentors. It creates a stronger community for everyone. You can fill out the volunteer forms online, or there are forms available at all the booths."

I glance at dad and Sarah, and they both nod, coming to center stage. I hand the microphone to dad. He turns to the crowd. "Sarah and I represent the company that built this great edifice. I wish I could say we got the job because I'm her dad, but..." He shakes his head with a chuckle. "Carmen didn't pick me. She did her research and found the best architect in Delmont." He nods to Sarah and hands her the mic.

She turns and looks at the sea of faces around us. She clears her throat. "When I was young, I would have given anything to have a safe place to be able to be myself and not be judged for it." The crowd goes silent at her words. "A lot of things have changed in the last twenty or thirty years. We're moving in the right direction. But there are still kids out there who are afraid to be themselves at home. Afraid to let their friends and family see them for who they are—that they won't be accepted in their own homes. That's hard. Really hard." She swallows.

"No kid should have to deal with that. Everyone should be accepted and valued for who they are. They should be empowered to be their best selves, not shamed or ridiculed for who they are." She takes a deep unsteady breath. I instinctively move toward her, but Lily is already by her side, arm wrapped around her waist. Sarah regains her strength. "That's why I'm so proud to be part of this project."

I step in and take the mic from Sarah, settling myself on the other side of Lily with my arm over her shoulder. "Let's officially open this safe space where everyone can be accepted and valued as they are, supported and empowered by this amazing community around them."

Dad hands me the ceremonial scissors, and Sarah and I do the honors of cutting the ribbon together. I turn back to the clapping crowd. "There are booths for many of our programs around the grounds, and food and drink around the north corner of the Center." I point in that direction, but I think most people already smell the meat on the grill. "Find something to eat, check out the booths, mingle with your neighbors. Introduce yourself to someone new. Enjoy the afternoon!"

As we mingle with the crowd, I notice dad head off to talk to some people I don't know, and Lily goes off with a group of her friends from school.

Sarah turns to me. "Do you have any idea how much of a difference you're going to make for all these kids?" She gives me a watery smile. "To have a safe place to be themselves, without judgment?" She looks around us, at a supportive community that wants to empower its young people. "Thank you for doing this."

"It's not about me, Sarah. It never was." I squeeze her hand. "If I can give just one kid a sense of pride in who they are, I'll be happy. Dozens, maybe even hundreds, in time? I'm all in."

I notice Lily's friend Chuck coming toward us with an adult couple and a young woman.

"Ms. Reynolds." Chuck comes directly to Sarah. "I'd like you to meet my parents. Charlie and Megan Montgomery. Mom, Dad, this is Lily's mom. I told you about her."

Sarah shakes hands with both his parents, then turns to the girl. "You must be..." She pauses for a moment, searching her memory. "Nancy, right? Chuck's older sister."

Chuck looks at Sarah like she grew a second head. "You remember her name?"

"It's my job to learn new things and remember them." She breaks into a grin.

"Well sure, but only important things," he says, still flabbergasted.

Sarah laughs, shaking her head. "Your sister is important. So are you."

Nancy snorts and pokes at her brother. "See, moron? The world doesn't revolve around you."

Megan Montgomery groans. "You two, go find something to eat. Don't kill each other in the process, please."

"Lily's around with a bunch of your friends," I tell Chuck. "I'm sure your sister would be welcome, too, whatever they're up to."

After the kids disappear, Megan turns back to Sarah. "I want to thank you for talking to Chuck, for encouraging him to talk to us. He was so scared at first that we wouldn't accept him for who he is."

Sarah offers a self-deprecating shrug. "I just helped him talk through some things and choose the best way for him. I'm glad you're supportive of him. It's not easy when your family doesn't accept you for who you are." I move closer to her, slipping an arm around her waist. I know it's still hard for her to talk about her parents.

"My sister's bisexual. She says maybe she's pan now. Is that a thing?" Megan asks curiously before dismissing her question. "As long as she's happy, she can love whoever she wants."

"I think her husband might take issue with that," Charlie mutters beside her, chuckling.

I snort out a laugh. "Mm, yes. If she's married, she can be a monogamous queer. Most of us are monogamous."

"I'm not sure the same can be said for straight people," Charlie mutters under his breath with a grin. His wife looks aghast at his comment until she realizes he's playing with her.

"Isn't queer a derogatory term?" Charlie asks, suddenly serious.

"It honestly depends on who's saying it. For LGBT+ allies, it's often used as an umbrella term. If I met your sister at a gay bar, it would be wrong of me to assume that she's a lesbian. Obviously if we got into a relationship, it would be wise to discuss that. But just like most hetero couples, you don't sit down and talk about your relationship history right away. You get to know each other first."

Sarah bumps shoulders with me. "You better not be going to gay bars and meeting her sister. Or anyone else's sister." Megan and Charlie both laugh at that.

I turn to Charlie. "Did I hear from Lily that you've become an ambassador of sorts for our Cultural Center?"

His ears turn pink. "I'm not sure what you heard. I needed to change jobs to leave a toxic work environment, and I wasn't shy about throwing my dad under the bus when I interviewed for new jobs. I never brought up Chuck, mind you. It was more the principle of the matter. I probably dropped a few words encouraging forward-thinking businesses to support the center, or any other cause they felt worth investing in."

"Good for you." My words are heartfelt. "We've seen an influx of long-term donation pledges from a lot of the financial sector the past few months. It'll make a significant difference for a lot of young people. Thank you."

Megan looks at Sarah, taking a step closer. "Thank you for being someone my son could trust, when he wasn't sure he could trust us," she whispers.

Sarah gives her a hug, and they hold on to each other for a long moment. "I'm glad I could be there for him," she whispers before letting go.

After they leave, Sarah turns to me. "He's just one person. It seems so small. It was just a simple conversation."

"One person, Sarah. Think of the life that boy has ahead of him, and the difference he can make in the world because the people in his life support him."

"Think of the dozens of people who can change the world because of what you've built," she turns it back on me. "All because of one person." She grins, lacing her fingers with mine.

EPILOG

LILY

3½ years later

I hang my keys up on the hook inside the door. Linda comes squealing at me before I see her. I pick her up and give her a playful raspberry on her cheek. "Hello, beautiful. How was your day?"

"Gah," she says, signing the word for *good*. I can't wait until she can talk to me beyond the handful of signs she can communicate with.

"Is mamá home?" I ask.

She nods, making the sign for Carmen. *"Mah."* Carmen is home.

"Mah-mah," I repeat to her, showing her Carmen's sign. "What about mom? Is she home yet?"

This time she makes the sign for mom. *"Mah,"* she says, shaking her head. So mom's not home yet.

I take Linda into the living room and drop my school bag onto the chair. I reach over and give Carmen a quick hug. "When's mom coming home?"

"Soon. I've got something for you once she gets home." She gives me a mysterious grin.

"Is it mail? Is it from California?" I applied to UCLA Early Decision for environmental sciences. When mom and I flew out there to visit the campus over the summer, the head of the dance department gave me information about applying for all the dance scholarships they offer, too. I want to continue ballet, but it's not something I want to major in.

Linda starts wiggling, so I let her down. She immediately crawls onto the couch like a monkey, curling up against Carmen's growing belly. Missy climbs up after her and sits on top of Carmen's huge stomach. "Did you two take a nap this afternoon?" I ask, raising an eyebrow.

Carman laughs. "For a grand total of five wiggly giggly minutes, then we just turned on Dora."

"Mah-mah," Linda looks up at Carmen in surprise, a hand on Carmen's belly. "Buh-buh."

I snicker loudly. "Is your brother already trying to kick you, beautiful?" I glance at Carmen. "Do you want me to watch her for an hour or two so you can touch base with the office?"

She shakes her head. "I already talked to Michael this morning. He's got everything under control."

"I can watch her if you want to take a nap," I tell her. She looks exhausted. She wasn't this tired when she was pregnant with Linda, but it seems like the twins are taking a lot more out of her. Mom says it's a lot of work to grow babies, especially with a wiggle worm like Linda trying to escape every time you turn around.

"You need to go get your homework done before ballet. You have exams before Christmas break, right?"

I groan. "Yes. Physics and Calculus. I have a Spanish essay I need to finish, too. Do you think you could proofread it for me when I'm done with it?"

She swats at me with a throw pillow. "Aren't you supposed to do it yourself?"

I shrug. "I am doing it myself. But an extra pair of eyes never hurts."

"You should ask abuela to help. She'll be over most of the day tomorrow."

I roll my eyes at her. "I don't know if it'll be done by then. We'll see." It's been harder to concentrate on school the last few months, since both Carmen and mom have been working from home part of the time. Even though mom works for Ella now, she still has a space at Richard's office, mostly because he has the room and she would miss everyone at the office, she says. That, and she needs to escape the chaos around here at least a few times a week. "Do you need anything before I disappear to the homework dungeon?" I ask Carmen.

SARAH

"Hey. Do you want me to make you a snack while Lily's at ballet? You look hungry." I glance over at Carmen.

"You know I'm capable of getting myself a snack, right?" She gently puts Missy on the couch next to a sleeping Linda before awkwardly getting up. "Don't you dare laugh at me," she murmurs.

"I wouldn't dream of it," I lie, trying to hide a smile. I pull her into a soft kiss. "How are you feeling today?" I turn her around. "Lean over a little. Let me rub your back."

"Like I'm growing two hungry monsters who want to sap all their mama's energy." She groans as my thumbs dig into her back. "Why am I so much more tired this time?"

I smack her in the ass playfully. "For one thing, your body is doing twice the work. For another thing, that angelic little creature over there."

"You mean Missy?" she asks with a laugh, straightening up and turning toward me. She takes my face in her hands and holds my eyes for a long moment. "I love you. Have I told you that today?"

She did, this morning before I left for work, but I shake my head. "Not enough," I whisper into her ear. She pulls me closer, her hands untucking the back of my shirt. Her fingernails trail up my back. "Okay, horny mama. Bug's home, right? Save it for tonight. Or at least when she's at ballet," I laugh.

We thought sex was complicated when Lily was younger, but with a baby that sleeps in our room, we have to get creative.

"You guys are gross," Lily says, coming out of her room. "Do you want me to drop her off at abuela's while I'm at dance?"

I shake my head. "No. I have to fly out to California tomorrow for a few days. I should be back on Friday, though." I miss them so much when I travel. All of them. I glance over at Linda. "How long has she been sleeping? She needs to sleep tonight."

"Only ten or fifteen minutes, Sarah. She wouldn't lay down for a nap earlier."

I pick her up gently, cradling her soft head against my chest. "Wake up, beautiful." I nudge the top of her head.

"Mah." She opens her eyes with a sleepy smile.

Lily rounds on Carmen, bouncing on the balls of her feet anxiously. "Mail. Where is it? Please don't make me wait."

Carmen gives me an apprehensive look, and I give her a hint of a shrug. I mentioned to Ella that Lily was applying, but didn't ask her to work whatever magic she might have. I'm not sure if Lily decided to have her write a letter of recommendation or not. I put my hand on Lily's back. "Temper your expectations, Lilybug."

"Mom." She draws out my name in a whine. "I know. I'm not expecting good news, but I want to know."

"Wanna know," Linda parrots, making all of us laugh.

Carmen reaches into the drawer and pulls out a big envelope. She puts it on the counter, pushing it toward Lily. Lily just stares at it for a long moment, then meets my eyes. "Will you open it for me? Please?"

I know she'll be okay either way, but she's had her heart set on UCLA since Ella and Alexi decided for certain that we'd be building in California. She's been stalking their dance program, and she's even doubled her private classes the past two years.

"Are you sure? We could put it back in the drawer until after ballet," I tease her.

"Don't make me kill you. Carmen couldn't handle three littles without you." She laughs, pushing the envelope toward me.

I shift Linda to my left hip and pick up the envelope. It feels thicker than a single piece of paper. I look at Lily, raising an eyebrow, and she nods. I slip my finger under the flap, carefully ripping it open, and pull it out of the envelope. I read the first paragraph, then raise my eyes to Carmen, trying to school my face. I hand her the letter.

Carmen does a good job of hiding her reaction, too, then reaches for the envelope and puts the letter back into it. Lily squeals when Carmen lays it back on the counter, pushing it toward her.

"Uggggggghhhhhh," she groans, reaching for the envelope. "You guys are horrible."

"You love us." Carmen laughs as Lily pulls the letter out and reads it for herself.

She squeals as she reads the acceptance. She starts bouncing lightly on her feet, but she keeps reading. I didn't read all of it, just the beginning. Carmen and I exchange a glimmer of pride between us.

"At the special urging of the Department of World Arts and Cultures/ Dance—" Lily tightens her fist around the letter and attacks me and Linda with a bear hug. "We did it! We did it!" She jumps up and down. She peels Linda out of my arms, dancing around the room with her. When she slows down after a few frenzied minutes, she grabs Carmen in a hug, too.

"I'm so proud of you, *mija.*"

Lily leans down to kiss Carmen's belly. Linda gives it a soft smooch, too. "These little peanuts are lucky to have you, too."

"They are *not* the size of peanuts anymore."

Lily snorts. "Yeah, well. I'm not commenting on your melons."
I bite back a laugh.

Carmen smacks her. "I appreciate your restraint." She's quiet
for a minute, before telling Lily, "Something else came in the mail
for you."

"Today? What is it?" she asks, genuinely concerned.

Carmen shakes her head, pulling out another envelope from
the drawer. "It came last week, but I was saving it for when you
heard back from UCLA."

"Just in case." Lily nods, taking the second envelope from
her. She looks at the return address and breaks into a grin. She
tears it open, then looks up at Carmen with tears in her eyes.
"I'm officially yours," she murmurs softly, sinking into Carmen's
arms.

"You've been mine for a long time, *mija.*"

I'm not sure what I did to be so blessed.

ALSO BY CASSIDY LANGUE

<u>as Cassidy Langue</u>
Sophie and the Sea
Freedom
Lasting Impressions

~

<u>Love Enough for More series</u>
(writing sapphic poly romance as Polly Emorie)
All the Oceans #1
All the Water #2
All the Words #3

~

To sign up for my newsletter to hear about new books
go to cassidylangue.com
If you enjoy a book, please consider leaving a rating or review.
It helps other readers find great books!

Printed in Great Britain
by Amazon